WAR OF THE MOONRHYMES

Also by the author

Guardians of the Singreale. Volume I in the Singreale Chronicles

Star Riders of Ren. Volume II in the Singreale Chronicles

WAR OF THE MOONRHYMES

Volume III in the Singreale Chronicles

Calvin Miller

1817

Harper & Row, Publishers, San Francisco

Cambridge, Hagerstown, New York, Philadelphia
London, Mexico City, São Paulo, Sydney

 For information address Harper & Row, Publishers, Inc., 10 East 53rd Street, New York, NY 10022. Published simultaneously in Canada by Fitzhenry & Whiteside, Limited, Toronto.

FIRST EDITION

Designed by Jim Mennick
Illustrations by Daniel San Souci

Library of Congress Cataloging in Publication Data

Miller, Calvin.
WAR OF THE MOONRHYMES.

(Volume III in The Singreale chronicles)
I. Title. II. Series: Miller, Calvin. Singreale chronicles ; v. 3.
PS3563.I376S53 1983 vol. 3 813′.54s 83-48428
ISBN 0-06-250579-3 [813′.54]

---

84 85 86 87 88 10 9 8 7 6 5 4 3 2 1

Contents

I. A Distant Roaring 1

II. The Ledge Too Far 17

III. The Return of the Graygills 37

IV. The Meeting of the Realms 53

V. The Unspoiled Valley 69

VI. The Blackgill's Journey 85

VII. Eastwall 101

VIII. Sammuron's Gift 119

IX. Ganarett's Treachery 137

X. The Strategy for Survival 153

XI. The Blazing Paradise 173

XII. The War of the Tunnels 187

XIII. The Return of the Guardians 201

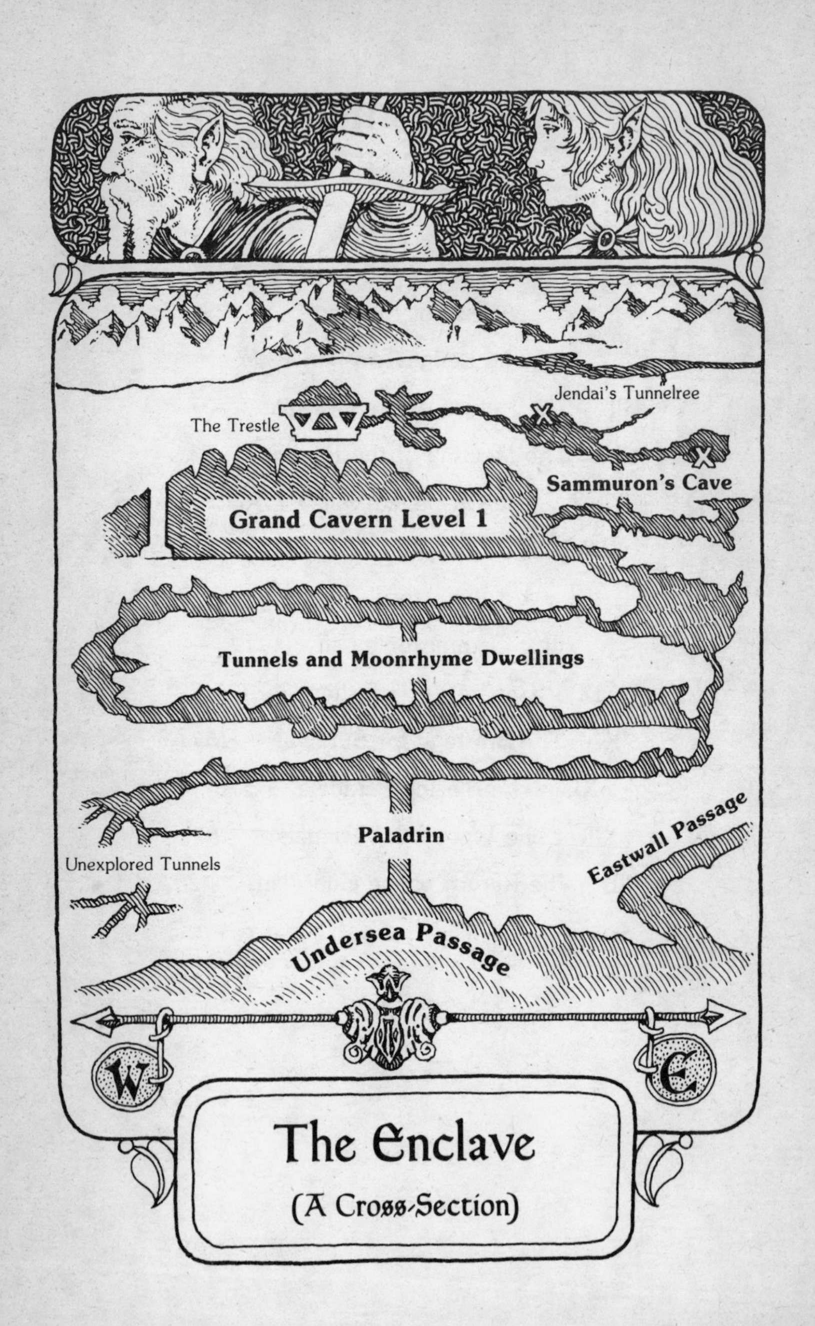
Jendai's Tunnelree
The Trestle
Sammuron's Cave
Grand Cavern Level 1
Tunnels and Moonrhyme Dwellings
Paladrin
Eastwall Passage
Unexplored Tunnels
Undersea Passage
W
E
The Enclave
(A Cross-Section)

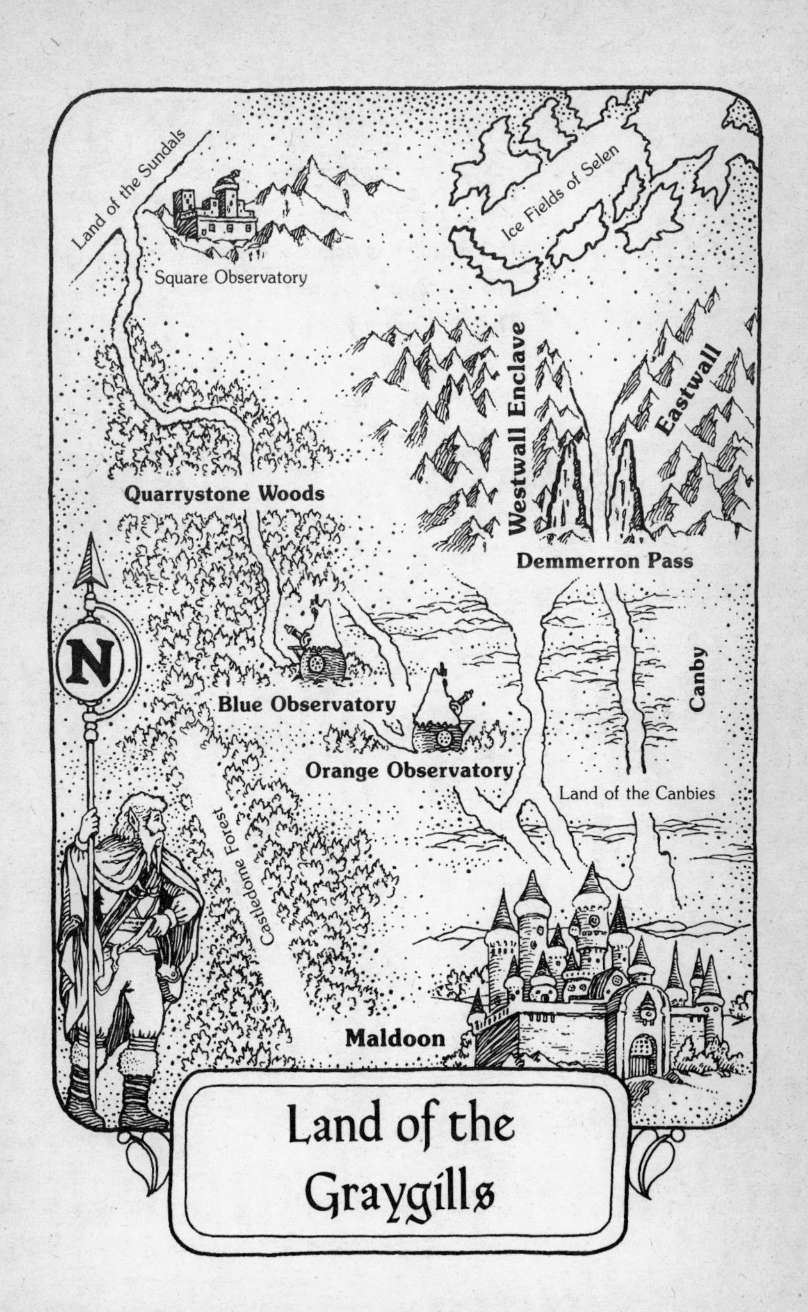
Land of the Sundals
Square Observatory
Ice Fields of Selen
Westwall Enclave
Eastwall
Quarrystone Woods
Demmerron Pass
Canby
Blue Observatory
Orange Observatory
Land of the Canbies
Castledome Forest
Maldoon
N
Land of the Graygills

There is a rending
In the earth.
The mountains heave—
The steppes are torn.
The swollen past
Is in travail.
Tomorrow comes:
An age is born.

CHAPTER I

A Distant Roaring

THE SAME MONTH that Raccoman and Velissa sailed for the troubled northern lands, a leathery old Moonrhyme heard the cry of the last Ganzinger fowl making its way to warmer lands. The cold of the northern winter held an icy prophecy. "It is the end, the end of all is at hand unless the stones can live," the Moonrhyme whispered to himself in the darkness.

Old he was, and blind. The light of day had not declared itself to him for a thousand years. He had lived longer and could remember more of life than anyone in the enclave. No one there could remember back to that time when he could see. Sammuron had dwelt in darkness since the Singreale had been stolen from the tower of Maldoon. The years had run down over his slight frame like dark wax, sealing him in shadows of the past. Most said it was impossible to survive in darkness so long. But Sammuron lived on in a sunless defiance of their argument.

He felt the heat of the torches that kept the enclave lit. His pale and delicate skin, unaccustomed to wind or light, felt the slightest change of temperature in his own small cavern. And though he saw nothing, he heard all. Too loudly he heard the private conversations of the other Moonrhymes, even those in the most remote caverns. His sensitive ears caught every whispered secret as if it were a shout.

He never joined the festivities that were held in the torch-lit Grand Cavern. He complained that the raucous music hurt his ears, which could detect even the sighs of Moonrhyme lovers or the whimpering of an infant in a cavern three levels below him. The distant arguments, the slightest gossip—all filtered through the tunnels, and Sammuron heard.

Some doubted that Sammuron was a Moonrhyme, but never did Sammuron doubt his heritage. The pale blood that flowed through his blue-white hands was as Moonrhyme as blood could be. His unkempt hair was as white as his skin and stuck out at wiry angles. Wrinkles coursed down his forehead and over his pinched nose. His useless eyes, which rarely blinked, rested on large wrinkled pouches that made his cheeks look small. He dressed in a kilt gathered around his thin abdomen. For one millennium, he had been unable to see if his tunic were tucked in or out. After two centuries, the proposition had ceased to be important to him. No aspect of his personal appearance was. His arms and legs were as thin as the reeds that flanked the lagoons where grumblebeaks fed in the summer.

He lived alone in the heart of the caverns and symbolized the life, indeed the existence, of the Moonrhymes. Throughout the sleeping centuries, they came to him to talk of the cataclysm. He had survived it, and his lower body was a mass of scars from the ordeal.

He complained of his own curse of having survived the centuries. He didn't hate being old; he only hated that being old went on so long. But his cursing of the years never brought him sympathy from the younger folk who passed his warm tunnel.

A small fire warmed his section of the cavern. Like himself, the fire seemed eternal. It had blackened his cave with ashes. Day after day, he moved the old cinders aside to make room for new fuel so the flame could burn on. His face was always smudged with soot from his fire.

There was a natural updraft in his cavern that drew off the thin smoke. The smoke spiraled upward and into the gray stones, through the crevasses and dry draughtways, until it billowed from his mountain furnace. Above his undying flame hung a kettle made of latticed straps of iron. The vessel contained two round stones. These were sooted to velvet.

Never had Sammuron permitted anyone to touch the stones. Though he had been blind for a millennium, he could hear the slightest creaking of the long black chains that held the kettle, or the softest footstep upon the stone floor. It was altogether impossible for anyone to slip by him and move his treasure. Even if someone had been able to sneak in undetected, he would have needed a special ladder to reach the warm black stones because they hung so high.

The connecting stone catacombs of Old Sam's dark world were a favorite place for the Moonrhyme children. The children loved the warm floor; they could walk barefoot in Sammuron's tunnels. They never loved the warm floors more than in winter when the snows lashed the surface of the outer cliffs.

Sammuron rarely became crotchety and short with the children, even in his latter centuries. He loved the little ones. And they adored him. They were forever begging him to tell his tales and sing his ballads about the cataclysm and about the happy days of the long past before the Moonrhymes first moved from the valleys to the enclave high in the western cliffs.

Only one adult spent much time with him, and that was Jendai, the wood-bearer. Like his father and his grandfather before him, Jendai served the blind fire-tender faithfully.

Throughout autumn, Jendai carried the wood they would need during the winter months. Sammuron's fire demanded his strength. Twenty times a day, Jendai scaled the cliffs with a burden of wood tied to his strong back.

The wood-bearer was large for a Moonrhyme, large enough and strong enough to climb like an insect up the sheer cliffs of Westwall. He was diligent. When tempted to be lazy in the summer, still he did not yield. He knew that in winter the handholds, chipped into the face of the cliffs, would be precariously slippery with ice. Wood-gathering would then be impossible.

By the time that winter blasted the Moonrhyme cliffs, he would have stored wood in a thousand niches and alcoves of Old Sam's tunnelree. The tunnelree was that portion of the cavern system that any Moonrhyme was allowed to claim as his or her own. It was a kind of property. As the Canbies south of Demmerron owned certain areas of their valley, so did the Moonrhymes have "rights of tunnelree" that made them sovereign owners of those niches or labyrinths given to them by time and the clan.

With the "rights of tunnelree," there were no restrictions. A Moonrhyme could use his own section of the burrows as he chose. Old Sam chose to fill every available section of his cave with wood so that the fire which blackened the stones from generation to generation could burn through every winter.

Jendai preferred to carry candolet bark, since it burned hotter and was lighter to transport in large bundles up the cliffs.

The two of them sat down before the fire one winter's eve. Sammuron spoke: "Jendai, the time has come to test the stones."

"Test?" asked the wood-bearer.

An interval of moments passed. Sammuron always spoke in an unhurried manner, and Jendai had grown used to their sluggish conversations.

"The Selendrenni wait in the frozen seas. Only they can test the stones," said Sammuron. "You must bring the Selendrenni."

It was not the first time that Old Sam had spoken of the Selendrenni. He spoke of them often, and whenever he did, the wrinkles that surrounded his blind eyes tightened into deep crevasses, revealing his excitement.

"All right, the Selendrenni. I will go to the Ice Fields of Selen. But when?" asked Jendai.

"Tomorrow, before the sun is up. Use the ice slide of the north wall and follow the Grand Dragon. That constellation now lies just above the fields of Selen. Dress warmly. If you get caught in the gales of Selen, you will need all that you can wear to survive."

"But, Sammuron," Jendai protested, "how will I find the Selendrenni once I have found the Ice Fields of Selen?"

"Wherever steam rises from the ice and falls again in torrents of frost, there you will find the Selendrenni. Yet, beware—and pray that you find them before they find you."

"Remember, you cannot touch them," the old man droned on. "I cannot tell you how to catch them, but we do not need many."

The old man stopped. Something had interrupted his instruction. He listened intently for what seemed like a very long time to Jendai.

"There is thunder in the earth. Can you hear it, Jendai?" asked Sammuron.

"No, Sammuron. I hear nothing." Both of them sat perfectly still. The old man's face tightened in the amber shadows of his millennial blaze. "Why can your young ears hear nothing, Jendai? *I tell you, there is a roaring in the earth!*"

It was no use. Jendai heard nothing.

The old man sighed. "Go to the Alkreede Tunnel," he said. "There you will find a metal door behind a pile of wood at the back of the tunnel. Open the little door and there you will find a strange pail. It was given to me by a Moonrhyme wizard who perished in the third fire storm."

"But where did he get the pail?" Jendai asked. His question went ignored. The truth was that Old Sam could not remember even the Moonrhyme wizard's name, much less where he had happened on the pail. While some of his memory failed him, his old mind stuck to the plan of the ages.

"Bring the pail, Jendai!" he insisted.

Jendai leapt to his feet and left the room. He turned and hurried to the Alkreede Tunnel. His fingers tore at the dark pile of wood he found there. At the base of the stone wall, his hands felt in the darkness a metal hasp. He pulled it open, and a rusty old key fell out. There was a miniature door. He opened it and reached inside the enclosure. His fingers touched what seemed to be a small, metal basket. He pulled it through the door and examined it. Candolet fibers covered the strange pail, and finely welded wind foil lined the inside. A snug lid fit tightly over the inner lining so that the bearer of the pail might not spill whatever substance it was designed to contain.

Jendai returned to Sammuron's fire chamber.

"I have the pail, Sammuron," he said.

"I must have four!" demanded the blind Moonrhyme.

"Pails?"

"Selendrenni!"

"How?"

"They love fire. Build a fire, and they will come to you. Keep them in water—they must have water to survive. Send for Jond."

Jendai knew why he wanted Jond. Someone must keep the fire going in Jendai's absence. The stones had to be kept hot. Jond had tended the fire on other occasions. He would not fail Old Sam now.

Jendai stoked the fire and looked again at the round black stones. Without speaking further to Sammuron, he turned and went to his own tunnelree. There he put together such things as he would need for his trip to the Ice Fields of Selen. It did not take long. As soon as he had prepared himself for the journey, he fell asleep.

Morning came. Its only announcement was a softening of the darkness in the tunnels. Before he left, Jendai returned to see if Sammuron was content. The old one spoke of hunger, and Jendai brought him such vegetables as were preserved in his larder. They drank some candolet tea at a small table in the tunnelree.

"Tell me of the cataclysm. Tell me of the stones."

"The cataclysm. My parents were killed in the first fire storm. There were no villagers left alive at the end of the second storm. I came to the mountains with others of the valley dwellers. We found these caves."

Sammuron was in no mood to talk, and thus he cut short his account. Whenever he did not feel inclined to conversation, he would abbreviate the tale they both knew and yet constantly rehearsed. There had been three fire storms. The fire had come from the skies and rolled through the valleys in volleys of flame. All of the villagers had been destroyed, and the intense heat had burned the animals into nothingness.

"And the stones?" asked Jendai.

The old man only repeated the words: "The stones!"

His glazed eyes seemed to be looking far away, and then he said, "Demmerron."

After that, Sammuron fell silent. It seemed, even to Jendai, an especially long silence. At last, Old Sam told Jendai that they could expect Parsky to return with siege ladders once the ice had melted from the cliffs in the spring.

"We must have the Selendrenni by then!" Old Sam insisted.

"But do you think Parsky can climb these cliffs and threaten us where even the flames of the cataclysm could not enter?" Jendai asked.

"He will come. As he once climbed the walls of Maldoon, he will climb the cliffs of Demmerron." The wrinkles surrounding the old man's eyes tightened with the grimness of the proposition. "Parsky will stop at nothing!"

Jendai waited while Sammuron stopped and listened again.

"Can't you hear it now?" the old man asked.

The earth was roaring again, he said. Jendai wondered if Old Sam could be imagining the strange roaring that only he could hear. A frequent saying circulated the tunnelrees, "Doubt Sam's eyes, but not his ears."

Long after they parted, Jendai listened hard for the roaring in the earth. He heard nothing.

Jendai dressed warmly. He checked to be sure he had his flint stones and bundle of small twigs in his back pouch. As he passed Sammuron's tunnelree, he could see the old one silhouetted against his fire. He knew that Jond would arrive before long. A strong draft in the tunnel kept the fire as bright as if it had been stoked all during the night. The strength of the draft made Jendai wonder if the frost sheets had already been broken from the entrance to their cave system.

When he reached the end of the tunnel, however, the intense darkness convinced him that ice still covered the entrance. He tied the strange pail to his waist, pulled on his gloves, and drew a warm hood around his face. Only his eyes showed but they sparkled in the thin morning light that filtered through the eerie ice sheet.

He braced himself as if against an unseen foe, then picked up his stone axe and swung it through the wall of ice. In an instant, the wall shattered and shards of ice flew both outward and inward. Brilliant light exploded around the wood-bearer. The gales howled through the opening. He threw the axe far away from the door and stepped out into the wind.

Inside the tunnelree, Old Sammuron heard the shattering of the ice. He also felt a blast of heat. The draft created by the free winds caused his flame to burst into vigorous burning. Jond, who had arrived to tend the fire, shivered in the draft and threw some more wood on the fire. As he did, he prayed for that happy hour when the ice wall would reseal itself.

Outside on the white cliff, Jendai smiled. Without losing any time, he turned and walked along the precipitous icy ledge. Delicate shapes of snow and ice twisted out before him creating a wonderland of frosted castles and crystal spires. The fury of the canyon winds made him hurry, stopping only here and there to turn his back toward them and catch his breath. Whenever he felt able to continue, he turned into the wind again.

Advancing in this manner, it was well after midday when he came to the end of the narrow ledges on which he had been walking. His heart quickened its pace; he was at the high rim of the North Slide. A stone trough had been built in the summer by chiseling the stone to a long slide that was smooth when frosted with ice.

He feared and anticipated the North Slide. It was a horrendous plunge of thousands of feet, but the gradual grade made the slide relatively safe. Besides, it had been lipped on either side to prevent the Moonrhymes who trusted it from flying off to an icy death.

Jendai turned his back on the wind to rest one last time. When he felt that he could face the winds again, he sat down and inched his way cautiously to the edge of the precipice where the slide began. Before him, the white slide descended, gradually disappearing into a hazy infinity of mists and fluffy clouds through which he himself would travel. When at last he reached the top, he swung his legs over the edge. Closing his eyes and imagining himself brave, he pushed himself down the slide.

The pail at his waist clattered on the surfaces just behind him, and they both flew at a marvelous rate down the long slide. When he had hurtled down the first thousand feet, the slide curved and turned behind a shaded section of wall. Here he was sheltered from the wind, and when the course of the slide straightened again, the wind had all but stopped. He felt as though it was suddenly summer. The icy wind howled above the thinner altitudes of the slide.

For nearly an hour, he plummeted downward and finally reached the frozen lagoon at the bottom of the cliffs. This was the greatest fun of all. He spun out awkwardly onto the ice, his legs upward for awhile and then his seat. His bright maroon clothes surprised him with their bold color. He had not seen them in outside light since the beginning of winter. Now they gave him the appearance of a colorful acrobat skating uncontrollably across the wide lagoon. Finally he skidded to a stop. He tried twice to stand, but slipped and fell both times.

When he was free of vertigo at last, he stood up firmly upon the ice and laughed into the morning sun. Then he turned his back on the slide and walked north for the rest of the day. There were places where the snows seemed to be crusted, and yet if he tried to walk on it, the crust would break, spilling him through the surface into the softer snow beneath. By nightfall he came to flat ice plains that made walking easier. Fortunately, there was no wind. He found a thicket of young shrubs and lay down behind them to take his first rest. They would protect him if any sudden storms arrived during the night.

None came, and Jendai awoke to the brightest sun shining upon the whitest snow he had ever seen. He made sure the pail remained tied to his waist. Then he picked up the bundle of wood in his back pouch, swung it over his shoulder, and started into the snow-bright morning. He ate only such provisions as he needed. His strong legs carried him north for three uneventful days until he came to the steppes.

Here the land rose slightly over the next three days. Traversing the rising wilderness, he reached the Ice Fields of Selen at last. Before sundown on the seventh day, he thought he saw a vapor rising in the field near his camp.

"I must be wrong," he mused. His eyes were burning badly from the strain of the sun-white wilderness through which he traveled. "I must find a place to rest." The vegetation was sparse, but he found a natural shelter of frosted stone. It could in no way be called a cave, but at least the projection of rock jutted out far enough to protect him from the winds, should they drop in fury to the fields. He slept well.

When he awoke in the morning, he was completely covered with frost. His heart started as he heard his mind echoing with Sammuron's warning: "The Selendrenni will find you."

He stood immediately. He felt warm. The rocky cove had served him well. He heard the sound of water lapping and that intrigued him. Either he had been driven mad by the silent wilderness or he was very near to the Selendrenni. He looked around, then stared in amazement. The lapping waters were bubbling up in a lagoon only a few feet from the rocky cove in which he had slept.

"I must get some of that warm water in my bucket," thought Jendai. It was an impulsive thought that he should have considered longer, but he had been cold for days. In his excitement, he ran to the edge of the cove. The water was boiling! He lowered his pail into the water. It filled, but as he lifted it, two eellike creatures sprang up out of the seething water and landed on his gloved hand. He had little time to observe their gray-pink forms before his glove caught fire.

In spite of his pain, he held onto the bucket until he had carried it a safe distance from the shoreline. Then he set it down hurriedly. He tried to swat the tiny eels with his free hand, and immediately the other glove caught fire. In an instant, he came to himself and buried both of his flaming gloves in the snow. When the fire was out, he smashed the wormlike creatures on the frozen rocks and crushed the life out of them.

Once they were dead, he examined them. They were only a little longer than his stubby hands. Their lifeless bodies soon cooled and became encased in ice.

Jendai was glad to see that while his gloves had flamed brilliantly, they were not badly burned. The water before him still seethed. "There must be thousands of the fiery creatures," he said to the frozen wastes around him.

He puzzled over how to get them out of the boiling lagoon and into the pail of water he had dipped from their midst. His brow furrowed as he turned the matter around in his mind. The he smiled with inspiration.

He took off his back pouch, removed a dozen of the candolet twigs, and walked back to within a few feet of the shore. He laid the twigs in a circle and struck the two flint stones together. Sparks shot out. Three of the Selendrenni flew out of the boiling water and struck his heavy mackinaw. It caught fire. Jendai ran blazing to a snow bank and jumped into it. The impact killed the flaming Selendrenni.

"I came too close to the water," he noted. He looked in the snow for the flint rocks. He found them both and moved back several feet from the edge of the water. Cautiously he struck the rocks together. Sparks shot out again, and while their light made the Selendrenni leap up from the water, they could not fly that far.

Jendai breathed deeply and rearranged the twigs.

This time he struck the flints vigorously.

The sparks caused the tiny eels to jump up out of the water in great excitement. Jendai smiled and wondered what made these icebound creatures so excited by fire? The sparks ignited the candolet shrubs. Now the fire eels were jumping out of the water to great heights like a fountain of fire.

Jendai watched as finally they stopped their frantic antics. One of them wriggled out of the boiling water and crawled up onto the land. It inched and then glided like a snake until it was in the fire, standing upon the burning twig and dancing in delight at the flames. Carefully Jendai lifted the twig on which the small creature wriggled and removed the lid from his pail of water. Then he shook the Selendrenni into the pot and quickly replaced the lid.

He heard the Selendrenni vault against the lid of the pail again and again. The fire eel was clearly angered at being taken from the fire and dumped into the water. It intended to break through the pail and escape, but its efforts were useless.

Jendai felt exhilarated and yet fearful. He had one eel, but he needed at least three more to fulfill Sammuron's instruction. He knew that the instant he opened the lid to put another fire eel in, the first would jump out. The problem would become more complex each time he tried to add another eel to those already imprisoned in the bucket.

A dozen more Selendrenni glided like fiery serpents across the frosty rocks. They plunged into the fire, squealing in delight. There were more of the beasts than Jendai could hope for. But how was he to get the other three that he must take back and not lose the one he had?

He had learned his pattern of thinking from Sammuron. While the excited creatures squealed in the joy of the arctic fire, Jendai's face lit again in inspiration. Holding the pail between his hands, he began swirling the bucket with the lid tightly fitted, creating a fast-moving whirlpool within. When he stopped this swirling, the fire eel was silent, no longer hitting the lid of the pail. He opened the bucket and saw that the whirlpool had stunned the Selendrenni or at least made it too dizzy and muddled to escape. Quickly Jendai snatched another twig from the fire and dumped two singing eels into the boiling water of the bucket. Instantly angry, they vaulted upward from the water, but only succeeded in hitting the lid of the bucket before they fell back again. Now Jendai had three.

Once more he swirled the sealed pail between his hands, again creating the whirlpool until all was silent within. When he opened the bucket, he saw all three of his captives floating alive but inert, waiting to regain some sense of equilibrium before they flew at him and exploded in fire against his clothing.

By this curious process, he soon captured three more of the creatures. He sealed and bolted the lid. Having all that he needed, he sat down at a distance to watch the other Selendrenni playing in the fire. They had a wonderful time in the flames, but as soon as the fire burned down, they became incensed. There were thirty or so of them, and all of them turned—not back toward the frozen lake they called home, but toward Jendai.

Jendai grabbed his pail of captives and started running across the fields to the south. The Selendrenni glided across the arctic waste, leaving trails of water where their hot little forms seared the frozen ground. Steam and vapor rose as they pursued Jendai. Several of them flew at him like flaming darts, but he ran with such giant strides that he left the angry fire eels far behind. The creatures at last turned in disappointment and started back toward the steaming hole they had left in the ice.

Jendai laughed and stopped running. The six Selendrenni in his pail were all furiously thumping against the top of the bucket, trying to get out. Jendai could feel the heat rising from their prison. Threads of steam seeped out around the lid. He knew the steam they were creating would blow the top of the pail away unless he put them quickly to rest. Again he grabbed the bucket between both hands. The heat was so intense that he could barely hold it even through his thick gloves. He rotated it furiously until all of the eels were quiet.

He felt proud as he walked southward across the frozen fields. He was determined not to let the Selendrenni get their sense of balance for the rest of the day. He stopped occasionally as he walked among the blue drifts, kicking the snow with his maroon boots, and swirling the dizzy fire eels.

That first night he slept until the Selendrenni awakened him, noisily thumping against the lid of their prison. Groggy with sleep, he rolled over in the snow, grabbed up the pail, which he had set upon a rock, and sent the six eels swirling in their dark prison. He repeated the process twice during the night and every night thereafter.

Within the week, he came in sight of the Stone Sentinels of Demmerron Pass. He moved to the icy handholds chiseled into the face of the Moonrhyme cliffs. He feared Westwall in winter. The cave openings in the solid ice cliffs were plastered with the ice sheets that had formed during the winter months.

Jendai knew that even the youngest and most sure of foot could slip on the icy heights and be lost. While he reckoned himself brave enough to begin the climb, he heard the Selendrenni thumping in protest against the lid. The bucket was hot again. Once more he held it between his hands and was about to swirl it, when it occurred to him to press the steaming vessel against the cliff. He was struck by his own ingenuity: not only did the icy cliff cool the fever of the pail, but the hot bucket melted the film of ice from the footholds. Step by step, he made his way upward, while the fire eels melted the ice that would have prevented his ascent. Soon he came to the upper reaches where there was no ice, just a cold granite outcropping that rose sharply from the snowy lower walls to the ice-crusted upper walls.

Here he swirled the steaming canister, putting the Selendrenni to sleep, and climbed on.

Suddenly he found himself in the middle of a shower of ice

shards. Someone had seen his approach and knocked away the ice to free a frozen cave opening.

Within moments, Jond and a host of others had lowered a long rope that ended in a double-braided loop. At least six Moonrhymes held the other end of it. Jendai smiled up at them. The treacherous upper ledges lay just within reach. Here the going would have been slow and dangerous in spite of the fire eels' assistance.

Gratefully he took the loop of rope and slipped it over his bright maroon mackinaw and under his arm. One final time, he swirled the pail. The eels grew silent.

"All right, friends of Sammuron," he cried, "bring me home!"

Hearing his shout, they pulled the rope taut and Jendai let go of the handholds. He dangled like a spider on a silken web as his friends took in the rope, coiling it on the floor of the ledge, and pulled him swiftly up the ice-slick heights. Up he rose, until at last his friends pulled him over the edge of their icebound haven.

"Jendai!" they cried.

"Did you bring the Selendrenni?" his friends asked eagerly.

"Listen," commanded Jendai.

There was silence on the ledge. They all could hear the mysterious thumping that had begun within the canister.

Jendai and Jond found Sammuron waiting for them as they walked into his tunnelree. The old Moonrhyme smiled when he heard the fire eels objecting to their captivity.

"Build the fire higher than it has ever been before!" cried Old Sam.

In a little while, the fire roared. The Selendrenni canister bristled with steam. The heat of the room nearly drove the Moonrhymes out. It was like an oven. Sweat coursed down their faces. Jendai had thrown his maroon mackinaw and boots in the corner. Finally the old man removed his shirt and then his boots. His kilt was soaked with sweat.

Sammuron picked up the bucket and tried to remove the band that sealed it.

The container was an inferno. It was so hot that the old man could barely touch it. Jendai grabbed an axe and chopped at the hot steel band that sealed the lid to the barrel of the pail. Hot sparks shot out as the iron band broke free and the lid flew off. All six of the eels leapt out upon the floor followed by blistering trails of fire. They shrieked in ecstasy and glided into the hot flames that warmed the large black stones still resting in the iron kettle. Never had the rocks been so hot.

The Selendrenni were delirious with joy. They sang in a high and whistling harmony for a while. Then they began leaping upward into the air. Gradually, one by one, they swam the crest of the flames until they reached the iron kettle. Smoke now billowed out the draftway, coloring the whole sky above Westwall.

The Selendrenni sang ecstatically. Fire broke around their bodies as they danced onto the boiling surface of the two hot stones. Attacking the surface of the stones, they bored into the very burning surface of the two great spheres. Around their tiny little bodies a fiery slime oozed. Then they disappeared inside the stones.

Jond and Jendai were amazed.

But not Sammuron. "Watch!" the old man cried.

His own blind eyes could not behold what the wide eyes of his two companions refused to believe.

"The black stones are glowing red," said Jendai. "It's as though there is light coming from inside the stones."

The old man grinned. "They're not stones, Jendai."

"Not stones?"

"They are eggs."

"What?" cried Jendai.

"Just keep them warm, friend Jendai," said Old Sam.

His broad grin dropped to a wan smile and then a thoughtful emptiness. For a long time, silence filled the cave. Then a strange shadow crossed the old one's face that had nothing to do with the Selendrenni or the eggs.

"I tell you, there is a strange roaring in the earth," said the survivor of the cataclysm.

Jendai didn't hear a thing, but for an instant he sensed a deep tremor within the hot tunnelree, like the sound of feet stamping out a dark threat. The sensation passed.

The two red spheres glowed above the fire.

Grief seldom walks
On nimble feet.
It stumbles out of
Step and late.
In crippled trust,
It clings in lust
To tears, and then
To bitterness and hate.

CHAPTER II
The Ledge Too Far

VELISSA MOUNTED THE FALCON. At once, the magnificent bird hurtled into the sky. While the women of Canby watched, Orkkan turned toward the North. Orkkan knew that the very lives of these last survivors depended on him. If he failed, there was no one else to lead them. In the eyes of this piteous band of exiles, Raccoman and Velissa had abandoned them at the worst possible moment.

The falling snow had begun to cover the ledges of their flight. Their mood was bleak. Melancholy settled over the Canbies as they watched Velissa sail away on Rexel. Something of their hopes flew with her. Their husbands had all died in the battle of Demmerron Pass and now they themselves faced extinction.

Through the haze of the lightly falling snow, they could see the ruins of their beloved Canby. There, in better times, they had reared their children and cared for their men.

Orkkan mounted Collinvar and, with a sense of foreboding, watched Velissa disappear. In an effort to preserve the morale of the women, he said with mock cheer, "Come, the day is early! We can walk several miles yet if we begin now."

Orkkan had barely spoken when he felt awkward and arrogant riding the centicorn. In the silver saddle, he towered above the exiles. Orkkan felt ashamed. They did not need his gallantry so much as his nearness. He placed his boot in the footlocks and dismounted. His boots hit the snow with an audible crunch. He released the reins of the centicorn. He knew Collinvar would follow on his own. The group walked, disconsolately, up the trail.

When they had gone only a short distance, they heard the roar of the coming tilt winds. They all thought of Velissa and wondered if, indeed, she had made it back to the Hall of Dakktare. The biting cold of the wind, as it came over the mountains, caused them to huddle against the face of the cliff. They pulled their heavy clothes tightly around themselves and continued along the narrow ledge that led up the walls of the western ridges.

The skies opened and snow fell with a fury none of them could remember. In those places where the trail grew too narrow for safety, Orkkan crossed the ledges first. In other places, he brushed the heavy drifts from the ledge to make it safer for the women and children to follow. On the third afternoon of their pilgrimage, one of the older women lost her footing and fell. She plummeted through the snow mists that gathered like floss at the base of the precipitous canyon walls.

This grandmother was the first to die in the frozen expanse. They felt sure that she would not be the last. Her death filled the others with discouragement. Lack of wood on the ledges prevented Orkkan from building a fire. He found a wide place in the ridges and the two hundred women and children clustered around him. The snow continued to fall and the brightly colored garments of the widows of Canby grew dull beneath the thin layer of winter frost that froze to their clothing.

Orkkan suffered most. He looked at Collinvar and wondered why he had brought the centicorn to the upper ridges. These narrow passages now twisted toward the icebound Sentinels of Demmerron Pass. He doubted whether the women could survive the ledges, and he was almost sure that Collinvar would sooner or later fall and be lost. He did not know if the gallant steed could make his way back down the precipitous trails, but Orkkan loosed his saddle and removed it and then his halter. Collinvar turned and walked away, retracing the trail.

The next morning, the women stirred from a dismal slumber and rose to dust the clean, cold frost from their garments. The snow had stopped falling, but the heavy gray skies left little doubt that it would soon begin again. The women were too exhausted to continue the climb. Against Orkkan's hopes for them, they rebelled. They decided that they must halt the impossible exodus and return to the lower altitudes where they and their children might better survive the cold. Orkkan quailed at the thought of meeting Parsky. Though the Blackgill might pardon the women, he would show Orkkan no mercy. All would have to cast themselves on his mercy and beg to be allowed to survive in his diabolic kingdom.

Grentana was one of the younger widows in the group. She had no children, and so perhaps had less to risk than the others, but she had no desire to comply with the women's wish to return. She was determined to make her way forward. She would never beg Parsky for anything, even her life.

The other women in the snowy upper campsite thought Grentana a proud fool. The most she could hope for, they said, was to die on the ledges or to slip from the trail and perish. Still, Grentana decided that whatever the cost of continuing on, she would rather beg for a place to stay from the peaceable Moonrhymes than face the despotic Parsky. Orkkan believed that Grentana could better hope for clemency from Parsky than he could, but it was the women who felt Orkkan should go on with Grentana. He agreed that they could make the descent without him, and his own best chance of survival was to accompany Grentana. He placed two of the younger women in charge of the group and sent them to retrace their arduous ascent. He knew they would find their descent less perilous than their climb had been.

So the women turned back, while Orkkan and Grentana walked upward on the slippery trails.

At the bottom of the ledges some two weeks later, the starved and frozen exiles met a large band of Parsky's drones. They begged for mercy and received mercy of a kind.

Many of the smaller children and older women had died in the extreme cold. The remaining survivors received an armed escort back across the snowcap to the south. The weather was kinder on the plains, but the women were so cold and hungry that they greeted the icy dungeons of Maldoon with some cheer. At least they were out of the weather. They felt that life under the chain and key was better than death on the frozen ledges.

Grentana and Orkkan struggled upward toward the Moonrhyme caverns. The tilt winds came again, and this time they were both so weakened by hunger that they did not know if they could reach the maximum elevations.

They were nearly parallel with the stone sentinels of Demmerron Pass when they at last reached the final barrier. The snow had not fallen in a week, but the bright sun made the stone walls of the upper granite cascades as slippery as glass. The sun on the canyon walls nearly blinded them at times. Orkkan took his sword and tried to chop the ice from the ledge before them.

Believing the ledge to be clear enough, he leaned full against the frosty face of the cliff and proceeded forward. His sword got in his way, so he drew it from its scabbard and handed it back to Grentana. She intended to follow him across the treacherous ice wall that barred the way to the descending path beyond. The trail there was free of ice and snow. A large outcropping of stone sheltered it from the winter weather. "If only we can reach that part of the trail," cried Grentana, "our headway will be rapid and sheltered from the wind!"

Orkkan worked his way across the rim of ice and was almost to the end of the section when he slipped. He reeled and flailed his arms, struggling to keep his balance. Unable to do so, he fell outward silently through the frozen air. He held his voice lest his dying scream unnerve the brave Grentana as she struggled forward. The last surviving man of Canby was no more.

Compounding her grief, Grentana felt a new terror in her aloneness. She had a slight advantage over Orkkan, for she was much smaller, and so she inched forward to the treacherous lip of ice that had cost Orkkan his life. Then as she came to the narrow and shinning shelf, she did an insane thing. Instead of facing into the cliff as Orkkan had done, she leaned against the cliff outward into space. Cautiously she inched forward, not daring to set her feet down too firmly.

She steeled herself against her risky maneuver. She could see the pinnacles of stone thrusting upward through the snow far below her. They looked like giant teeth firmly planted in the jaws of death. She held her breath as she came to the place where Orkkan slipped. She took three uncertain steps. A tightness gathered beneath her heart. She felt herself beginning to slide, but she was strong and her lightness and strength now served her well. She thrust her delicate boots against the side of the cliff in a daring leap and passed above the gaping crevice that separated the icy ledge from the wider, sheltered, ice-free rim of stone. Below her passed the sharp stone spires that threatened to impale her.

She was not going to make it! The dry stones stuck her in the chest and her gloved hands grasped at and then closed upon the firm ridge of stone. She dangled above the abyss, begging her arms to be strong.

"Oh, Singreale!" she cried. "Not for this!"

Gathering strength from the name of Singreale, she drew her thin form upward. Her body writhed in her attempt to pull herself to the ledge. Her legs flailed the cold air, as she struggled upward with utter determination. She lifted her body till her elbows at last came up over the dry ledge and caught. Then she wriggled onto the sunlit ledge that felt warm beneath her body. With joy, she faced the morning sun and cried, "Singreale, Singreale!" Her love and exultation echoed through the snowy void and disappeared.

She rested before moving on. In less than half a day, the Moonrhyme cliffs loomed before her. They were free of ice for the most part. The ice had broken away from one of the windows, and she decided to enter the caverns through that opening.

She was still three hundred feet too low. She would have to gain access to the open window by using the handholds and toeholds chiseled into the face of the cliffs. Climbing had become a customary way of life for Moonrhymes, but Grentana was a Canby and not at all used to the steep ascent.

Undaunted, she began the upward climb until she had reached an outcropping of stone only a hundred feet below the open window in the face of the cliff. The afternoon sun had melted enough of the upper ice that a small rivulet of water crossed the cliff, staining the rock. Now she knew she would never be able to reach the window, since all the handholds would be sealed and packed with ice. She yelled a single word, "Hello!" Her bold greeting vaulted around the canyons, but no one appeared in the window.

She determined to wait a while before she tried to call again. She repeated her cry at intervals, each time daring to hope that someone inside the cliffs would hear. In late afternoon, she braced herself for a night on the ledge. It was wide enough to rest upon, and she felt that surely someone would be up on the morrow.

Daylight came all at once to the ledge. The night had been warmer than the previous one, and now the sun exploded on the cliffs, glaring directly into the open window. Grentana began her pleas for help once again.

Old Sammuron bade all to be quiet on that morning as Grentana yelled upward. "Listen," Old Sam commanded. "Do you hear nothing?"

"Is the earth roaring again?" asked Jendai.

"There is someone on the ledges—a woman" said Old Sam.

Jendai could hardly believe Old Sam, yet he had never known him to be wrong. The wood-bearer raced through the tunnelree and came at last to the opening. He stared downward.

Grentana smiled upward.

"Just a moment!" cried Jendai. He disappeared from the opening. In a few moments, he returned with a group of husky Moonrhymes and a rope. They lowered the familiar rope from the opening. Grentana, with relief and joy, slipped the loop down over her upper torso and fastened it beneath her arms.

"Don't let go!" cried one of the Moonrhymes who assisted Jendai.

"You may be sure of it!" Grentana called back.

"Here we lift!" Jendai yelled downward into the cold but sunny air.

The Moonrhymes began to hoist her up, passing sections of the rope from one hand to the other. They pulled her up until she passed by another frozen, glazed tunnelree. At last, she swung gently only a few feet beneath Jendai and the others. She swayed a thousand feet above the canyon floor only a moment before they drew her in.

She was saved!

These Moonrhymes were all strangers to her, but her gratitude was so great that she clasped Jendai. He was delighted that he happened to be the closest to her when she stood at last in the tunnelree opening.

"I'm saved!" she cried.

"Indeed you are," answered Jendai.

It seemed to Jendai that she was winter's special gift to him. In her excitement, she hugged him again, and again Jendai was glad that he was nearest at hand. Her embrace was firm and he felt exalted as he looked upon her beautiful face. Jendai wondered if it was because he had kept Old Sam company for so many years that she seemed especially pretty. Whatever the reason for his fascination, Grentana seemed to him the most beautiful woman he had ever seen.

Well, perhaps her face was a little squarer than he might have liked. Still, her eyes were soft and her brow noble and high. Her hair fell free about her face and her sidelocks were a delicate caress to her soft yet strong features. They stared at each other for quite some time before he managed the presence of mind to ask,

"Where have you come from?"

Her lips parted for a moment before she answered, and he had a sudden urge to embrace her once again. He set the urge aside as she answered simply, "I have come from Canby, across the western ledges."

"But how?" Jendai was overwhelmed by his inner vision of the treachery of the upper ledges near Demmerron. "How?" he repeated. "Surely not across the ledges of Demmerron?"

As he spoke, Grentana was remembering with horror the sight of the silent Orkkan falling . . . falling . . . falling. The image paralyzed her, forbidding her to speak. "I am alive! Alive, by Singreale's mercy—I am alive!" she cried at last.

She closed her eyes to stop the tears prompted by all that she had seen. Now, finally, she knew she was free to fall, and she fell forward, unconscious. Jendai caught her. He was powerful from his seasons of hauling wood up the same cliffs that Grentana had just ascended, and she seemed light to him. Those who had helped him in lifting her to safety departed to their own tunnelrees and reported to all they met in the stone corridors that a woman from Canby had arrived in the Moonrhyme settlement.

Jendai carried her easily to his own tunnelree, placed her silent form on his bed, and studied her. In the dim light of the torches, he again affirmed her striking beauty.

In her unconscious delirium, Grentana saw only summer. The heat of Old Sam's fire made her feel its warmth and set her visions in sunny fields. Jendai could in no way know what prompted her smile, but it pleased him. The sleeping Grentana smiled because she was with her husband again, working in the warm fields of Canby. She carried a basket through an untroubled land of sunshine. She and her young husband were filling the basket with vegetables and fruit against the cheerful winter when there would be fireplaces and hot tea and dancing.

Grentana slept for hours. When finally she awoke, her consciousness returned too suddenly. In the dark tunnelree, she looked puzzled, unable to recall how she had come to this place.

"Where am I?" she demanded.

"In my home," answered Jendai, gesturing toward the ceiling of his tunnelree.

"Oh, my darling Ganarett!" she cried and threw herself at him, nearly knocking him over. "They told me you were killed at Demmerron!" She held Jendai close, and his closeness brought back for a moment the lost reality she had just been dreaming of. Then she pushed him away.

"You are not Ganarett!" she cried.

"I would that I were," answered Jendai, "for you have just embraced me as you must have often embraced him. Who is he?"

"He is—or was . . ." She began before her voice flattened and refused to punctuate her sad ending with finality.

"All right, who was he?"

"He *was* my husband!"

"Was? Why not *is*?" asked Jendai, daring to probe more deeply.

She did not answer.

"You have a husband," Jendai declared, allowing his disappointment to show.

"I had a husband," Grentana corrected him. "Like all the others, he was killed by the catterlobs at Demmerron."

"Oh, I'm sorry," said Jendai. Yet, he was not altogether sorry. He could tell that Grentana had married young and was still young.

"And what happened to your children?" he asked.

"We had no children," answered Grentana. "But my Ganarett so wanted me to give him a daughter. I used to pray to Singreale to give us a daughter. He never did. But if we had been married longer, I am sure he would have. It is so warm in here."

"It is Old Sam's fire. He is incubating the eggs."

"What?" asked Grentana. "Old Sam's eggs make it warm?"

"No, it is the fire that warms the eggs that also warms all the tunnelrees in this section of the Moonrhyme dwellings."

Grentana began to shiver uncontrollably.

Jendai reached out to touch her forehead. She shrank back, but did not manage to withdraw before he had felt her brow. She was burning with fever.

"You're not well," he said. "I will get Old Sam to tell me what herbs to give you. You will be well before long." Grentana's eyes grew wide with fear.

"Leave me alone!" she screamed and then fell unconscious once again. Jendai brought handfuls of ice and placed them around her face. The wood-bearer attended her while her sickness continued into night and into day. After three days, her fever had subsided, but not her delirium.

By the light of a dim lamp, she awoke as Jendai was leaning over her to change the poultice Old Sam had created for her. Grentana once again looked into his strong and handsome face and cried from her delirium: "Ganarett . . . oh, Ganarett, I love you." She reached up to him so imploringly that Jendai was torn between pity and desire. He fell into her embrace, and she clutched him as strongly as her weak arms would allow. At last, she fell back exhausted and slept the remainder of the night.

Jendai could not sleep.

There were many bachelors in the cavern of the Moonrhymes. Like Canby, the Moonrhyme enclave had three men for every woman. Thus two-thirds of all their men were doomed to bachelorhood. Jendai was among that cursed lot. He had never been embraced by a beautiful woman before. Ganarett—whoever he had been—was dead. Jendai was glad. Jendai also felt ashamed that her grief was such a consolation to him. Yet, right or wrong, he could not help how he felt.

Grentana's arrival in Jendai's tunnelree caused a great deal of interest among the other Moonrhymes. Several bachelors came just to stare at the woman who slept there.

"Singreale just dropped you a woman upon the ledge, did he?" remarked one of the envious bachelors.

"That he did," laughed Jendai. "But listen, lads, before this Grentana fell unconscious, she told me that her husband, like all the other men of Canby, had been killed by the catterlobs at Demmerron."

"What's that she said?" asked one of the older bachelors.

"A city of widows! A city of widows!" cried another of the bachelors in a moment of insight.

Jendai fell silent as he considered that the other women of Canby, like Grentana, must also be overwhelmed by grief. However, his mood could not remain gray for long. His face brightened, and he exclaimed, "Do you know what that means, good fellows? In the valley, there is a city of women without any men, and here are we in this enclave, a city of men with very few women. Why, we must see what we can do to bring the two cities together."

"The idea is exhilarating!" exclaimed another Moonrhyme bachelor.

"We could bring a little more cheer to these tunnelrees. We need dances where the men can dance with women. What do you say to that, my good Moonrhymes?"

A cry of assent rose, making it clear that the prospect created no little excitement.

Unfortunately, the cheer caused Grentana to stir in her slumber, and so Jendai drove the others away to allow her to sleep undisturbed. He knew that if her progress continued, she would soon be well. He could hardly wait till then.

By morning, she felt better. Old Sam, blind as he was, prepared the sleeping widow a bright bowl of broth. The aroma came as a delight after her weary struggles. The effects of her ordeal on the icy ledges also passed as the fever left her.

Her clear state of mind held one disadvantage for Jendai: she never again confused him with Ganarett, her late husband. He sat and visited with her while she gained strength from Old Sam's broth. At length, she smiled and said as one who had confused things in a troubled sleep, "Are you the one they call Sammuron?"

"No, Sammuron is the old man who keeps the fire," he laughed.

"And you mentioned eggs—the old man who keeps eggs?" ventured Grentana.

"Yes. Sammuron is incubating the eggs."

"What sort of eggs?"

"Before the cataclysm, there were salamanders abundant in these canyons and caves. Old Sam believes these two eggs are the last around."

"Will they hatch?" asked Grentana.

"Old Sam believes they will. And I myself brought the fire eels back from the Ice Fields of Selen. I watched the eels fertilize the eggs."

"Eels fertilize eggs?" asked Grentana.

"They are part of the life cycle. The Selendrenni thrive by the millions in the summer sluices in the Ice Fields of Selen. The great salamanders that once deposited their eggs in the icy lakes are gone now, but the eels remain."

"Will you take me to the tunnelree of Old Sammuron?" asked the beautiful Grentana.

"When you are stronger. But today you must rest." For personal reasons, Jendai hesitated to bring his patient into the fuller life of the community. She was already the main subject of conversation among the other young bachelors of the enclave. He wanted to keep her to himself as long as he possibly could.

"Tell me," he said, "while you rest, of the battle of Demmerron

Pass." His suggestion stirred an old grudge to life.

"I do not blame Raccoman Dakktare, altogether," began Grentana. "But he was the one who suggested that our husbands try the long and cold autumn march to the north. He felt that if we could dig a trench across the narrow canyon between the Sentinels of Demmerron, we could keep the catterlobs away from our border. His plan went awry. All the men, including my Ganarett, were killed. I cannot forget the last night he held me before he left. He seemed to sense that Raccoman's venture would end unfavorably. He confessed to me that he feared the Sentinels of Demmerron more than all else and that he. . . ." She could not go on.

In the long silence that followed, Jendai sensed the weight on her soul. She could not have been more than one hundred and eighty-five years old, yet she seemed as bent and weary as Old Sam when he picked up a bundle of candolet bark for his aging fire.

Jendai knew what he had to ask. "How did you get to the ledges through the ice and heavy snows? There are places in the canyon where the snow would bury an entire catterlob. How did you make it through?"

"Raccoman and Velissa and Orkkan suggested that we follow the upper ledges and try to reach the caverns of the Moonrhymes. We might have succeeded, except that the snows came early and would not cease. I can only hope that the rest of the widows and children made it safely back to the plains of Canby."

"But they'll be killed there by Parsky!" Jendai exclaimed. "What hope have they in the unprotected plains?"

"They would have died on the ledges, anyway. I cannot imagine the older widows and the grandmothers and the children ever surviving the leap that I myself barely made when I traversed the last of the ledges. Even Orkkan was lost."

"Orkkan of Canby—lost?"

"Yes, he slipped and fell. But he remained brave to the end, refusing to cry out even in the moment of his death. I think if he had, I would never have had the courage to go on."

"Ah, but you did have the courage, Grentana," said Jendai. "And now you are here in my tunnelree. I am glad!"

"I, too, am glad," Grentana acknowledged, then abruptly returned to her tale. "Velissa flew away."

"The star-watcher's daughter?"

"Yes, she and Raccoman shared the golden glider, providing she and Rexel were able to make it back."

"Why would you doubt that she made it back?" asked the woodbearer.

"Because shortly after Velissa left, the tilt winds came in fury. I wonder that anyone could survive those winds, especially in flight."

Grentana ceased talking. Jendai could tell that she felt a great deal of antipathy for Raccoman and Velissa. Graygills rarely harbored resentment for anyone, yet she seemed to have a great deal for the welder and his wife.

Jendai had long known of Raccoman. His father, Garrod, had been a famous Moonrhyme, as had his Uncle Krepel. Jendai had resented Raccoman for choosing to live in the plains rather than staying in the enclave. Somehow he felt that although Raccoman was only half Moonrhyme, he should have stayed with his father's people.

Jendai had further reason for resenting Raccoman. He had seen Velissa at Krepel's observatory several times and had been intrigued by feelings of love for her. He thought that she was beautiful beyond all others. He loved the way she looked in her blue dress and boots. He loved her saucy, flirtatious ways. He had considered the idea of bringing her home one day as his own bride, to the caverns of the Moonrhymes.

Jendai had gone to Krepel's party the evening that the house was attacked by the armed catterlob. Like Velissa, he refused to eat Parsky's evil stew, and so he remained uncontaminated. Having eaten no meat, his gills were still as gray as Raccoman's. However, Raccoman could dance and sing and make ballads. Even at the fateful party, Jendai felt inept and prosaic as he watched the thousand-year-old Raccoman dance and sing so enchantingly that the lithe and youthful Graygill lass was caught in his spell. Jendai fled into the darkness as they were attacked, and he only learned much later what befell Raccoman and Velissa. The tragedy of that terrible night was mixed with his disappointment at watching them leave the party together.

Wherever the welder and his wife were now, however, was a matter of small consequence to him, for he had Grentana with him in his own tunnelree.

Seeing the weak and tired Graygill lass before him, Jendai finally put his animosities for Raccoman aside.

Grentana slept.

When she awoke in the afternoon, they discussed the sailplane that Raccoman had built and how he and Velissa intended to avoid Parsky's awful war. It seemed that the Dakktares lacked compassion. They had abandoned the widows to seek their own safety. Grentana had her own reasons for resenting Raccoman.

In the days that followed, the entire Moonrhyme enclave learned of the Paradise Falcon and of Raccoman and Velissa's planned escape. None knew for sure that they had reached safety, but that was of secondary importance. The great tragedy lay in their desire to escape during the thick of the fray. Grentana blamed Raccoman's bad counsel for the destruction of the village of the plains. No one knew what had become of the widows of Canby. The Moonrhyme men were intensely interested in the fate of those women.

The months passed.

On the first day of spring, Jendai felt a strong sense of elation. Although Grentana had selected an empty tunnelree as her home, she never abandoned her interest in the Moonrhyme who had first shown her so much concern. Her affection for Jendai was plain to see. Their relationship deepened to the point that Grentana showed little interest in any of the other Moonrhymes.

The sun had been warm for so many days that the upper snows melted from the ledges. Old Sam's wood-bearer and Ganarett's widow walked upon the sunny ledges. They talked and smiled and filled these bright middays with talk of the future and what possible offensive the cliff-dwellers might launch against Parsky of Maldoon. They both wondered where the widows were and if any of them had survived.

Nestled back against the rocks, they surveyed the snowy valleys below. Jendai slipped his arm around his companion's waist and smiled into her eyes. They were alone. In the distance, a ganzinger that had been flying toward them turned its head and tipped its wings in approval before it turned its flight in another direction. Nothing beheld them but the sun, and Jendai, knowing the sun would not tell, turned to Grentana and kissed her.

For a moment, she seemed to enjoy it, but then she quickly pulled away and stood up.

She turned from Jendai, but he followed her.

"I love you, Grentana." He spoke the words into her hair.

She replied only two words, "Please . . . Ganarett."

Her two words were enough to tell Jendai he had been too bold. He now hoped his boldness would not dampen their future relationship. He saw that Grentana needed more time. She had barely been a widow for six months. It was too soon to expect her to turn from those memories that had been her life for so many years. Such memories had once steeled her to endure a future that was not entirely secure.

"I only thought," Jendai began, "that since Ganarett was killed at Demmerron Pass, you might be open to a new. . . ."

"Please, please!" Now Grentana was growing angry.

Jendai stopped, realizing that he had only made matters worse by trying to straighten them out. How he wished that he could learn the proper way of dealing with women! Yet, how was he to learn about these matters? No woman had ever shown any interest in him before. He had long ago decided that if the opportunity presented itself, he would be as aggressive as he needed to be. He had seen the lonely majority of the men who lived without families, and he knew he did not want their disconsolate existence. Now his aggressive determination not to be wifeless had led him instead to be crass.

Even so, he knew—and he sensed Grentana knew it, too—that he did not want just any woman. Only Grentana would do. He had determined she would be his, and he felt she wanted him to pursue her. Still, the ghost of Ganarett made her feel guilty for allowing Jendai to kiss her.

As the weeks passed, Grentana more and more wanted Jendai to be hers as she had once been Ganarett's. Even though she did not feel secure at the heights, she was adjusting to the cliffs and felt in time she might even learn to climb them and help with the farming of the valleys. This spring the farming would be dangerous, for as soon as the snow disappeared from the valleys, Parsky would be likely to bring his war to the canyons.

At last, Jendai approached her and said, "I'm most sorry, Grentana. I have been so forward. Can you forgive me?"

She smiled, and it seemed to him she was about to speak when they heard a cry.

It was one of the men of the enclave. "Come, Jendai! Old Sammuron needs you!"

Jendai ran down the ledge and climbed the seventy or more feet up the face of the cliff as quickly as he could. Grentana admired his agility on the face of the cliff. He flew up the handholds as few in the enclave could do. He was clearly motivated by fear that something might be wrong with Old Sammuron.

He had already reached the top of the cliff when he looked down and saw Grentana. "Wait!" he cried. He disappeared, and in a little while four Moonrhymes appeared and lowered a looped rope to lift Grentana to the window ledge. Grentana removed the rope and hurried down the sunless cave corridor.

In a moment she arrived at the hot labyrinth and turned directly into Sammuron's tunnelree. She was greatly relieved to see Jendai's blind friend standing, talking with his wood-bearer.

"Listen," the old man was saying. "Do you hear anything, young Jendai?"

"The crackling of the flames," came the reply, although the flames burned lower than before.

"Not the flames, my boy!"

Jendai looked upward. The crackling noises now seemed to be coming from the iron kettle.

"My vigil is at an end," Sammuron declared.

What can he mean? Jendai wondered. Yes, he thought, it must be—no, it cannot be! After all these centuries. Since the very cataclysm, the old man has been heating these stones—the eggs. Could it be?

"Lower the kettle." Old Sam spoke with resolve now.

Jendai went to the kettle and loosened the chains. They were hot—made hot by the flames that had seared them for centuries.

"Owww!" he cried, quickly wrapping the chains back around the double pegs. He ran to the back of the cave and found a pair of ash-smudged gloves. Slipping them on quickly, he returned to the chains and unbound them, gently easing the tension.

Dutifully, the high iron kettle descended. More and more Jendai fed the sooted chains through the high crane. Lower and lower the basket dropped, until at last the black spheres lay at the very feet of Old Sam.

Jendai left his gloves on. He had never realized the eggs were so large. They were half his size, but tied to the remote ceiling for so long, Jendai never had occasion to measure them.

"May I look?" asked Grentana, cautiously approaching.

The old man and the young man studied the eggs. The old man studied only with his ears, while the young man stared in disbelief. So did Grentana.

"Take them out of the kettle and lay them on the floor!" commanded Sammuron. The eggs were heavy and hot, and Jendai found them most difficult to lift out of the searing container. Their cumbersome immensity meant that Jendai could handle only one at a time. Each hot black egg rolled against his chest and darkly sooted his tunic as he picked it up. One after the other, he laid the eggs down as gently as he could, seeing that they nearly burned his hands to touch them.

"We won't need the iron kettle or the chains anymore," prophesied Old Sam.

Jendai pulled the hot chains and raised the empty iron basket over the fire again just to get it out of the way. He returned to Old Sam and Grentana, and all of them sat down to wait and watch. They did not have to wait long until they heard the same odd, cracking sound again. The black egg on the left began to rock. In a little while, so did the egg on the right. Both of them rocked with an exaggerated motion and then lay perfectly still. But as soon as they were still, the cracking noise began all over again.

Then the unbelievable occurred. A white and jagged line appeared upon the surface of one of the sooted spheres. A loud cracking sound accompanied the ever-growing fissure in the egg. Other cracks shot out like jagged bolts of lightning. Soon both the sooted balls were crossed and then crisscrossed in response to some inner pressure that broke their blackened crusts.

A large segment of the shell on the left fell away, and a claw thrust through the pink opening. Another segment of the shell broke, and a bony tail, still covered with birth slime, turned outward and struck Jendai's boot. The slime was hot, and as he reached down to brush it away, flame shot out upon his gloves.

Jendai wisely backed away and drew Old Sammuron and Grentana with him. He remembered the fiery sequence he had endured upon the Ice Fields of Selen.

More of the shell fell away from both spheres. Jendai did not know whether to run or to remain. Now the eggs seemed to disintegrate before their astonished eyes. There was more steam and slime. Pieces of the shells smouldered as they broke free, then caught fire. At last, the egg on the left was gone except for the cap of the shell that rested oddly upon the head of the lizardlike creature that had emerged.

When both of the creatures were liberated, Jendai could see that they were twice as long as he was tall. He wondered how the huge creatures ever had fit inside the confining black shells.

"Lizards?" asked Grentana.

Old Sam corrected her. "Not lizards—salamanders."

The salamanders had dusky, red skin and were spotted along their sides and backs with red speckles that glowed like fire. Their powerful forelegs ended in heavy claws that scratched sparks on the floor as they writhed in the newness of life. They looked first at the old man who had been so faithful in the long process of their incubation.

Their eyes stared steadfastly into the old eyes of Sammuron and seemed to be lit by some fire that blazed within. Sammuron could not see them, but Jendai could see that their fierce eyes held fire. A forked tongue issued out of each of their huge mouths, which opened all the way back to their hinged heads. Their tongues seemed to sparkle with brilliant light that fell and then exploded into flame on the cave floor. Grentana's guess that they were lizards was not far amiss.

Their appearance was lizardlike and their eyes, which sat far back on their heads, looked both evil and friendly.

"I am glad our friends have come at last," said Sammuron.

Jendai wondered why he called the evil-looking creatures his friends. "Whatever shall we do with them?" Jendai questioned.

"They have come to us from across the cataclysm," replied Old Sammuron.

"Yes, but how will we keep them? How will we tend them? Whatever shall we do with them?" Jendai's questions came rapidly together.

"They have come to us in a time of war!" Sammuron rejoiced.

"Yes, I know they have come to us in a time of war, but can they answer Parsky of Castledome?" Jendai looked at the creatures even as he asked the question.

He tried to imagine how the salamanders would ever be able to scale the castle walls of Maldoon. He could not wonder without protesting, "How will they help in the war? Can they climb the castle walls of Maldoon? They seem so ugly and powerless."

One of the ugly beasts apparently heard Jendai's innocent insult. He turned and opened his mouth. Fire shot out around his forked tongue, forcing Jendai to leap backward to avoid being burned.

"I'm sorry—you're not all that ugly," he told the offended salamander. "Still, Sammuron, how will they help us win the war against Parsky?"

The old man stood silent a moment. At length he spoke.

"Not that war!" he said. "Not the war with Parsky. They have not come for *that* war. They have come for the war we shall fight in the tunnelrees."

"What war in the tunnelrees?" asked Jendai.

"They have come to answer the roaring in the earth!"

The huge beasts slithered and crawled into the fire and lay there looking at those who had attended their hatching.

Fear is
A leering jackal,
Which haunts
The minds of men
And on the
Threshold snarls at boys
Who would
Turn home again.

CHAPTER III
The Return of the Graygills

TWO LONG WINTERS had come and gone since Velissa left the widows of Canby high on the ledges of Westwall. The ashes were two years old. Black cinders and old debris fouled the snow. The bright yellow wind foils of the Paradise Falcon stood in sunny contrast to the dull gray soil.

Velissa was home! The charred remains of the house where she had once lived marred the spirit that should have attended her homecoming. The red trees did not cheer her, for Quarrystone Woods now seemed ominous and unfriendly. Behind the bright glider grazed a condorg. As far as Velissa knew, it was the first time that any of the beasts had ever landed on the continent.

The sleek leathery wings of the condorg were folded comfortably at its sides as it nibbled the longer grass that protruded through the snow. In the Southern Continent, Velissa had always believed that the flying beasts were white. Now as she watched this one grazing in the snow field, she realized how wrong she had been. In the bleak, blue-white of the Northern Continent, she saw that the condorg was grayish pink, tinged with brown.

The night would show this one's true color as the daylight faded. For then it would begin to glow in the mysterious fashion of all condorgs. Its inner light would come through its skin, and at midnight it would glow diamond-white. Condorgs loved dark skies. Their strong inner light complemented the bright incandescence of the stars.

Raccoman was gone. He had decided to fly wide across the middle lands of Canby. He did not want Parsky of Maldoon to have the slightest inkling that the Dakktares had arrived home. Raccoman shivered at the memory of his friendship with Parsky. They would never be friends again.

In their return, Raccoman and Velissa had taken strong precautions against the Blackgill knowing they were home. They soared the night sky in a wide circle beyond the stone sentinels of Demmerron to fly west of the ridges and land unseen in Quarrystone Woods. It grieved Velissa when she remembered how happy Quarrystone

Woods had been until Parsky had discovered that Velissa's father kept the all-powerful Singreale.

Raccoman returned on the condorg and interrupted Velissa's reverie.

"Raccoman, I'm cold!" she exclaimed. It was not her nature to be short, and yet it sounded almost as if she were blaming Raccoman for her shivering. A bright frost bit the air. "I had forgotten how cold the winters are," she said.

Raccoman shrugged and replied:

I thought you liked the winterlands.
How can you scold
What once you called "the glorious cold"?

As he took the halter from the condorg he had only lately ridden, Raccoman knew his small rebuke would call his wife back to reality. She scooped a handful of snow, molded it into a loose ball, and hurled it at him. She aimed the white missile well, and it struck her Graygill husband full in the ear, fusing his sidelocks to his furry gills.

Velissa ran to him laughing. She embraced him fully, throwing her arms around his yellow mackinaw, and exclaimed:

This is a glorious snow—I never shall complain again.
Oh, Raccoman, I do declare, the candolet trees
Have never blazed so red!

"We are home!" cried Raccoman, as though it needed to be said.

"Raccoman, the slide!" shouted Velissa.

She remembered what he had never known. She ran to the back of the blue barn. There, a steep incline, frosted with new snow, beckoned to Velissa. She stood smiling at the top when her husband reached her side. Raccoman, a weary eight centuries older than his wife, arrived much later than she.

"So, this is the slide," he said.

Yes, yes, Raccoman!
How often I have seen this sight
Washed in the joys of winter light.
I love you!

She embraced him again and then pulled him to the ground. They kissed. Suddenly Raccoman felt himself sliding on the icy stones. They had moved too near the incline. He tumbled over the slide, dragging Velissa with him. Velissa's bright blue dress and boots twisted inseparably with his own clothes. They became a blue and yellow dervish, whirling out of control. They rolled until they thudded into a frozen bank of red grass and lay there laughing at the marvelous mishap. When the metal-worker gained control of his laughter, he declared:

Velissa Dakktare, we are home.
But maybe
We should be less athletic—
Remember the baby.

Raccoman patted her stomach. Velissa could not forget that she was carrying his child. He wanted a girl and she wanted a boy, but neither would get his or her wish for many, many months to come.

"How could I forget your son?" she asked, blowing the snow out of his shaggy eyebrows.

"No, how can you forget my *daughter*?" he corrected her, brushing the snow from her hair.

"Son!" she insisted.

"Daughter!" He was firm.

"Son! You'll see—son! SON!"

"Daughter! DAUGHTER! Whoop—Halloo! Behold!"

Orange-red fur had appeared in the red grass, and six sets of eyes watched them. Half a dozen creatures had formed a welcoming committee.

"Congrels!" Velissa exclaimed. She ran toward them. At first, the animals scampered away, but then slowly returned to her. She extended her hand, and they crept up to sniff her upturned palm. She picked up one gently and stroked it. Then they all ran bravely to her, begging her to touch them. They were happy that the Graygills had returned. Velissa and Raccoman played with the congrels, tossing them gently back and forth to each other and rolling them in the soft new snow.

From the top of the incline, two long shadows fell across them. A tall and handsome man cleared his throat and asked, "How can you frolic in the snow which makes us shiver just to walk through it?"

It was Hallidan who had spoken. He and Raenna, his new wife, had flown on their condorgs to this icebound land that Raccoman and Velissa loved, but the Star Riders found uncomfortably cold for all its beauty. Raccoman had assured them that they would soon become adjusted to the extreme temperatures of his beloved winterland. Both Hallidan and Raenna had brought heavy clothes to warm them against the northern winter. Hallidan had flown over the winterland many times at thin upper altitudes; he knew how to dress for survival and even enjoyed the northern climate. Still, it appeared that their complete adjustment would take more time than they had originally guessed.

"Join us! Come down the slide!" cried Velissa.

Hallidan shook his head. Raenna and Hallidan were twice the size of the Graygills, and their tall dignity was not well suited for the kind of frolicking tumble that delighted the Graygills.

Raccoman, seeing that his friends were in no mood for such a tumble, called up to them, "Well, then—here!" and threw a warm, orange bundle of fur to Hallidan. The congrel could hardly have been more surprised than the knight who caught the creature easily, stroked it, and handed it to his wife.

"What is this?" he asked Velissa who had scooped up another armful of the cuddly animals.

"Congrels!" cried Raccoman.

"The forest abounds with them," said Velissa. "Even the plains."

Raenna stroked the furry animal with her narrow, gloved hand and held it to her frost-tinged cheek. She was delighted by its incredible softness.

When the foursome had enjoyed quite enough of their homecoming antics, they put down the congrels, which followed them, cavorting at their heels all the way back to the pile of ashes.

"Velissa, where shall we stay?" asked Raccoman.

On their long flight back from Rensland, they had spoken of it over and over, finally deciding to stay in the observatory if it still stood. This would allow them to stable the condorgs in Collinvar's barn and, at the same time, take advantage of the fireplace that warmed the Blue Observatory. Seeing that the observatory was intact, they made their way to it.

Raccoman and Velissa entered the Blue Observatory through the weathered door. Hallidan and Raenna began to sense the difficulties that would be theirs in sharing the small observatory with the Dakktares. They realized how confining the place would be when they had to drop to their knees just to pass through the observatory door. Fortunately, the second level inside was more open and accommodating. It had been built to allow the barrel of the huge scope to swing upward and outward through the domed roof. The floor area, however, was small. Built by a race of people half the size of the Star Riders, the building, with its stonework and gabling, was only half the size that it needed to be to fit Hallidan and Raenna.

A heavy layer of dust covered everything. House cleaning would be the first necessity. The women agreed to go and look for wood, while the men began the dirtier work of sweeping and dusting and washing the floors and walls of the neglected enclosure. Raccoman and Hallidan cleaned the delicate mechanisms of the telescope meticulously. Raccoman saw at once that the observatory remained in excellent condition, and he hoped that in future days he would be able to clean the lenses and use the old telescope again. He had always enjoyed studying the night skies, but inwardly he desired to direct the old scope toward the distant and remote promontory of Maldoon. He knew the scope would reveal whatever news there was of Parsky.

While they were cleaning the old scope, Raccoman came across the small, hairline fissure that he had once been asked to weld. Now he regretted that he had never taken care of the simple assignment.

They next scrubbed the walls and shelves of the observatory. Hallidan was so tall that he could reach the top of the walls without even stretching. The shorter Graygill finished cleaning the portion of the wall that lay nearer the floor. Within another hour, they had washed even the quaint oval windowsills that decorated the sidewalls and let in the light from the snow-white candolet groves beyond the house.

The floors proved the most arduous task of all. They had tracked in much snow and ash from the remains of the burned house that stood directly between the observatory and the blue barn. The powdery ashes had been mortared with snow-water and took them nearly three hours to scrub clean.

With an hour of daylight remaining to them, the two men moved to the lower level of the observatory and began to clean the floor. At this first level, there was much structural bracing beneath the floor to support the great scope. The work here was most difficult for Hallidan. The ceiling was low, and he found that he was forced to kneel to handle the broom and brush, both of which were made for smaller men than him. Still, the pair worked at it, determined to surprise their wives with all that they had accomplished.

Meanwhile, Raenna and Velissa searched the area west of the barn for dead branches from the red trees of Quarrystone. Though the cold made their job unpleasant, they found many large fragments and, within a short time, had collected a great deal of wood. They dragged the chunks of bark west of the charred ruins of the old house. Velissa found an axe in back of the blue stable and chopped the wood into lengths that would fit the small fireplace. Within three hours, they had enough wood to warm the observatory for a month. Candolet burned slowly, and only a few chunks of the soft, hot-burning wood would give them the comfort of warm mornings at a time of year that the knight and his lady would find hard to endure. Once the sun had set, the foursome would be plunged into a fierce coldness that would be intolerable without heat.

When the women brought in the first armloads of wood, they cried in delight at the sight of the transformation in the observatory.

"Oh!" gasped Velissa. "It looks just like it used to—as if Father had just stepped out of it for a moment."

The others remained silent, not daring to interrupt her reverie.

"Well," said Dakktare at last, "it is just like it was then. Now, however, it must also serve as a bedchamber for four."

"Without any beds," laughed Hallidan.

"At least, for tonight," Raccoman replied. His face grew wistful, then brightened with inspiration. "Velissa, do you suppose any of the old beds would have remained undamaged at Krepel's?" he asked.

"Who can say?" she answered.

"For tonight," said Hallidan, "we'll sleep on the hard floor just as we did when we stayed in the cave and waited for Grendelynden."

"It will be the same, except here we'll have a fire."

They were all very hungry, for their provisions had been exhausted on their flight from Rensland, but none of them mentioned this. By mutual consent, they had learned that the best way to deal with hunger was to ignore it. To speak of food seemed to increase their need and add to their discomfort.

Raccoman ended their conversation by selecting several chunks of candolet wood and starting a fire. Velissa took a chunk also and separated the outer bark from the soft fibers beneath. Then from between the two layers, she peeled the thin inner bark and smiled.

"Raccoman," she laughed, "are there any vessels in the barn?"

It was nearly dark, but he dutifully drew his yellow mackinaw around him and left the house. Velissa had not realized until that instant how threadbare and ragged his old coat had become. The color had not faded, but years of wear had frayed the garment. She could only hope that before long a new age would begin and there would be cloth-workers who could make a new one.

Raccoman returned soon, carrying a large, deep kettle. It was half full of clean water. The unspoiled well outside the blue barn yielded up crystalline water.

"I used to feed Collinvar with this," she laughed, taking the kettle from Raccoman, and both remembered the proud steed with his arrogant silver horns.

Gradually, the couples were adjusting to life in the observatory. The women set the candolet tea to boiling and poured it into the same small alabaster flasks that had been their source of water for the flight.

The men took the condorgs into the blue barn. Taller than Collinvar, the large beasts could barely get through the door. Once inside, however, they found plenty of room. Raccoman also discovered that a sufficient supply of provender remained. The old place looked as if it had been left completely undisturbed since Velissa had last stabled the centicorn there. When the beasts were cared for, Hallidan hung their saddles across an idle beam, then stooped greatly and walked back out into the cold night.

The wind was beginning to blow.

The condorgs glowed softly in the scant interior light of the blue barn.

Raccoman remained inside the barn and felt his way along the string loft. All old barns had such lofts, where the Estermannians hung great strings of dried fruits and vegetables for the winter. In the darkness, his hand touched great welcome hulks of substance.

"This larder is still filled with dried foods!" he cried. "The old astronomer must have left them." Raccoman tore loose two strings that contained several pounds each. "This is glorious—there is an abundance left! Halloo, Hallidan, we are saved! The string loft is filled!"

Hallidan, well outside the barn, heard Raccoman crying the good news. Soon both of the starving men were rejoicing at the find. They called Velissa and Raenna to join in their excitement.

They had uncovered abundance, and their hunger was the only formal invitation they needed to guide themselves to the feast. They warmed the vegetables and ate the fruit, which they laid on the small observatory table. The candolet tea issued bright green vapors from its opaque red liquid.

Raccoman exalted some of the food and spoke the words that the men of his race had used for centuries:

To the maker of the feast
To the power of loaf and yeast
Till the broth and bread have ceased
Gratefulness is joy.

There was neither broth nor bread, but it was a feast indeed.

"Do you suppose," Velissa asked cautiously, "that the old handmill might have a store of unmade grist nearby?"

There was a lantern still hanging in the observatory. Raccoman took it from the wall.

"The lantern is full of collen oil!" he exulted. He struck a small flint stick and ignited the lantern.

Velissa's question about the possibility of unmilled grist had stirred him. He dashed to the barn, in too great a hurry to button his mackinaw, and ran to a rough gallery past the open vault of the barn. The condorgs were only slightly disturbed by his sudden entrance. He knocked open the door to the milling room. Bags of grist—some ground, some waiting their turn to be ground—filled the room that lay sunken into a stone floor. Raccoman turned the handle of the handmill and laughed out loud in the dim light. Then he dipped into a nearby yeast crock and smiled again.

"Bread in the morning!" he cried as he re-entered the house and saw the bewildered faces of his guests. He snuffed the lantern and hung it next to the hearth.

Soon they were all enjoying with relish the hot food and brisk tea. The fire flickered throughout their cheerful conversation. As they sipped their second cups of tea after dinner, Hallidan walked to the hearth and threw another chunk of candolet wood on the fire. Then he returned to his place and sat down once more.

"So this is life in the winterland," he mused as they all watched the fire. Raenna snuggled against his broad chest. The Graygills nestled themselves into a similar twosome.

"Life in the winterlands has a charm I could grow to like," said Raenna as she snuggled further into the slumping form of her husband. She pulled his great arm around her waist.

"Wait till you smell the bread in the morning. There is nothing like the smell of hot bread on a cold morning," Velissa told her with a smile, then added, "And the morning will be cold. Doldeen never ceased to complain."

Her voice trailed off. The amber flickering of the fire colored her mind and mood as she remembered Doldeen. Her old friend. The old days. Her father. Collinvar. Where were they now? Her mind was full of demons and ghosts of things that used to be, but were no more.

The four travelers watched the fire in silence, but their thoughts raced. What were they doing here? Why had they come back?

"Hallidan," asked Raccoman, "why did you come back with us?

Was it just the war
Or something more
that made you soar
the studded sky?

Raccoman's jingle was a fair question.

"Who can say, friend Raccoman?"

"You can say, friend Hallidan." Raccoman was insistent.

"All right, I will say. I have an old account to settle. My brother."

"So, it's Thanevial, then," Raenna interjected. "You're going to have to settle your account with Thanevial."

"I will not have him ruining two worlds!" Hallidan grew angry.

"It's been six months since he left the summerlands. It will be six months more before he reaches the winterlands," said Velissa. "So we have time. At least it took your father a year to make the trip," she continued, turning to Raccoman.

Raccoman spoke a sombre rhyme:

We must go to the caverns of the Moonrhymes
To inform them that these are desperate times.
The Moonrhymes are not fighters.
I'm afraid they will submit—yes, succumb
When the Drogs begin to come.

Raccoman was right. The fact that the Moonrhymes lived in the cliffs declared to the whole world that they would avoid open conflict whenever they could. Their rocky caverns had served as their armor. Now they were trapped between the foes in the valleys and a dark and ruthless enemy in the sunless tunnelrees they called home.

"Are you sure it took my father a year to walk the undersea passageway?" Raccoman asked Hallidan.

"Eleven months," replied Hallidan as he slumped before the fire.

"Then we do have time to warn the Moonrhymes," said Raccoman.

"Time," agreed the slouching knight.

A silence had fallen over the group, when all of a sudden Raccoman started up from his comfortable position.

"But they're faster!" he cried. "Oh, no—we forgot, Hallidan!"

"Whose faster?" Velissa asked.

"The Drogs," Raccoman explained. "The Drogs are twice my father's size. They are bound to make the trip faster than he did."

"You're right!" Now Hallidan sat up, too.

"They could be there sooner, perhaps twice as fast!" Raccoman cried.

"Perhaps they are—" the knight began.

"Already there!" said the Graygill, completing his thought.

"Tomorrow we must go to the caverns and try to warn the unsuspecting Moonrhymes."

The new urgency with which Raccoman spoke dominated the mood. The conversation stopped for a few minutes as each of the four tried to visualize what might now be taking place if the Drogs were already in the Moonrhymes' enclave.

"Do you suppose that Parsky has any idea that we've returned to Quarrystone Woods?" asked Velissa at last.

"Certainly not yet," said Raccoman.

So many things had happened to them on this single day of their homecoming. Raccoman, who had settled a bit after his last interjection, suddenly sat up again, and Velissa realized what her husband was thinking, for the same thought had just come to her.

"The scope!" she cried.

Hallidan and Raenna were puzzled as they watched the two

Graygills run to the barrel of the great scope. The rain had kept the upper end clean. Raccoman wiped the eyepiece quickly with his sleeve. He lowered his face, peered through the tiny glass, and smiled. By this time, Hallidan was at his side. His great size almost intimidated the Graygill into giving up his place at the scope.

"Velissa," cried Dakktare, "I've forgotten how beautiful the heavens are at night!"

The sight of Hallidan's belt buckle in his face, however, brought Raccoman back to the real issue. With some reluctance, he moved away and let his gigantic friend look at the night sky. Hallidan looked for a long time, as though his eager eyes could not quickly drink in the majesty of the heavens he had recently traversed. Though Hallidan knew the sky well, he could not withdraw from its overpowering nearness.

The Star Rider dropped to one knee to accommodate the low level of the eyepiece. "I see the universe now in a new way, though I have ridden it a hundred thousand times. Nothing changes up there," he said, pointing up toward the ceiling of the observatory. "They never move, the stars. How constant they travel and yet never travel!"

For a long time after that, he said nothing until Raccoman cleared his throat. Then the skies were shattered for the reluctant Hallidan as Raccoman took possession of the scope once more.

"Suspend the vertical rotor, Velissa," he said.

Velissa obeyed his request, pulling the pin from the barrel of the scope. The cradle of the telescope groaned and then tipped an inch or so. Velissa knew what her husband was looking for.

"Can you see Maldoon?" she asked.

The hulk of the old castle appeared to Raccoman as a dark blur upon the horizon.

"I can," answered her husband. "There are torch fires burning on the upper towers, but it is too dark to see anything more than a silhouette against the stars. We shall have to wait till morning to have a better look."

The foursome agreed to have a final cup of candolet tea before they retired.

"You know, my dear, the Moonrhymes are in a most lamentable position." Raccoman was now thinking out loud:

Unless they band together,
They might be trapped
Between the Changelings and the weather.

"There are only four of us," said Raenna. "But maybe we can somehow conceive a plan to keep the Moonrhymes safe. Oh, that we had a hundred of Ren's best knights—and soon."

"Or the Miserians," offered her husband.

"Perhaps the knights and the Miserians are too tall to fight in the tunnelrees of the Moonrhymes," objected Velissa.

"They are no taller than the Drogs," insisted Hallidan. It was a point well made. "Many of the tunnelrees are too short to accommodate either the knights or Changelings," Raccoman observed. "Still, the Drogs will find a way through, and they must be stopped!"

"We will find a way." Velissa was nearly pleading. "If the Moonrhymes stay in their high cliffs, they will certainly be slaughtered by the Drogs. If they leave, they will be eaten by Parsky's catterlobs. In the caves, they face certain death—but in the valleys, they would fare as badly as the Canbies did before the monstrous beasts."

Raccoman began again. "We should all be safe at the Blue Observatory until winter is finished," he said. "But once it is, we must think of a way to liberate Maldoon and put an end to Parsky's control."

They all agreed.

"There is an old man among the Moonrhymes. He is blind," said Raccoman, turning the conversation in a new direction. "His name is Sammuron. He is well known throughout all the winterlands, for he knows all the secrets of the earth. He has been blind for a thousand years, but he hears everything. He will know if the Drogs are in the nearer tunnelrees of the high cliffs. He keeps a fire."

"A fire?" asked Raenna.

"A fire," repeated Raccoman. "He has kept it since first the cataclysm receded. There he warms two old stones as though his life depended upon them. The stones are black with the soot of the centuries and no one knows why he keeps them warm. In his blindness, he is attended by a young man who brings him wood in the summer to store in the tunnelrees, so that the fire will never go out and his stones will never cool."

"Why?" asked Hallidan.

"I do not know," said the Graygill welder. "What is important is that he alone may be aware of the coming of the Changelings. I will go to him. We can use Rexel to summon some of the Moonrhymes to the windows of the cliffs to lower us a rope. Otherwise, we cannot make it to the upper chambers this time of year. It is the only way."

"So Rexel will travel with us?" Hallidan asked.

"Rexel—where is he?" asked Raenna.

Suddenly, they all realized they had not seen the falcon since the landing or even before. But Rexel was never in real danger. He flew high, sighting every danger ahead of time. Knowing this, they all slept soundly.

At breakfast time, Velissa took two huge loaves of bread from the fireplace. She was about to call the foursome together for tea and bread when she heard a fluttering of wings above her. In the narrow opening of the observatory dome, Rexel had landed on the barrel of the scope.

"Parsky has the women!" croaked the falcon.

"The women?" asked Raenna.

"Then the exodus failed!" cried Velissa.

"But what of Orkkan?" Raccoman pressed anxiously.

"He was killed in a snow slide only a few miles from the cliffs of the Moonrhymes," replied the Falcon, regaining his breath.

"And Collinvar—what of him?" Velissa asked.

"They say he is alive. Some even saw him on the ridges before winter came. He may be roaming these parts."

"If he is in Quarrystone Woods, he'll come here," said Velissa. She couldn't help but believe that they were in the right place. She felt the great centicorn would not stray far from Quarrystone if he were free.

Her faith was rewarded. By afternoon, she saw her beloved centicorn nibbling the tall red grass at the edge of the candolet groves.

"Collinvar!" she cried. The centicorn wheeled in joy and raced to her with long, glassy strides.

"Oh, Collinvar! You're alive, alive!" she exulted.

The proud mount threw back his head and his five silver horns glinted like tinsel above the gleaming snowfields.

Grace is a gift,
And friendship is shared.
All tears and laughter
Are owned by the day.
Allegiance can sometimes be bought,
So they say.
But trust must be given away.

CHAPTER IV

The Meeting of the Realms

RACCOMAN DECIDED that it would be easier to have the condorg Zephrett deposit him atop the Moonrhyme cliffs directly above the opening to the enclave. He secured a long fiber cable to the trunk of an oversized candolet tree, musing over the strength of its red bark. He smiled, for he knew that the fibers that composed the rope had once been a smaller candolet tree. He suspended his rope from the tree and it fell free upon the sheer icy front of the cliff.

Raccoman walked to the edge of the precipice. Ordinarily, he was not afraid of heights, but now as he looked down the vertical wall of ice-covered rock, his heart nearly stopped. Suddenly, he understood, better than he ever had before, why the Moonrhymes felt so secure in their mountain dwellings. None but the boldest would dare to ascend the precipice that the Moonrhymes climbed daily. Below him, white fleecy clouds nestled like fluffy down next to the cliff. Raccoman looked away for a moment or two, remembering that his own father had been a cliff-climber. The thought gave him courage and he was suddenly ashamed to have been afraid at all.

He sat down on the overhang of the towering precipice. The top was free of ice, and he scooted until his yellow boots dangled out over the void. His rope hung below him like a glistening thread, until it, too, disappeared into the mists.

In a moment of resolve, Raccoman grasped the rope in both hands and flung himself over the edge. Clutching the strong cable, he moved hand under hand until he had lowered himself a long way.

Hallidan, who had delivered him to the starting point of his descent, stood on the top of the cliff and watched Raccoman disappear below the clouds. When he saw the rope go limp, he knew that Raccoman had reached a ledge below the level of the clouds.

The clouds were much thicker than Raccoman had supposed, and it took him a while to lower himself. When at last he broke through them, he caught his breath at the vision that greeted him.

Below him a thousand feet, he saw two people—apparently, a man and a woman—riding toward him on some snakelike creatures directly up the ice-covered wall of the cliff.

What a magnificent pair they were! The great lizard creatures moved with incredible ease. The two who rode them had locked their strong legs around the broad necks of the beasts and were leaning backward into space against the long backracks of primitive saddles that supported them. They rode comfortably, looking straight upward into the underside of the low-hanging snowy clouds that shielded the sky and the upper cliffs from view.

The speed at which the huge lizards shot up the vertical cliffs amazed Raccoman. Their sure-footed claws dug with certainty into the ice and soft rock, and they moved with swiftness oblivious to any exertion. At first, Raccoman thought that they were heading directly toward him, but just when his fears were the greatest, the two beasts turned and darted horizontally into the face of the cliff. Raccoman hung above them at such a height that he could not see the huge window through which they had disappeared.

Suddenly he was afraid to lower himself any further. He had known of the Moonrhyme dwellings for years, but he had never heard of any such creatures existing in them. The two riders had appeared to be Moonrhymes. But what of the beasts? Were there more of them? Did the riders have full control over their mounts? Would they attack strangers? Their forbidding appearance and immense size terrified the Graygill welder.

Nonetheless, Raccoman realized that he had little choice. He knew that he did not possess the strength to climb back up the rope, and so he continued to lower himself down the face of the cliff. Within a few moments, he found himself dangling on the rope directly before the cavern into which the lizard beasts had disappeared. The hole was dark and forbidding, but Raccoman decided that however forbidding, this was a good place to enter the enclave.

He began to sway gently back and forth until his rope pendulum swung him into the opening in the cliff and he dropped onto the dark stone floor. He wondered where the beasts had gone as he rested for a moment to recover from the exhaustion of his rigorous descent. He wanted to complete his mission as soon as possible for he knew that above him, Hallidan awaited.

His mind reeled. Surely the Drogs had not reached the canyon.

The beasts he had seen were not the lumbersome sauroids of the other continent. These lizard beasts were quick beyond belief and so sure-footed that they could traverse canyon walls with ease. The primary problem to be solved, however, was where he should begin his search for the Moonrhymes. He had not been to the enclave in centuries, and his best attempt to recall the scheme of their complex system of caves eluded him.

As he pondered the issue, a huge bulk appeared, thrusting itself out of the darkness. The sleek, snakelike head was as large as he. "This surely must be one of the beasts I just saw disappear into the darkness," he thought. Behind the red eyes of the monster there smoldered a fire. The denizen opened its mouth, and the two forks of its tongue slithered out as though they were separate beasts. Fire shot out from its nostrils, then from its mouth and played about Raccoman's feet. The entire tunnelree was washed in amber shadows. Raccoman jumped backward to keep from being burnt.

The beast came on another step and opened its mouth again. Once more, fire issued out around the Graygill's feet as he took another step backward. Another step . . . again, the fire . . . and again the Graygill retreated. The menacing and intelligent lizard intended to back him out the door of the cave.

Soon the fire that played around his feet spilled over the edge of the ledge and out into the snow mist, brightening the clouds with orange mystery. Raccoman's heart raced in terror. He could back away no further. The canyon lay directly behind him now. The lizard beast opened its mouth once more and out shot a hot blast of fire.

The season of reason ended. With daring, Raccoman turned and faced the mocking heights. Then he jumped into the icy void, barely managing to grasp the rope on which he had so recently lowered himself. He hung there for a moment, before the advancing beast approached the edge of the tunnelree and stood resplendent in the gray light of morning. Raccoman admired its majestic head and hated it at the same time. The beast looked at the section of rope just above Raccoman's head and opened its mouth with a grisly intent that Raccoman clearly understood. Flame shot out around the rope.

"Stop, Goronzo!" cried a voice behind the monster.

The beast withdrew into the darkness of the tunnelree and in its place stood Jendai.

"Are you all right?" Jendai asked Raccoman.

"So far!" said Raccoman. "May I come in again?"

Jendai laughed, "Please, Goronzo didn't mean to be so unfriendly—He's one of the nicest salamanders around." He laughed again and motioned Raccoman back into the opening. His laughter was welcome. The Graygill began swinging once more on the rope until his slight trapeze swayed in an arc that landed him a second time on the floor of the cave.

"Welcome to my tunnelree," said Jendai.

"Thank you, Jendai!"

"I'm glad to see a Canby," Jendai affirmed. "There are few of them left since the war."

"Yes!" was Raccoman's only reply.

Raccoman wanted to ask so many things at once. He had resolved to take all the time necessary to ask about the Drogs. The whole subject needed to be approached in security at the right time. Later they would talk about the unseen evil that waited in the lower caves. Later he would try to tell the Moonrhymes about Star Riders and Drogs and about the Southern Continent. He knew that he must find a way to convince them that all of these things existed. How hard it would be for them to accept their existence and yet how utterly important it was for them to believe. Unless they believed, the entire enclave could be destroyed.

One question, however, could not wait: "Jendai, what was that creature that nearly burned me into nonexistence?"

"They are fire salamanders—there are two of them. They were hatched here in the enclave less than a year ago. Grentana and I have learned to ride them."

"Grentana? Grentana of Canby is here in the enclave? Grentana, the wife of the late Ganarett?" Raccoman realized he was asking too many questions at once.

"Grentana is the only woman to survive the migration," said Jendai.

"I've learned since my return that the widows who turned back are imprisoned now in Maldoon," said Raccoman. "Were many of them lost in the exodus attempt?"

"Grentana believes so. After Orkkan's death, she continued the migration and thus knows nothing of the fate of the others. It is a miracle that she survived the high ledges near Demmerron. Now, she is here, Raccoman." His exultation told volumes about their relationship. Raccoman could see a new light in Jendai's eyes.

"We are in love. We plan to marry in the spring, when the snow is gone."

"Jendai, I congratulate the both of you!"

Jendai modestly lowered his eyes before continuing. "Grentana was here when the salamanders hatched, and together we have cared for them. It took a while to adjust to their swiftness, but now I ride Goronzo and Grentana rides Calaranz. We experimented with various saddles." Jendai stopped a moment and then broke into laughter. "Friend Raccoman, you should have seen the pair of us the first day that we traveled the cliff walls. We were riding in the tunnelrees when all of a sudden the salamanders bolted outside and flew down the face of the cliff. Old Sammuron—"

"Praise to Singreale! Then he is still alive?"

"Sammuron? Yes indeed, he is alive. Quite alive. He warned us about the sudden and strange behavior of the salamanders, and so we were prepared from the very first time we rode them."

"If you were prepared, why did it frighten you?" asked Raccoman.

"When I say we were prepared, I mean we had built special saddles fitted with safety straps so we could not fall out. But, Raccoman, we were not all prepared for that horrible first plunge down Westwall. Poor Grentana screamed, thinking that the beasts had gone too far and were falling. Such was not the case. It amazed both of us how fleet and sure-footed the salamanders are. Goronzo seems to take the lead, setting the direction and velocity with which the two of them dash up and down these cliffs. Our terror gradually dissolved in delight. Now we enjoy the exhilaration of sweeping down the walls for a thousand feet."

The very thought of sweeping down a cliff at the unbelievable velocity that the salamanders traveled froze Raccoman's blood. He felt relieved when Jendai finished his description of salamander riding, and for a while, both of them were quiet.

"But, Jendai," said the Canby Graygill, at last.

"Yes?" said the Moonrhyme Graygill.

"How did you—where did you get the salamanders?"

"Raccoman, before the cataclysm of fire, such beasts played in great numbers upon these cliffs. Old Sammuron says that these beasts once dug the caverns and burrows of our enclave."

Jendai stopped. He realized that he still had not answered Raccoman's question as to where these two particular salamanders had come from.

"Remember Old Sam's fire and the stones he had been warming since long before the siege of Maldoon?"

Raccoman nodded.

"Those weren't stones."

"Not stones?"

"They were eggs."

"But they were all blackened and burnt in the flames. Eggs would be burnt up," Raccoman argued.

"Not salamander eggs. They must have heat, though not so much as their race was subjected to in the great cataclysm. Those earlier beasts and most of their eggs were destroyed in the fire storms. Old Sammuron rescued two of them. I, like my father before me, brought him wood, and thus his fire has burned. I didn't know it at the time, but I was helping him save a race of noble creatures."

"But why didn't the fire destroy the eggs?" Raccoman still persisted with his old logic.

"No, no—they have to have fire. Even after the little salamanders hatched," Jendai said, pausing as he remembered how big the salamanders were at the time they hatched, "they jumped right back into the fire, only gradually moving out of the flames to cool down so we could touch them. Even now, they love fire and will move compulsively toward it. Last summer in the canyon, we built big fires for them to play and sing in."

"They sing?" asked Raccoman, dumbfounded.

"Well, squeal with delight," replied Jendai, bringing the tone of his story down to a more moderate truth. "They squeal and roar in their delight of the flames, just like the Selendrenni who sired them."

"The Selendrenni?" Raccoman's brow knotted again in puzzlement.

The Selendrenni were another story. Jendai began to tell of the

Ice Fields of Selen, but before he had gone on long, Raccoman interrupted him:

"The Ice Fields of Selen are the last frontiers of the glacial north. In Canby, we spoke of them as a barren and forbidden world from which no traveler ever returns."

"Ah," protested Jendai, "at least one has returned. I myself have been to the ice fields, and as you see, I have returned. In the dead of winter, too!" With this preface, Jendai went on with his story, telling of his strange pilgrimage and how he captured the Selendrenni using only the lure of fire.

When Jendai finished recounting all that had transpired in the past two years, he inquired what had become of the welder and his wife. Raccoman told him of the flight of the Paradise Falcon and of the transference of Velissa from the talons of the giant Rexel to her own seat beside him on the upper deck of their marvelous, high-flying glider.

Jendai's tales of life in the enclave could hardly have been wilder to Raccoman than Raccoman's tales were to Jendai. The adventures of each seemed incredible to the other. But when Raccoman finished with his story of the war in Rensland, he felt compelled to tell Old Sam's wood-bearer that the peril of the Southern Continent would soon visit the North.

"Jendai," he said, "the enclave is in the greatest danger possible. The Westwall can no longer protect you. An enemy more terrible than any can imagine will come from within."

"You see, wood-bearer," he continued, "the Southern and the Northern Continents are one. They are made so by a long passageway that connects the two worlds. This passageway once took a year for my father, Garrod, to traverse. But the Drogs are twice our size, and though they appear to be large and slow, in fact they move at nearly twice our speed. Parsky and the catterlobs are no longer the greatest enemy we face."

"The catterlobs!" cried Jendai, suddenly remembering. "That's what I forgot to tell you."

"The catterlobs?" Raccoman repeated. "Listen, Jendai," he insisted, refusing to be interrupted, "the Changelings will soon be here in the enclave, and they have with them the greatest force in all Estermann—the Singreale."

"The catterlobs!" cried Jendai again. "They are gone!"

"Gone?"

"Gone, dead, killed! Most of them, anyway."

"Killed?"

"The fire salamanders! They are swift and relentless in their hatred of the large beasts. While the salamanders are small by comparison, they are lightning swift and can tear away the flesh of the catterlobs in an instant! Parsky brought his entire herd to the valley last summer to terrorize the enclave. When Goronzo and Calaranz saw them, they behaved as if they had seen fire. They rushed out of these openings, down the cliffs, and tore furiously into Parsky's denizens. In less than an hour, they killed most of the catterlobs while our people gazed from the windows of the enclave and cheered."

"But Parsky was riding a catterlob in armor!" Raccoman remembered the spectre that had so haunted Velissa in another time.

"When Parsky saw that most of the beasts were gone, he turned and fled with no more than half a dozen of the catterlobs. The bewildered beasts ran at full speed toward the South and out of the canyon. Goronzo and Calaranz chased them as far as the Sentinels of Demmerron Pass."

"Has Parsky come back?"

"Not yet," said Jendai. "I have the feeling that he will not. He seems to fear the enclave's steep tower of stone. We are hoping that his double fear of the steep cliffs and the fierce salamanders will keep him from returning. Besides, he knows full well that we do not have the Singreale, so there would be little reason for him to risk his army of drones on Westwall."

"Don't be too sure about Parsky," Raccoman warned the woodbearer. Raccoman somehow felt that Jendai's diversion to speak of the catterlobs had been deliberate. He began again the stern warning that Jendai had interrupted. "Jendai, you must see that your people are warned. Even if you are safe from Parsky and the catterlobs, you are not safe from the evil that will soon be invading your caverns. Don't you see, Jendai? There could be as many as a thousand of these beast-warriors. They will all be armed, and they will be carrying the Singreale as well."

"The Singreale!" Jendai exclaimed.

"Yes, they stole it from the knight Hallidan at the end of the war in Rensland," replied Raccoman. He was about to go on with his explanation, when a soft, sweet voice behind them interrupted him.

"Jendai."

"Grentana," said the wood-bearer, "Raccoman has come back."

"Oh, hello," she said, without enthusiasm. In fact, her greeting was so icy that Raccoman recoiled.

Raccoman asked Jendai if there was to be a council in the enclave soon.

"We will have no more gatherings for the remainder of the winter," said Jendai, "until the cliffs are free of ice. In the winter, we are so shut in by our moods that we become intolerable to each other. Especially the oldest ones."

"You do not have till the winter is over!" Raccoman insisted.

"Then does the great Raccoman Dakktare see some other desperate set of circumstances and wish to promise some equally desperate way out of them?" Grentana snapped.

Now even Jendai felt uncomfortable with Grentana's tone. "Grentana, hospitality is the law of the tunnelrees," the wood-bearer reminded her.

"I'm sorry, Jendai. Certainly, Raccoman is welcome."

Grentana had turned to leave when Raccoman spoke, "Grentana, please speak, for if there is some possibility that you do not see the danger that now faces the enclave, the whole Moonrhyme community could be lost."

"What danger?" Grentana demanded.

"The Drogs from the Southern Continent are already enroute to the enclave. Soon—perhaps very soon—they will be here and death will stalk every tunnelree and Moonrhyme blood will flow throughout these caves."

"Drogs? Southern Continent?" asked Grentana with less skepticism. "Surely, Jendai, you do not believe that there is a Southern Continent. Have we not always learned, 'Estermann is a perfect world built perfectly. Estermann—one continent, one sea.'"

"But that proverb is false!" Raccoman cried. "Estermann has at least two continents. The southern one is called Rensland. Until recently, Rensland was troubled and ripped by war. Now the fugitives who survived the conflict are enroute to the enclave of the Moonrhymes."

"And you have seen this world you would have us fear?" Grentana questioned.

"I have been there," said Raccoman firmly.

"On your golden glider?"

"Yes," said Raccoman, "exactly!"

"Why should we trust you or believe you? You were a Blackgill once, even as Parsky is now a Blackgill. All Blackgills lie," said Grentana.

"I am a Graygill," countered Raccoman, angered at having his evil past resurrected.

"But what if Raccoman speaks the truth?" Jendai asked, joining the debate.

"As he spoke the truth to the men of Canby? Our husbands were all killed because of his 'truth.'"

"I tell you, Grentana, I speak the truth now, and you must believe it or the enclave will perish."

"Our husbands perished at Demmerron, and many of their women perished on the ledges as well." Grentana had become savage. "I think you lie, Raccoman. I think there is no Southern Continent. I think you never sailed anywhere on the tilt winds. And most of all, I do not believe that any danger is coming through the heart of the earth. Get out of this enclave! Leave us to life and peace!"

"Please, Grentana. There are only two choices: either the Moonrhymes must fight or they must leave these caverns till the danger is past."

Suddenly the full weight of Raccoman's suggestion settled heavily on Jendai. "But it is winter. The cliffs are icebound. Where could we go in the winter?"

"Where the women went!" cried Grentana. "To be frozen to death while following the advice of a former Blackgill. Your lies destroyed the Canbies. Leave the Moonrhymes alone!"

Raccoman saw the hopelessness of his task. He had hoped to move to the Grand Cavern and plead for some concerted defense of the tunnelrees. Grentana made him realize that the Moonrhymes would never believe his heavy prophecy. Raccoman had never before considered how much his ill advice had cost the men and women of Canby. Now a wave of disconsolation washed over him.

He had already turned back to the opening of the enclave when he was struck by a kind of evidence he could yet submit to the skeptical widow.

"Grentana, you will believe. If I can show you evidence that there is a Southern Continent, will you call a meeting of the council?" asked Raccoman.

After a moment of thought, Grentana and Jendai both nodded.

Raccoman had remembered that Hallidan still waited for him on the cliff top. Because they faced the intense light in the opening of the cave, neither Grentana nor Jendai could see Raccoman's eyes dance as they lit up with sudden hope. He stopped for a moment and then made as though he would leap out to grasp the rope that still dangled before the opening of the cave.

"No, don't leave!" cried Jendai. "Please, Raccoman, we have not meant to be so inhospitable."

Though Raccoman knew that the kind of treatment he had just received was unusual for the Moonrhymes, he was firm. "No, I must leave. I am not welcome here. Nor will my truth be believed. I am going to climb up and out of here. Yes, I will climb up and be free—up to the sunlight of the top of the cliffs."

He had chosen his words well. He had used the word *up* three times so that the Moonrhyme Jendai might make his own discovery. Moonrhymes never liked being told an outright truth. They preferred to discover it themselves.

"Did you say 'up,' Raccoman?" Jendai asked. "Of course, you did. You had to say 'up,' for you came down to the opening of the tunnelree on a rope suspended from above. Look, Grentana, don't you see? He did not climb up from the valley floor. He lowered himself down from the top of the cliff."

Grentana's expression turned from hostility to doubt. "But how? Even our best climbers have never been to the top of the cliffs in winter."

Raccoman faced them both, but now he spoke only to Grentana. "Suppose I told you that there is on top of the cliff, waiting for me right now, a giant who is twice the height of Jendai. And suppose I told you that not only is there a giant up there, but there is at this moment near him a winged animal big enough to carry four Moonrhymes into the sky at once—would you believe me?"

"Certainly not!" snapped Grentana.

"But if there was, would you then allow me to speak without interruption to all of the men of the enclave at once?"

"It would be hard to refuse a man who could produce such evidence," she said.

"Then mount Goronzo and Calaranz and have a look for yourselves!" Raccoman exulted. "Only promise me that you will not let the fire salamanders attack Hallidan or the condorg that he flies."

Goronzo and Calaranz were soon fitted with saddles.

"My saddle is strong enough for two. Ride with me, Raccoman," said Jendai.

"It is strong enough for two, but is it big enough?" asked the welder. "And will it not be too heavy a load for Goronzo?"

Jendai only laughed at Raccoman's naiveté. "Wait till you ride this beast upon the cliffs," was all he said.

So Raccoman found himself strapped into the high-backed saddle behind Jendai. The great fire salamander slithered outward and swung his low and snakelike torso out of the opening. The leap to the outer cliff took the welder by surprise. Raccoman's breath stopped. He hung vertically in the saddle so that his chest was pressed against the back of Jendai, who rode in the forward part of the saddle. Raccoman peered over the wood-bearer's shoulder and faced an icy cliff with a thousand feet of snowy canyon, but the fiber straps that held him to the back of the saddle were secure and kept both of them from pitching over the head of their mount.

Still, the horror of the vision would not leave Raccoman. Raccoman turned his head nearly half around to look back. Above him, on the side of the cliff, hung Goronzo's huge body. It seemed uncanny to Raccoman that the serpentine salamander, which must have weighed more than three or four condorgs, could cling so lithely to the wall of sheer ice. Raccoman's eyes followed the body as it protruded from the cliff wall. The huge claws clung firmly to the cold stone, and before long, Raccoman began to breathe again. Just then, Calaranz, carrying Grentana on its back, shoved its way out of the opening and rushed down beside Goronzo. Jendai and Grentana looked at each other only a moment before Grentana spoke: "Jendai, we rarely ride the salamanders through the snow clouds. Will they do it?"

It made Raccoman uncomfortable for the two of them to be looking straight down and discussing whether their mounts were capable of traversing the snowy cloud that hung above them. Raccoman looked up again. Although the fleecy clouds hid Hallidan and Zephrett, he felt sure they were still there, far above him and his serpentine mount.

Jendai answered Grentana's doubt. "Upward, Goronzo!" he shouted.

The beast flipped its huge, scaly tail.

"Watch the tail!" cried Jendai. The heavy tail barely missed Raccoman. If the Moonrhyme had had any doubts about Goronzo traveling through clouds, he dared not voice them now. The salamander dashed into the clouds, scrambling upward.

Goronzo's claws dislodged some loose stones on the front of the cliff and sent them knifing through the clouds. The rocks flew all about Calaranz, who followed Jendai's beast.

In but a moment, they had all broken through the clouds and raced to the very pinnacle of the great cliff. Raccoman looked back over his shoulder just as Calaranz and Grentana broke through the cloud. Below the beasts and their riders, the clouds stretched in a fleecy white blanket over all the entire world. It was as if the great salamanders had found a way to leave the Moonrhyme's world completely.

They rushed on to the upper cliff, and just as Goronzo slithered over the edge, there greeted the unbelieving Jendai all that Raccoman had promised. Then Calaranz came over the top as well and both of the great salamanders stopped.

Hallidan was as surprised as they were. The condorg shied at the sudden appearance of the salamanders. Hallidan drew his sword. He could not see Raccoman, who was seated squarely behind Jendai, and Hallidan felt for a moment that the beasts would attack him before he could get to Zephrett and escape.

"No!" cried Raccoman. "Put away your sword, friend Hallidan!"

Terror gave way to friendship. On the summit of the cliff, they all sat down to confer. Grentana could not take her eyes from the kind and handsome Star Rider. Around their lonely pinnacle of stone, there was nothing but sky and clouds. The salamanders enjoyed lying in the winter sun that bleached the clouds while Zephrett wandered around them. The Titan and the Graygills sat on a rock that appeared to float on an endless sea of clouds. They talked for nearly two hours, and by the end of that time, they had a plan. Hallidan stood. Jendai and Grentana marveled at the grace and beauty of this giant who came from a land that all those who dwelt in the mountains doubted.

Hallidan mounted the condorg alone and cried "Skie-ho!" The

animal stretched its wings and lifted vertically in a powerful surging till it disappeared into the blue. The Graygill watched him go. Secretly, Jendai had a desire to fly with the great Star Rider, but his own unique mount required a kind of courage that even those who flew might not manage.

The clouds rose until just the pinpoint of the mountain was visible, and when Hallidan looked back for the last time, the three seemed to be sitting on their beasts in an immense white nest large enough to hatch a great, new dream. That was indeed what had happened.

No virtue is safe
With a scoundrel.
Each Eden is
Paradise frail.
No Heaven was
Ever too lofty
For devils with
Ladders to scale.

CHAPTER V
The Unspoiled Valley

A LOW BANK of snow clouds obscured the northern and eastern skies. A bold blue claimed the remainder of the sky. The sun blazed upon the snow. While Raenna's eyes had not fully adjusted to the glare, she and Velissa decided to fly northwest and use the day for exploring.

In all of her one hundred and seventy-five years, Velissa had never traveled very far in that direction. Now they soared on bright new wings past large fuchsia splashes of candolet groves, where colorful fingerlets of the forest interlaced with the white of winter. Within an hour, they had flown so far that nothing they saw was the least bit familiar to Velissa. In the distance, she could see a thin strand of silver forest.

"Ginjons," Velissa said rather softly.

"What did you say?" asked her companion over her shoulder.

"Ginjons!" repeated Velissa. "They are the principle trees of Castledome Forest." She paused for a moment before going on. "It's odd," she mused, "how little we know." Miles of uncharted terrain flashed by beneath her. "Yes, how little we know. We always have thought that Castledome was the only ginjon forest on the continent. Now we know there are at least two. I wonder if there could be other peoples as well?" With this, she quit speaking out loud, but the inner turmoil of her thoughts continued to roll. She realized how much larger the world was than she had originally imagined. If there were two continents and two ginjon forests, then there might be other continents and other forests and other lands filled with other kinds of animals and people.

In the distance beyond the silver trees, Velissa could see what appeared to be blue vegetation. Surely not trees? Yes, trees! What kind of trees, she could not say, for she had never heard of blue trees. They were not so bright a blue as her own clothes, but they were not so pale as the evening sky. She looked beyond the trees and saw dwellings—a whole valley of homes.

They flew on, yet Raenna turned the condorg upward so as not to be visible from the ground.

"Houses," remarked Velissa, as she continued studying the landscape. Then she burst into laughter.

"What is so funny?" asked Raenna.

"Those houses—they're square!" The very idea of square houses amused Velissa.

At a great height, they circled the valley filled with a village of square houses. When at last Velissa had seen enough of the village, they flew southward over the upper valley and disappeared over the forest's edge. They were ready, by this time, to stop and rest for a while, and yet they could see no break in the forest floor. They circled for another fifteen minutes before they spotted a clearing. In the middle of it was a house.

"Look, Raenna! There are star-watchers in this valley of square houses!" cried Velissa.

An observatory with the same typical scope sticking out of the snow-covered roof adjoined the lonely house. The scope was obviously in use, for the snow had been cleared from the upper lens. The tube of the scope, the scope house, and the star-watcher's dwelling were all oddly square. The color of the remote houses, like those that Velissa had seen earlier in the nearby village, were not so bright as the dwellings of Canby.

"Raenna, let's get to know the resident of this lonely outpost!" Velissa shouted into the draft of headwind created by the condorg's flight pattern of rapid circling above the square observatory.

Raenna reined back the tapered head of her mount so that it slowed its wing beats and turned downward. The flying beast circled wide over the trees and touched the ground behind the observatory. By using this method of arrival, Raenna seemed satisfied that they had not yet been noticed.

When the condorg landed, the women dismounted and walked over to the corner of the observatory. They paused momentarily to watch some congrels frolicking in the sun. Velissa laughed softly as they approached the dwelling.

"Even the windows are square," she commented. Raenna felt Velissa was making too much of the architecture. She herself did not find the geometry of their expedition nearly as humorous.

Velissa knocked hesitantly at the odd square door.

In a moment, the door swung open. They were greeted by a Graygill. He was only a little shorter than Raccoman, and crowning his head was stiff wiry hair that looked like it could not be combed. He wore red spectacles. They were so dark that Velissa wondered how he could see anything past the end of his rather bulbous nose.

"Mandra!" he called, alarmed at Raenna's great size.

A small woman quickly appeared beside him. She, too, wore spectacles, but hers were tinted a deep blue—again, so deep a blue that it was a wonder that she could see through them at all. Her hair was as gray as that of her Graygill companion and nearly as wiry. Though Velissa could tell that they were Graygills, they were unlike either the Canbies or the Moonrhymes. While they stood in the doorway looking out, two orange-gray animals appeared at their heels and sat up in an attitude of begging.

The sight was more than Raenna could stand—two Graygills with wiry hair and colored spectacles, flanked by an honor guard of little animals. It was as though the doorway held its own reception committee. She could not help but laugh at the odd appearance of the four that greeted them.

But the old man and woman, in beholding the two women at their door, whose sizes stood in sharp contrast, could only suppress their own amusement for a moment. Put to ease by Raenna's mirth, soon all four of them were laughing. Their small hosts even chuckled with strange syllables of laughter: "Halla, Halla, Halla!"

"Well, Hindra, invite them in," exclaimed the woman.

"Yes, yes—do come in," cried Hindra.

Velissa and Raenna entered the square rooms and found places on square furniture.

"I'm so relieved," Velissa told the pair, "that you speak Canby."

"Oh, no," said Hindra. "Not nearly so relieved as I am that you speak Sundalese."

"Sundalese?" asked Velissa.

"What else should a Sundal speak?" Hindra's spectacles vibrated behind the ball at the end of his nose.

Mandra turned to Raenna, "You are a tall Graygill." The statement seemed sudden and tactless. Still, Raenna was taller sitting than either Mandra or Hindra as they brought tea. Mandra tried to change the subject by asking Velissa if she was from some outpost of the Sundal Valley.

"I am from Quarrystone Woods," said Velissa.

"Where is that?" asked Hindra.

"If you could fly," replied Velissa, "you could go there quickly."

"Fly?" asked Mandra. "Who can fly? Do you try to tell us that there is another valley with another race of Graygills?" asked the old woman most seriously. "Can that be, Hindra?"

"That is what he said, too," said her husband, the skin wrinkling around his bulbous nose. His square spectacles moved up and then down again. "Yes, he said that there was another valley. I cannot believe it. Still, Mandra, in one week we have had two visitors, who have come from beyond the lands of the Sundals to tell us that there is another valley of life."

"Two visitors in one week?" asked Raenna.

"Yes," said Hindra, "two visitors. Still, I cannot accept that there is another whole valley with its own village and other kinds of Graygills."

Velissa found their accents intriguing as they debated the existence of the Valley of the Canbies.

"But who was the other visitor?" Velissa asked, echoing Raenna's question.

"How is it that you and Raenna are such different types of Graygills?" asked Mandra, ignoring Velissa's question.

"Oh, I am not a Graygill," Raenna insisted. "I am—."

"Now, now, Raenna. There is little use in rehearsing our lands and people." Velissa had deliberately interrupted Raenna, realizing that she had been about to tell Mandra and Hindra about Rensland. Their square-spectacled hosts would never be able to understand that another continent existed with a kind of life they could never imagine.

"Mandra," Velissa pressed, refusing to let her host ignore her original question, "you had another visitor from beyond the valley of the Sundals this very week?"

Just then the door flew open. An urge to laugh seized Raenna once more. She had never before seen a Graygill child. The Sundal boy stood scarcely as high as her knee, and yet he ran with enthusiasm to Hindra, who picked him up and tossed him in play toward the flat ceiling of the square room. "Ho, ho, my little Abbon, look! We have company!"

The boy looked and obviously found Raenna as intriguing as she found him. "Papa, she is so tall! Halla, halla!" laughed the boy. Raenna now could restrain herself no longer. She laughed, too, and they all broke into laughter. The little boy was wearing dark green spectacles, as square as those worn by his parents.

His hair was gray and wiry like that of Mandra and Hindra, but he had no sidelocks and, of course, he was far too young to have the customary gills that typified the Sundals as well as the Canbies. Velissa had seen Canby children, but never a Sundal child. He was, by her standard, an impish-looking youngster. He couldn't have been more than twenty years old and, therefore, barely out of the nursery.

"Papa, I hope he comes today. He promised me he would!"

Whoever "he" was, Velissa could see that the child was most excited.

"Oh, I wish he would come now! He promised me that I could ride with him."

"Well, he will be here before long, and then we shall see about your riding with him!" Hindra was firm. "You cannot be patient, can you, boy?"

Mandra turned to Velissa and Raenna. "The boy is much like his papa, I am afraid. He cannot wait for anything."

"Why don't you go out and play with the congrels?" Hindra suggested.

"All right," answered Abbon. "But, Papa, could I wear my red spectacles instead? I am so excited!"

"Green will be fine," answered his mother. "No, perhaps you should wear your blue ones—they will cool you down a bit. Help yourself to patience, son."

Abbon accepted this wisdom without protest. He scampered out of the room and in an instant returned with his blue spectacles on. He ran much slower now than when he had been wearing his red ones. Velissa was greatly intrigued to see how the color of the spectacles could change both the mood and the vigor of the boy.

"Well, now you must stay for dinner," Mandra told the two women. "We're having baked kamma."

"Yes, yes," said Hindra. "We harvested these early last spring and have been keeping them all through the winter. This would be an excellent time to enjoy them."

Mandra left through a side door and went out into the snow. She found a door in the drift, entered an ice chamber, and removed two large vegetable stalks, which she brought back into the house.

Velissa and Raenna had no idea what baked kamma was, but they watched as Mandra and Hindra worked together to prepare the stalks with certain seasonings, cooking them on an open fire. Velissa was glad to see that, like the Canbies, the Sundals were apparently vegetarian.

While the huge vegetables cooked, Velissa had to ask, "Does anyone eat meat?"

"Meat?" asked Hindra. "Is meat anything like kamma?"

Velissa decided not to pursue the question, delighted that meat was yet unknown here.

For the first time in many months, Velissa enjoyed the aroma of a meal in the process of being prepared, and it intoxicated her with anticipation. She did not have to wait long. Just as they were about to sit down to eat, Abbon burst through the door.

"Dearest Abbon," commented Mandra, "I thought sure that the blue glasses would slow your mood. But they have not."

"Well, it is time to change glasses now, anyway!" This injunction, which made no sense at all to Velissa and Raenna, seemed to make excellent sense to Hindra and Mandra. Hindra said nothing, since he was already wearing red spectacles, but Mandra and Abbon both removed their green and blue spectacles, went to a little box, and selected red pairs.

When they all were in their red spectacles, Hindra turned to Raenna and Velissa and said, "We would like you to join us in the meal." So saying, he produced two other pairs of red spectacles and gave them to Raenna and Velissa. The practice seemed odd, but the women did not want to offend and so they put them on. Raenna's broad face was so much larger than the faces of the Graygills that her glasses sat high on her nose. Her eyelashes swept the lens each time she blinked.

"Now," said Mandra, "You will be able to really enjoy the meal. Red always makes the world pretty and the conversation warm."

Both Raenna and Velissa were thinking that the red color washed naturalness from the world. But to every home its single joy, Velissa thought. For her, the world held, suddenly, an unnatural glow. The fire leapt up in a dazzling red. Mandra, Hindra, Abbon and Raenna were also red. Each of them reached for a red chair, pulled it out with their red hands, and sat before a red table laden with red dishes filled with glowing kamma.

Life was as red as it was square.

They gathered around the square table set with square utensils. Hindra traced a square in the air while he raised his other hand. As his stubby finger drew the top of the invisible square, he said:

From the snow and from the rain,

His hand then traced the descending side of the square:

Comes the harvest of our grain,

His finger stopped and drew the bottom of the unseen square:

From the skies comes bread again,

Once more his finger stopped, then rose upward to complete the remaining side of the invisible square.

To teach us we are loved.

They then began to eat, and while they ate, they spoke of many things.

"Papa, when I am finished, can I look through the scope?"

"Yes, Abbon, if there are no snow clouds."

"There will be no clouds tonight. I could see the stars even before I came in."

It was easy to tell that Abbon derived a great deal of joy from looking through Hindra's scope.

"My father was a star-watcher once," said Velissa as they ate.

"Is he not still?" asked Hindra.

"Papa, can I have some more kamma?" asked Abbon. The father responded by serving his son a rather generous second helping while reminding him, "Abbon, it is not polite to interrupt someone who is speaking."

Velissa continued. "Not any more," she said, then paused. "No, he was killed."

"Killed?" asked Hindra, "What's killed?"

Velissa again felt that she had mentioned something unknown in the valley of the Sundals.

"Killing is what happens when one person causes another to die," she said.

Velissa could see Hindra's eyes above the dark red lens. She could see that he understood the possibility of killing, even how it could occur. Still, he was unfamiliar with how or why anybody would ever want to make another die. The whole concept seemed unfamiliar to him. Now she wished she had not brought up the subject of her father. She could tell her statement had depressed the whole Sundal family. Hindra confirmed this by removing his red spectacles and quickly replacing them with blue ones.

Mandra asked, "Who caused your father to die?"

Abbon pushed away his kamma. The conversation was not one that these Sundals could pursue while continuing to eat. Little Abbon reached for his blue glasses and listened, while his parents laid down their square spoons. Velissa felt terrible. She decided to change the subject.

"Well, in our valley we used to have congrels and ganzinger fowls and serpents."

"Serpents!" shouted Abbon in glee. "You had serpents in your valley? Mama and Papa, can it be that they had serpents in their valley? I once saw a small nest of them near the northern woods, but I was not able to catch one. I love serpents!" Abbon was so excited that he ripped off his blue glasses and replaced his red ones. "Papa, when the snow is gone, could we go to the rocky dens and see if we could find a serpent for me?"

Hindra and Mandra were so joyous to see Abbon's delight that they changed glasses again.

"Mandra, we must get this boy a pet in the spring," said Hindra. "I think we can find you a serpent, Abbon."

"Oh, oh!" cried Abbon, then turned to Velissa and said, "Were your serpents hard to catch?"

"Not at all," replied Velissa. "I had my own. She was named Doldeen. My father got her for me before I was even born. We grew up together.

We used to play in the fields and ride the centicorn together, and we would have long talks on winter afternoons just like this one."

"This must be the greatest joy of all—to own your own serpent! Do you ever take her in the snow?" asked Abbon.

"Oh, no," said Velissa. "Serpents can't stand too much cold. My Doldeen would never go out in winter unless she had to. Oh, how I wish I had her back!"

"What do you mean?" asked Abbon.

"I mean, I don't have her any more," said Velissa. Raenna winced.

"But why?" asked Abbon.

"Because she was killed," lamented Velissa without thinking of the consequences of what she had just said.

Mandra and Hindra reached for their blue glasses at the word *killed.* But they only reached for them, because Velissa went on to say, "But there are still dens north of Demmerron, and someday I'm going to have another serpent." The statement was warm—so warm that Mandra and Hindra laid their blue glasses back down.

While Velissa and Abbon had been talking, Raenna found it hard to believe that these Sundals weren't at all familiar with killing or hatred or meat. Raenna knew that the fearsome image of the Drogs and their bloody war against Rensgaard would have put the Sundals in blue spectacles for a decade. But she could see Velissa learning to measure her words as the conversation progressed.

When the kamma was all gone, Hindra cleared the table. Mandra played a reedy pipe and Abbon danced, stepping brightly across the floor.

The low ceiling of the square room prevented Raenna from standing. She sat in a corner, clapping as elfin Abbon stomped out the cadence that Mandra played upon her pipe. The lively dance made Velissa and Raenna tired just to watch.

Mandra stopped playing long enough to ask her son to sing.

"Yes, yes!" agreed Hindra. "Abbon, you must sing for our guests. Sing 'The Bumbleganter's Song.'"

"Well, all right." Abbon reluctantly agreed to sing what was apparently his parents' favorite song, but not necessarily his.

"And do the actions, too," insisted his father.

"All right, Papa." Abbon walked to a square chair and sat down, taking off his heavy boots. Whatever the song was, it required him to be barefoot. He then took off his shirt so that he wore only his trousers. His bristly hair seemed to widen his whole boyish head. He stuck out his chin like the mandible of some unknown insect—possibly a Bumbleganter—and began to sing.

Oh, a Bumbleganter fell in love with a
winter Flutterby.
He decided he would marry her and carry
her away.
But she declined, and he resigned
that he would surely die—
And for his final meal he chose to eat
a three-pound pie.

He dined, then pined, then pined and dined
and wept to see his love.
He ate a dozen loaves of bread with twenty
pots of tea.
The Flutterby was most chagrined and
circled high above:
"You have no manners, Bumbleganter. I loathe
your gluttony."

"Oh, fly on by, you Flutterby. You surely
now can see,
I would as lief forget my grief by loosing
you above—
By drinking up a hundred cups and eating
berry-dees.
You'll rue the day you cast away the
Bumbleganter's love."

He had resolved that he would eat himself
to death—
And thus the guilty Flutterby would really bear
the blame
Of having stolen evermore the Bumbleganter's
breath.
She'd cry and sigh to live a life of tears and shame.

And so he ate and ate and ate, and then he
ate some more.
And when the camadons were gone and all the
cupboards bare,
He ate the roof and then the walls
and then devoured the floor,
After he had swallowed whole the table and
the chair.

During each of these verses, Abbon imitated the Bumbleganter eating the various artifacts he described. With each verse, he puffed his naked belly toward the laughing guests until his childish frame was quite distended with his song.

He ate the forest and a chorus
of singing schools of eels.
He ate the trees and hives of bees
And swallowed all the snakes.

He ate the ground, then turned around
And gobbled down the fields.
He ate the sky and said, "Oh, my
I'm so thirsty now, I think as how
I'd like to drink the lakes."

He drank a lake and then a stream and
then ate all the ground.
He gobbled rills and rocks and hills
and all the grass around.

Made fat and full by all he ate,
He did admit the hour was late
and he would likely die,
When there at last, she fluttered past—
the winter Flutterby.

He cried and tried to get his bride
to fly again his way.
But he had eaten everything—she found no place
to land.
So finally, sky weary, she lit upon his
hand.

"All right, all right, I'll marry you,
I'll marry you," she said.
"Oh, never mind, I've grieved and pined,
and now I've eaten all.
Dear Flutterby, I'm hungry—I'd rather
eat than wed."
Then he popped her in his mouth and found
her sweet as bread.

"Ah, now at last, my love, we're one.
We should have married soon,
Before I ate the wedding guests.
Now that I've gobbled down the bride—
I think I'll eat the groom."
And looking hungry at his leg,
He laid aside his spoon.
So standing on his narrow shelf,
He nipped his leg, then ate himself.

Now wherever Bumbleganters fly
or Flutterbys are kept—

When Bumbleganters do propose,
the Flutterbys accept.

It was a child's song. It was winter, and the snowy season of the Sundals invited long songs to keep the mood warm. Abbon now was tired of dancing. He took off his rosey spectacles and put on his black ones. Mandra was tired, too, and they all decided to take a short nap. Being perfectly gracious hosts, they extended pairs of black spectacles to both Velissa and Raenna, and all of them, by common consent, napped.

When they awoke, it was nearly dark, and Raenna and Velissa were preparing to leave.

"We must go," said Raenna, trying to stand but finding that she was just too tall for the room. She sat back down for the moment.

An obvious question suddenly occurred to Hindra. "How will you go and where will you go?"

Velissa bound up her winter coat. "Come outside, Hindra. You, too, Mandra—if you like." Velissa didn't realize that she had not made the invitation all inclusive until she saw Abbon's chin quivering.

"You can come, too," Raenna told the boy.

His face broke into a smile, and he looked to Hindra for the final approval, which he immediately gave. He pulled on a heavy coat and the boots he had kicked aside for the dancing. Then the entire party, dressed for winter, walked out into the young and starry night. They walked briskly and soon rounded the corner of the observatory, where they found the condorg waiting patiently.

"Papa, what is it?" asked Abbon.

Hindra had not the slightest idea.

Raenna climbed up into the saddle, secured her boots in the foot locks, and cried, "Skie-ho!" The giant wings stretched out and the condorg bolted into the starry sky. Even the darkness of the night could not obscure them. The opaque light of the giant mount was clear and beautiful against the stars. The Sundal star-watcher was envious and wished that he, too, might fly the heavens as the tall lady now was doing.

"Papa, would the tall lady take me on the gondorg?" cried Abbon, unable to contain his excitement.

"Condorg," corrected Velissa.

"Velissa, do you think that our Abbon could ride?" Hindra asked.

Velissa smiled.

Soon Raenna returned. The luminous steed dropped from the sky and landed at their very feet.

"Raenna, Abbon would—" Velissa began her plea.

She had no need to finish, however, for Raenna had already motioned to the boy to come closer.

She reached down to receive the boy as his papa lifted him up. She sat Abbon in the saddle in front of herself, then took a section of the saddle strap from behind her and lashed the small, heavily bundled boy to her body.

"Skie-ho!" she cried.

"Skie-ho," repeated Abbon in a weaker, thinner voice.

Abbon's eyes grew large as the condorg swept through the cold thin air. They flew and flew, soaring high above the village of Sundal Graygills. They soared until all the stars seemed to smile and their sparkling natures were reflected in the bright and shining eyes of young Abbon. They returned all too soon.

Hindra wanted to fly, too, but he could not bring himself to ask. Raenna could see the request in his eyes, however, and promised that she and Velissa would return and take the astronomer to the underside of the stars where he nightly trained his square scope. The promise was good enough, and old Hindra would wait till the promise could be kept.

"Now, Papa, I shall have so much to tell my friend when he comes!"

"Yes, you will, my son."

"I shall tell him of Raenna and Velissa and all that we have seen tonight."

So often during their time together, young Abbon had referred to this unnamed guest. Now Velissa could no longer refrain from asking about his friend.

"Who is this stranger who has come to you?"

"His name is Parsky," the boy's father replied. "He can sing and dance and—" The look on Velissa's face stopped Hindra mid-sentence. Her eyes filled with silent agony.

"Do you know this Parsky?" Mandra inquired.

"He came to our village once," said Velissa. "And now there is no village."

"No, you are mistaken," said old Hindra. "He loves us, and

Abbon best of all. He gave our Abbon a present."

"What was it?" Velissa asked earnestly.

Abbon, however, was too excited to be content with telling about it. He ran instead to get his gift. In a moment, he had come back and was hiding it behind his back.

"Let her see it," commanded Mandra.

"No, mama, let us see if she can guess what it is."

"Is it a knife?"

Velissa had guessed correctly, and Abbon was dumbfounded that she knew.

"When will he be back, Hindra?" Velissa asked.

"In a few weeks. He is coming back so our Abbon can ride his—"

"Catterlob!" shouted Velissa. "No, Hindra, no! Mandra, you must not let Abbon have anything to do with him."

"Papa, why doesn't Velissa like my friend?" asked Abbon.

Velissa grabbed up the boy and hugged him. She said nothing, but turned on her boot and swung into the saddle of the condorg behind Raenna. Then they flew away, trembling that this unspoiled valley had met the Blackgill Parsky.

When the galaxies
Hold council
In the early
Morning sky,
The planets clap their
Hands and sing
That day is
Standing by.

CHAPTER VI
The Blackgill's
Journey

HALLIDAN FLEW BACK to the Blue Observatory in Quarrystone Woods. When he arrived, he was surprised that Raenna and Velissa were not there. He had been home for hours and had begun a roaring fire before the women came through the door. After the condorgs were stabled, there were many things that had to be discussed.

Hallidan explained that Raccoman had elected to remain at the Moonrhyme enclave to warn them of their peril. Hallidan agreed to meet the Star Riders on their surveillance flight the following night. He intended to ask them to seek from Ren a group of knights who could help with the defense of the Moonrhymes against Thanevial.

Hallidan and Raccoman believed that the Moonrhymes, who were unused to fighting, would be in danger if they remained in the caves. They surmised that Maldoon was defended by many drones, but probably could be taken if an entire group of Star Riders landed within the crumbling walls of the old castle. Once they had liberated the fortress of the Moonrhymes, they could move from the Westwall enclave to the lands south of Canby.

Velissa frowned, for she knew what Raccoman, above all the others, would be risking. She knew that if Thanevial arrived before the Moonrhymes could be evacuated, there would be little hope for her husband's survival.

"Still," explained Hallidan, "he is determined to stay. He cannot help feeling guilty about the battle of Demmerron Pass in which the men of Canby perished. He feels even worse about the failure of the exodus and the imprisonment of the widows. Now he wants to make whatever sacrifices are necessary to defend the Moonrhymes."

Velissa felt lonely as she heard Hallidan and Raenna climb into their makeshift beds on the lower floor of the old observatory. She and Raccoman were separated—perhaps for a long time—as her gallant husband waited with the other Moonrhymes. On the lower level, Raenna listened for Velissa's customary night-humming, but did not hear it. She knew Velissa was not sleeping. Two or three times, she thought she heard Velissa crying. The following morning, however, Velissa appeared as refreshed as if she had slept the entire night. It was she who made the suggestion:

"Hallidan, Raenna, let us survey the path around the western ridges to see if there are any signs of Parsky or the catterlobs. Whatever the cost, we must not allow Parsky to return to the valley of the Sundals."

They flew on the two condorgs across the ridges and finally soared so high above the walls of Maldoon that they were invisible from the ground. There was little evidence of life around the old castle. It seemed that even Parsky had abandoned the site. Yet inside the open-court enclosure, there were five or six catterlobs lying on the snow. An odd mound of snow lay in the center of the castle court with black iron brackets sticking out of it at odd angles.

"The Iron Destroyer," Velissa commented to Raenna. She spoke into the artificial wind created by the rapid flight of the condorgs.

"The Iron Destroyer?"

Velissa realized then that she had never specifically mentioned the death machine to Raenna. It seemed to her that she had spoken of it in the Southern Continent, but never in Raenna's presence. Still, the roar of the wind made conversation extremely difficult, especially at the altitude they had chosen to fly. They circled lower, above the courtyard of the castle, taking a great risk of being seen. Still, they had to know.

"Look!" cried Raenna, as they passed over the structure.

From a side door in the inner court of the castle a file of warmly dressed figures were issuing with pails. They moved to a large receptacle near the center of the court, poured some water into it, and then backed away.

No sooner had they emptied the contents of the pails than the catterlobs moved toward the trough to drink. A second file of women, also dressed in black, approached the catterlobs. They were carrying what appeared to be chunks of meat. At the sight of this second group, the catterlobs turned from drinking.

The women appeared to be terrified as the heads of the monsters swiveled their way. They dropped the meat and ran. The catterlobs lumbered up to the meat and ate. The sight made Velissa more determined not to let the unspoiled valley of the Sundals be ravaged by Parsky's deceptions.

Raenna felt that she already knew the answer to the question she now asked Velissa, "Are these the remaining widows of Canby?"

"Who else could they be, Raenna?"

All of a sudden, Hallidan came flying at a furious rate toward them.

"Ho-lay-ho!" he cried. "Follow me!"

Without asking for an explanation, Raenna turned her condorg to follow her husband. They had not gone far when they caught sight of a rider on a lone catterlob making his way from Maldoon along the southern trail leading to the road that went around the western ridges.

"That catterlob is armed!" cried Raenna.

"Then its rider has to be Parsky!" cried Velissa.

"You must follow him to be sure that he is not headed for the land of the Sundals west of Quarrystone," said Hallidan. "I fear you must make the trip alone, for tonight I must meet the Star Riders and ask them to tell King Ren we need his knights to deal with Thanevial's Drogs when they arrive."

Velissa felt sure that Ren would help, but she had other fears that the enchantment of sun on snow could not erase. Raccoman could not hope to remain safe if the Drogs reached the enclave before reinforcements came from Rensland. If that happened, she and Raenna would have to act alone to stop Parsky's devious plan.

Raenna and Velissa circled higher as they watched the lone figure far below them in the snow. His lumbering, forward progress never halted even for an instant, but his pace was so slow that Raenna and Velissa decided to fly north to survey the ruins of the Orange Observatory. They abandoned their circular flight pattern and headed in a straight line to the ridges. When they were far north and west of the catterlob and its rider where they could no longer be seen, Raenna began settling in. Soon she brought the condorg to a lower, level flight. At last, they reached the Orange Observatory.

The buildings were in rubble, and the shattered, splintered roof of the great hall was filled with snow. Icicles hung in every room of the once-proud house.

Yet except for the ice and snow, it was as if the party had just stepped out. The bowls that Parsky had used for his stew still sat upon the table, now covered with shards of glass and bits of wood.

Great beams had fallen from the ceiling and were lying at odd angles over the table top.

Velissa gasped.

In one corner of the room, there lay a partly decayed form still holding a spoon in one hand and a great bowl in the other. His near-skeletal form was still clothed, but encrusted with snow and ice. On the clear span of floor that had been used for dancing, there were half a dozen other forms. Both of the women felt uneasy in the old room. They did not stay long.

They walked outside and were glad once again to be in the sun.

They made their way next to Old Krepel's Observatory. Raenna lifted the latch and tugged to pull the door open. The snow bunched up, forming a natural doorstop and making it impossible for the door to swing very wide. Raenna kicked the snow with her foot and cleared enough of it away to permit her and Velissa to enter.

As many times as Velissa had been to see Krepel, she had never entered the Orange Observatory. She was amazed that it was so similar to her father's. She started to peer through the eyepiece when she remembered that Krepel had, of his own accord, broken the upper lens. She turned from the telescope and looked around the room.

There was an odd clump of snow near the observatory window. It was bigger than all of the rest of the clots of ice and snow that had settled around the opening where the tube had jutted through the roof. Out of one section of the irregular clump of snow stuck a long black feather.

It was Raenna who saw it first. "Velissa!" she exclaimed. "Come here!" Velissa obeyed. Raenna kicked the snow away from the clump. More black feathers appeared. Both of the women fell to their knees and began clearing away the snow as rapidly as they could.

"Rexel!" cried Velissa in unbelief, then turned her head. She could not bring herself to look at her old friend.

"Velissa," Raenna said. She paused, still working with the snow until it was all cleared away. "Velissa," Raenna repeated. "Look, there is a broken arrow sticking out of the falcon's breast."

When Velissa had summoned all of the courage that she needed, she looked.

"Oh, Raenna! One by one, the Guardians have been killed. First, the white falcon, then Doldeen, now Rexel. All the guardians are dead!"

"Now we are the guardians," said Raenna.

"But how did it happen? How did Rexel get to the Orange Observatory?" asked Velissa.

"Rexel must have stopped to rest here on his way back from Maldoon."

"But could he have flown this far with an arrow in his chest?" asked Velissa.

"It seems unlikely," admitted Raenna. "Perhaps he just stopped to rest and was wounded here."

They heard a crunching outside in the snow. Both of the women froze.

Then Raenna laughed. "It's only our condorg. This old site is deserted."

Velissa turned again to Rexel.

She thought of how the gallant falcon once had been an ambassador of two worlds. She thought of how he once had served in the courts of Maldoon and then Rensland. She couldn't help remembering how she herself had ridden the giant falcon when he was filled with the essence of the Singreale.

"Oh, Raenna." Velissa spoke softly and with a faraway expression. "Raenna, he's gone forever. There is no Rexel, no guardian."

Raenna's reply was firm. "I say, *we* are the guardians."

"Still, Rexel didn't have time to reach Rensland. It must have happened here in the lost land of the Canbies."

"Parsky?" asked Raenna.

"I can't believe that Rexel would get close enough to Parsky of Maldoon to permit this to happen. Perhaps it was one of Parsky's drones," said Velissa.

"Do they range this far from Maldoon?" asked Raenna.

"They didn't when we were a part of the land, but we have been gone for a long time. They could be anywhere now."

As the Graygill stood, an arrow whizzed past her and stuck in a nearby beam. The shaft of the arrow quivered and snow trembled and fell from the top of the beam.

"What?" Velissa exclaimed. She turned to see where the arrow came from, but Raenna grabbed her and threw her to the floor. A second arrow shattered the air just above them.

Raenna looked in time to see a Blackgill standing in the door. The Blackgill was hurriedly working to fit a third arrow to his bowstring. Raenna decided not to give him the chance.

The valiant Raenna drew her fire-glass sword, which she had not used in many months. She swung the shaft and cut the bow in two. The Blackgill, who was only half her size, was terrified as soon as she stood up. He drew his much shorter sword and tried to face her.

The Blackgill and the Titan woman began circling each other in the small confines of the Orange Observatory. Several times he was within easy reach of Raenna's hot blade. Still, she could do nothing to make herself act. Velissa noticed that she had passed by two opportunities to dispatch her foe. When the third occasion presented itself, Velissa cried, "Now, Raenna!"

"I can't, Velissa!" Raenna shouted back. "He is so small!"

Velissa understood now that Raenna was troubled by the Blackgill's size and rather handsome appearance. Raenna had never killed a handsome foe. She had only dispatched the beastly and ugly Changelings, all her size or larger.

"It's no use," said Raenna. "I cannot do it."

The Blackgill smiled to see her intention so weakened.

When Raenna lowered her sword, he rushed upon her. His determination equalled that of the Drogs. He swung his short sword and caught the ribbing on Raenna's heavy coat. The garment took the brunt of the swing, but Raenna knew she would not be so lucky next time.

Velissa leapt to Raenna's defense and wrenched the hilt of the hot blade from her friend's hand. Raenna was powerless in that moment, but Velissa was not. Her mind flashed to the past. She imagined her friend, Doldeen, slain by a Blackgill sword. She imagined, as she had a hundred times before, her father dying from Blackgill treachery. She thought of the men of Canby and of Demmerron.

Now she wielded the hot blade with vengeance. She flew at the drone. It was his very arrow, she was sure, that had killed Rexel. This last thought provided all the motivation she needed. She swung the sword in a hot, red arc. The blade slashed through the Blackgill's mackinaw and came to rest in the searing center of his abdomen.

The heat of the blade prevented any blood from flowing, but the Blackgill's dying body fell across that of the falcon, frozen in the snow. Velissa and Raenna turned from the sight momentarily before they advanced to the dead drone, no doubt left on duty by Parsky at the Orange Observatory against the day of the Graygills' return. That day had come, but this drone would carry no word to his master.

They pushed the body of the Blackgill aside and removed the falcon, placing him in a basket made of candolet webbing. They found a patch of ground, and Raenna's blade cut away the frosty snow and earth until the burial basket could be laid inside.

Velissa sang the anthem of the Canbies:

We shall sing at the base of the ginjon tree,
For Canby's fields are the fields of the free.
And beasts and men are timeless friends
In the ageless land of Estermann.

Raenna thought of all of Rexel's years in the court of Ren and she, too, looked wistfully away as she repeated the words of the requiem:

This is the land
where honor reigns.
This is the land
where truth is king.
Here is the kingdom,
void of change,
Where men live free forever.

Velissa wanted so badly to get a message to Raccoman, but there was no messenger to send. Hallidan was on his way to the encounter with the Star Riders with a plea for help. She and Raenna must continue to follow Parsky. At all odds, they must prevent his deceiving the Sundal Graygills.

They turned away from the pathetic mound of snow Rexel's grave had created. Soon they were on the condorg, flying south to survey Parsky's progress.

The snow was growing deeper on the southern road ridge, and it was clear that Parsky's going was becoming even slower. They watched him long enough to realize that the Blackgill was determined to take the south road around Quarrystone Woods and make the long trip that would lead him at last to the valley of the Sundals.

They both knew what he wanted with the Sundals. They thought of Abbon and shuddered.

Raccoman and Old Sammuron became friends the very instant that Raccoman disclosed to the blind Moonrhyme that he was the son of Garrod. During the long afternoon that Velissa and Raenna spent in the unspoiled valley, Sammuron told Raccoman much of the history of the Moonrhymes. It was not boring to Raccoman, since he had sprung from the very stock that had produced life at the enclave.

Old Sammuron could not shed any light on what had caused the cataclysm. Nor did he know how life had returned to the desolate and burned-out valleys. But Sammuron assured him that the return to life had taken centuries. Further, the blind man reminded Raccoman that life in the valley south of the enclave was destroyed when Blackgill marauders entered Maldoon. Raccoman thought of Parsky and how he had deceived the people. He had once believed that Parsky was the friend of all who could sing and dance and bless the peace that marked the valley of Canby.

Then old Sammuron told him of the salamander eggs and how they had lived for years until Jendai brought the Selendrenni from the high cliffs.

"Goronzo is a male and Calaranz is a female," Old Sammuron exulted. "Yes, Raccoman, there will someday be salamanders again in these valleys. Oh, what I would give if my old eyes could see them for even an instant."

"They are indeed formidable," agreed Raccoman.

The conversation turned from the salamanders to life as Raccoman had last observed it in Rensland. Now the old man seemed perplexed. His brow rose and wrinkled several times during Raccoman's recounting of the war and the disappearance of the Drogs. Raccoman seemed to encounter no resistance in Old Sammuron as he continued his tale of the Singreale and Thanevial and the host the Drog lord had led into tunnel four of the Caverns of Smeade.

"So that is the roaring in the earth!" cried the old man. It was clear he was delighted to know the reason for the strange rumblings that his more-than-sensitive ears had heard. His excitement turned soon to despair, however.

"Alas, the Moonrhymes have never learned to fight," said Old Sam. "They have always depended upon the safety of the enclave to protect them from their foes."

"But their foe has always been in the valley. Now the foe will be issuing from these very tunnels," said Raccoman.

The Graygill asked if Old Sam had ever heard of the undersea passage that linked the continents.

He had not.

"Then the hopes I have had that you might be able to help us with some ancientbound disclosure are for nought. We have no hope!" Raccoman despaired.

"There is a kind of hope. It lies here." Old Sammuron's index finger, wrinkled and thin as it was, pointed to his ear. "I can hear the demon horde approaching these caverns. I have no idea when the Drogs will arrive, but the death noise of their approaching is all about us in the air."

"Can you hear them even now?" Raccoman grew alarmed.

"Raccoman, you are so like Jendai. He, too, hears nothing. I tell you, the roar of their approach is all about us in the caverns. And even could I not hear that, I would still be shaken by the tremor that now moves through this very tunnelree."

While Raccoman and Sammuron talked, Grentana and Jendai decided to take their boredom to the face of the cliffs. They climbed into the strong saddles of Goronzo and Calaranz and then spurred the salamanders to leap out of the high opening. The day was marvelous, and the great beasts raced down the sheer cliffs until they reached the lower canyon.

The salamanders desperately hated to run in the snow, which had collected in soggy, thawing drifts. They kept to the shallows at the very base of the Moonrhyme cliffs. It was a beautiful day, and Grentana and Jendai tied the reins of their mounts loosely to the fronts of their saddles, then set the salamanders free to play.

The beasts knew the gesture. A kind of capriciousness led them to race down the canyon with their riders toward the Sentinels of Demmerron. Grentana wondered if they would try to do what seemed to her impossible. The stone pillars from the base looked like titan spearheads stabbing the sky, but the beasts did not hesitate.

Goronzo first leapt to the spire and raced up the wide needle. Jendai could not believe his eyes. The stone appeared a large white icy nail standing vertical in the earth. Goronzo sped skyward and Jendai felt exhilarated by the swift ascent. Soon he looked over to the other stone tower and saw Calaranz also racing upward into sky. Grentana and Jendai glanced at each other at the same time. They were too far separated to see each other's expressions, but they could tell that their salamanders were enjoying the outing.

In a magnificent moment, Goronzo topped the stone and stopped so suddenly that Jendai lunged forward in the saddle. The salamander sat poised and gazed out at the long valley before him. To the left were the western ridges. To the right were the eastern highlands. To the southeast lay the formidable ruins of the once-proud castle of the dead King Singreale.

Calaranz sat atop the other pinnacle of stone. Grentana thrilled to feel the sky. She had never been so high.

The sun was warm on top of the snowy spires, and the salamanders sunned themselves. Calaranz closed her leathery eyelids and slept. Grentana yelled across the clear thin void:

"I love you, Jendai!"

"And I, you!" Jendai called back.

He checked his saddle girths, feeling suddenly very silly in his insecurity. Then he smiled to see that Grentana was checking hers as well.

"I'll never be able to look when they start down," she confessed.

"Let's hope they keep their eyes wide open," laughed Jendai.

They rested on the twin spires until late afternoon. By this time, snow clouds were rolling in behind them. The heavy clouds collected beneath them, but remained well above the valley floor so that the pair presided over an endless field of white mist pierced by the high, proud needles of Demmerron. Goronzo and Calaranz didn't seem to mind. They looked disinterested and continued to enjoy their sunlit spires. Below the mists, a fierce blizzard began to coat the upper cliffs with ice.

Finally Goronzo opened his eyes, signalling that his nap was over. Grentana's mount did the same.

"We let them come up on their own!" Jendai called to Grentana. "Let's give them the same freedom going down. Believe me, it will be the safest for all of us."

"All right!" shouted Grentana. "But I have the feeling this is going to be a very fast ride."

Goronzo turned on the tip of the Sentinel Stone, then abruptly and furiously, as was his custom, he fell over the edge and began plunging downward with gigantic strides. In an instant, the salamander pierced the clouds. Jendai wondered if the beasts did not derive some fiendish pleasure from terrorizing their riders.

The valley floor, which was a scramble of stones and snow drifts, rushed up at Grentana. Never had she seen the ground rise so rapidly. She was too terrified to watch, and yet she was afraid not to watch. When they had reached the bottom, the salamanders raced toward the east cliffs. The snow was falling heavily now and the wind was blowing. Jendai and Grentana decided to get out of the wind and the snow for a little while, so they reined their salamanders into an empty cave on Eastwall.

The caves on Eastwall were empty. They were too near the ground and too accessible to enemies for the Moonrhymes ever to inhabit them. Goronzo dashed into the cave and Calaranz followed. The moment they entered, the wind was broken and they felt warmer. They both dismounted.

Jendai found some dry twigs near the entrance to the cave, and he took his flints from his mackinaw and built a fire. The fire-loving salamanders drew their huge hulks as close as they could get. They put their beautiful heads right in front of the fire and delighted to inhale the small flames Jendai had nurtured. They breathed so heavily that they nearly extinguished the little fire.

Jendai and Grentana discussed the meaning of Raccoman's return and the strange report of the Changeling army. Gradually, however, their conversation turned to lighter subjects, and they talked about what they would do once the danger passed, if indeed any of them survived it. Grentana snuggled close to the warm front of Jendai's mackinaw. Soon they would be out in the snow again, but for now they were alone together and warm.

Jendai was almost ready to repeat the affirmations he made to Grentana atop the sentinel stones, but he decided not to. There was little point in saying it again, and yet he could not resist telling her:

"Grentana, I meant what I said on the sentinel stone."

"And I did, too," she replied before she saw two bright eyes glowing from a niche in the cave.

"Look, Jendai! We are not alone," she said.

"What is it?" asked the wood-bearer.

"Who can say?" Her answer was no answer.

Jendai stood suddenly, took up one of the pieces of burning wood from the fire, and approached the eyes. He laughed out loud. "It's a serpent!"

"A serpent!" laughed Grentana.

"We've stumbled upon her nest."

The great snake was glad to see the fire and had advanced from the back of the cave toward Jendai and Grentana. She hissed in friendly tones and curled up close to the fire.

They had made a friend.

"In the spring, she will lay her eggs," said Grentana. "We must mark the opening of this cave."

"We must," agreed Jendai. "Serpents are ever a sign of good fortune. Grentana, can you still have any doubt about our relationship?"

"Velissa Dakktare used to own a serpent," mused Grentana in a quiet voice.

"Hers was a guardian to Singreale," replied Jendai.

"Serpents can be taught to talk, you know," said Grentana. "Can we come again? You build the fires, and I'll teach her to talk."

The snow fell that day as far south as Maldoon.

Well before sundown, Velissa and Raenna were back in the Blue Observatory. A fire was roaring as Velissa prepared some of the preserved vegetables that Raccoman had found in the barn. Their minds were not on dinner, however. Now that Rexel was dead, it was critical that Hallidan get through and that Parsky be stopped as well.

The observatory grew warm as the fire grew hotter. Velissa was glad to know that the old scope was working. She scanned the skies. She was looking for a nearer star . . . Hallidan. She knew she would be able to tell the condorg from the other stars.

At length, it happened. Through her father's scope, she caught sight of a moving star. She cranked the focus wheel until the bright blur of the moving light became the incandescent form of the Star Rider Hallidan.

"I see him! I have found your husband!" she cried.

"Have you? Have you?" Raenna could hardly wait for her turn at the scope. They watched, each taking turns at the eyepiece until the tiny form of Hallidan had traversed the eastern span of the late night sky. Suddenly he dipped too near the low horizon and disappeared from their field of vision. As she had done before, Velissa suspended the vertical rotor and pulled the pin. Now the tube moved lower so that they could continue to follow the starry miniature messenger.

Near midnight, Velissa cried, "There they come!"

Raenna took the scope and watched. An entire starfield was moving toward Hallidan. With enchantment, Raenna watched as the single, migrating star met the wandering battalion of light. Somewhere beyond Maldoon, the skies held council, and that council would be the life of the enclave.

The grass grows green
Where red has flowed.
A loss of life
Is wisdom's gain,
And battle trenches
Line the face
Of those who wield
The mace and chain.

CHAPTER VII
Eastwall

WHILE OTHERS HEARD NOTHING, Old Sam had complained regularly of the roaring in the tunnelrees. Raccoman's gloomy prophecy, coupled with Sammuron's report, caused those who shared the enclave to shudder before an uncertain future.

The Moonrhymes knew that the times were perilous. Sammuron, early one afternoon, sent some of the children of the enclave home in the middle of a story. For longer than any could remember, he had been the Moonrhymes' storyteller, and never in the enclave's existence had he refused to finish a tale.

Raccoman was troubled, for he knew that the Moonrhymes could not even imagine a Drog. Winter was old, but an abundance of ice still clogged the ladder holds on the cliffs. He had hoped for an early spring so they could evacuate the enclave before the Drogs arrived. Now he had doubts.

His doubts were compounded by the uncertainty of how and when the Drogs would come. The chambers and tunnels of the enclave lay on seven separate levels. Sammuron's tunnelree was on the upper layer of the labyrinth, which gave him the freedom of his fire. His and a few of the other, uppermost tunnelrees had ventilating fissures that allowed smoke to move through the stone passageways and escape.

The lower levels had not been explored. These levels, reasoned Raccoman, were the ones most likely to connect to the undersea shaft that his father, Garrod—and later, the beast-warriors of Thanevial—had taken.

Connecting the lowest level and level four was an incredibly deep pit that had been named the Paladrin shaft. *Paladrin* was an old Moonrhyme term that meant "bottomless abyss." The Paladrin Shaft had the same kind of ladder-notching as the outer cliffs. The notches had been cut there by the earliest of the Moonrhymes. Being inside the cave, these handholds and footholds never iced over, and those enclave-dwellers who dared could descend the abyss to the lowest known and explored tunnelrees. The pit was twice as deep as the outer cliffs were high. Many of the Moonrhymes had descended the shaft from time to time, hoping to chart undiscovered tunnelrees.

The Moonrhymes feared the Paladrin. They were not afraid of heights, for they had long overcome that fear in their centuries of dealing with the outer cliffs. However, the Paladrin led to a world that was perilous and uncertain. Those who had been to the lowest levels of the enclave forbade their children ever to play there. Tales were told of other shafts in the unexplored labyrinths where children, and even adults like Garrod, had ventured, never to return.

Old Sam agreed to walk with Raccoman to the dreadful opening in the floor of level four. Raccoman felt that the old Moonrhyme's sensitive ears might be able to detect if the Paladrin was the source of the horrible roar that only he could hear. The torch they carried was for Raccoman's benefit as he led Old Sam along. Through the dark tunnels, they descended. As they reached each successive level, Raccoman became less certain. They were in the tunnelrees that connected levels three and four when Raccoman stopped dead still. There was a horrible crashing behind them.

"Drogs!" gasped Raccoman in terror.

"Goronzo!" croaked Sammuron.

The old man was right. The salamander had trailed after them from the upper level where he slept in Sammuron's fire to the third level that wound downward to the level of the Paladrin Shaft. The salamander breathed a column of satisfied flame into the darkness. Where the ceiling of the tunnelree was low, the swift Goronzo was able to flatten his bulk and move with ease through the small opening.

Raccoman, serving as eyes for the both of them, needed the torch. The pungent odor of the oil that fueled it masked the dankness of some areas of level three.

Near the end of level three, they passed four or five slime pits. Raccoman took careful note of their location in case he should ever have to pass that way in darkness. The tunnelree contained mounted torches only to the entrance of level four.

The last dwellings of the enclave were on level three. Each level of the caverns constituted a unit of the enclave. It was the responsibility of each unit to keep its own torches lit. In his concern for the safety of all levels, Raccoman found himself wishing that various levels of the enclave were connected by a single hallway. The Moonrhymes could then defend the entire enclave by blocking the stone corridors that connected all levels. This was not the case, however. The main corridors were lighted between levels, but miles of adjoining tunnelrees were not. All the burrows were latticed and honeycombed by complex and uncharted connecting tubes. No defense could be made by sealing any one corridor, for it would take their enemies only a little while to locate some alternative burrow to the next level.

One thing could be done to gain time: every torch could be extinguished along the way to the Grand Cavern on the uppermost level. The Grand Cavern was so large that it extended all the way to the outer crust of the mountain that was its outer dome. The Moonrhymes—industrious as they were—had paved the huge room and cavescaped it with benches, walkways, and an abundance of torches. It resembled a very large, indoor park.

Raccoman knew that the Grand Cavern would be unsafe when the Drogs came. It was too open and held no hiding places. The Moonrhymes' best defense was the one most natural to them. They knew well the courses of the inner labyrinths and which of them ended in blind corridors. This ancient knowledge of the enclave would serve them well when the Drogs invaded their subterranean world. After Raccoman's warning, the Moonrhymes had busied themselves digging new, small passageways through which Graygills could pass but not their giant foes. Indeed, many had already filled their secret hiding places with water and food and other necessities.

The Moonrhymes were superior to the Drogs in speed and agility. Under ordinary conditions they walked at only half the speed of the Drogs, but they could outrun almost any kind of beast or being on the planet. The centuries of cliff-climbing had strengthened their short frames. Moonrhyme Graygills were even a little smaller than Canby Graygills, and their size had deceived Raccoman at first. He had been surprised to find that they could move much faster than the quickest Drog he had ever seen. In most ways, however, they were ill prepared to fight. They had no weapons, having always depended upon the enclave as their defense. Raccoman shuddered to realize that besides Hallidan's blade, his was the only sword he had seen among the Moonrhymes.

With the shortage of weapons in mind, Raccoman felt that the best strategy might be to evacuate the enclave. Fleeing was not a good answer, but it seemed better than trying to defend Westwall without weapons. At first, the idea of leaving the sanctuary of the enclave had been abhorrent to the Moonrhymes. Gradually they became more open to Raccoman's logic. "If we cannot fight," they reasoned, "perhaps flight is best."

The Moonrhymes trusted Raccoman, and he wondered why. Perhaps, he thought, it was because the name of his father inspired trust in two worlds. Perhaps it was because they knew so little of war that they felt a need to trust. Perhaps it was because desperate times always require desperate answers.

The question now became: where would they go when they evacuated?

The best suggestion was Eastwall. Eastwall, too, was latticed with chambers and tunnels. The Moonrhymes had turned from living there in the early days for many reasons. Primarily, it did not catch the full warmth of the sun in winter. Every window of the shrouded eastern cliffs opened into the shadows of the canyon. Besides, there were few natural fissures in the rocks by which to ascend. A new set of foot holds would have to be cut to make the windows of Eastwall accessible. Besides, very few of Eastwall's tunnels and caverns had been charted. Finally, there was no guarantee that the undersea tunnel might not empty into the caverns of Eastwall just as it did on the western side.

Goronzo interrupted Raccoman's thoughts with a grunt. Raccoman stopped and turned to look at the salamander. Old Sam's face tightened. Raccoman had the feeling that they both sensed something he had missed. He held up his torch, flooding the walls of level four with light. Seeing nothing, he moved on. Old Sam clung to his elbow and moved with him, but not willingly. The old man's frail fingers seemed to draw Raccoman back.

"Is anything the matter?" asked Raccoman.

The old man said nothing, but pressed his free hand against his ear, as though the roaring in the cave had suddenly become too much for him. Raccoman was now becoming afraid, and still they moved forward, until they reached a bend in the corridor.

Raccoman blinked. His eyes perceived a blue incandescence that was different from the orange light that fell from his own torch. This blue light flooded the large cavern ahead.

They had reached the cavern of the Paladrin Shaft. The blue light shone upward out of the opening of the famed abyss. Raccoman had seen such light only once before. It was the glow of the Singreale! Suddenly, terror gripped him as he remembered that the Singreale was in the hands of Thanevial.

Sammuron and Raccoman retreated around the corner of a stone outcropping to listen. They heard a dull kind of militant singing coming from the pit. Now that Raccoman's eyes were accustomed to the new light, he could see bulky shadows dancing on the ceiling of the cavern. The shadows were those of great creatures, apparently climbing the shaft. They listened to the monotonous chant of the shaft climbers.

Counga Halka lin condungra!
Kalkamanga minn Ka Mungra!
Thanevial gukka Thanevial gukka!

The Graygill drew his sword and shuddered to think that others might have already cleared the abyss and were wandering in the enclave. Still, he reassured himself, he had seen no evidences of the Drogs anywhere else in the caves.

He knew if this was their first appearance after their long undersea march, they would be dreadfully hungry. Having eaten their own kind for several months, they would now be ready to devour anything they found. Remembering their cannibalism, Raccoman shuddered.

"Wait here," Raccoman whispered to his blind companion.

He pried Old Sam's desperate, bony fingers from his elbow and promised, "I'll come back for you. I'm going closer to the shaft."

Leaving his companion, he crawled slowly to the great opening in the floor, pushing himself along like one of the salamanders. Even before he arrived at the brink of the Paladrin Shaft, he could smell them. He had forgotten the stench that accompanied the beast-warriors.

Now he was close, and he inched his way cautiously and silently on his belly to the brink. There he listened to the scraping sound their claws made as they scratched the sides of the shaft to gain leverage for their climb. Once they stopped singing, he could even hear their labored breathing.

Raccoman peered over the edge of the opening in the floor. The shaft was bathed in the blue-white light of Singreale. From his prone position, the Paladrin Shaft extended downward so far that it appeared to be just another of the many caves opening into the cavern. Only the sweating, grunting Drogs convinced him that the tube was really vertical and a challenge to the monsters climbing up before his eyes.

Raccoman was relieved to see that they were still a long way from the top. He could only assume that the Singreale was still at the bottom of the shaft in the hands of Lord Thanevial. In the blue, shifting incandescence, it was hard to determine the source of the blinding light. Raccoman worried that they might see even his short brow and shaded eyes peering down at them. But they were spending every last ounce of their energy in the rigors of their climb.

Suddenly Raccoman drew back in terror. One of the Drogs was near the top on the far side of the shaft! Raccoman trembled when he saw him, for the Changeling would shortly clear the rim of the pit. The hunched monster was struggling so hard to climb that he had not seen the prone Graygill observing him. Raccoman crept away from the edge of the pit and followed the shadows to the far side. Then he moved toward the ledge of the abyss again and waited, drawing his fire-glass blade.

He heard the labored breathing of the Drog. His heart quickened as he saw the first of the Drog's two clawed hands come over the edge of the pit. He steeled himself and moved closer, raising his fire-glass blade. The second claw appeared, and the Drog rested for a final moment and prepared to swing his ugly hulk up out of the abyss. His pause for breath was overlong.

Raccoman ran to the edge of the shaft and brought his sword down in a fiery, red arc. Both of the Drog's hands were severed from his body. While the hands still clung to the rim of the shaft, the rest of the beast-warrior pitched backward into the blue light. His scream melted in a decrescendo of terror. His body became a missile, striking a clean swath down the side of the shaft, sweeping twenty Drogs with him into a wailing plunge to death.

Raccoman kicked the two sweaty, clawed hands away from the edge. He dared not look over the brink now. He knew he would be seen. Most of the Drogs would probably think that the falling Drog had only slipped in the ascent. However, it would not take them long to discover that one of the falling Drogs had had his claws severed. They would know then that their undersea journey was over and that they had arrived in the caverns of their enemies.

While Raccoman was occupied in thought, Goronzo rushed over the edge of the pit. Suddenly Raccoman knew he had to see. He threw himself back onto the floor and crawled swiftly to the rim. Goronzo's dark hulk flew down the shaft, while the climbing Drogs blinked up in wide-eyed terror. By the flawless light of Singreale, the Changeling warriors watched as the salamander raced on sure feet. The terrified Drogs, who had just witnessed their companions swept from one side of the shaft, now watched as the salamander cut a swath through more of the Drogs and sent them catapulting down the opposite side of the pit. From Goronzo's mouth issued a stream of fire as he blazed downward. Many of the Drogs were burnt, others were knocked aside, but all of them fell away in carnage.

The Drogs had pursued an uneventful march for several months. If they had been bored, their boredom now ended. Raccoman watched in amazement. The enemy had been caught so unaware that even those at the bottom of the shaft had no time to draw their weapons, and it was impossible for those already climbing up the side of the shaft to draw their swords, for they needed both hands to manage the perilous and lengthy ascent.

Whoever held Singreale at the bottom of the Paladrin Shaft must have realized, from the rain of falling Drogs, that something had gone wrong. The bearer of the Singreale quickly fled into an adjoining cavern at the bottom of the shaft. The shaft and level four above it were plunged instantly into darkness. The torch that Raccoman had been carrying was now a welcome source of amber light once the blue incandescence of the Singreale was gone. Old Sammuron held the torch, though it meant nothing to him. Raccoman smiled to see the old Moonrhyme there, blind as a rock, holding the light for his friend.

Raccoman stared into the black pit. He could hear the whirring of the air as Goronzo stirred it. It sounded as though the salamander had reached the bottom of the pit. Now and then, Raccoman watched for flashes of fire from Goronzo's mouth. But these scorching blasts of flame appeared only as weak flickers from the top and then ceased entirely. Raccoman strained to see into the black pit. He could hear the sounds of more falling Drogs. Their agonized wails were depressingly audible as Goronzo rose back to the top in blackness. The salamander, who had cut a wide swath going down, was cutting yet another swath through a terrible column of Drogs who were still clinging desperately to the walls. Raccoman knew he was coming back, for he could hear him racing up the stone shaft, but he saw no fire issuing from his mouth. By the scant, amber light of the torches, Raccoman at last saw a huge bulk in the dark and cheered. Goronzo was back!

Raccoman edged away from the shaft, ran to Sammuron, and seized the torch. When he returned, he could see the reason that Goronzo was not breathing fire. In his mouth, he carried the body of a Drog. The beast-warrior was dead, crushed between the giant jaws of Goronzo. Raccoman exulted that the salamander, acting alone, had repulsed the first wave of Drogs. Best of all, Raccoman now had evidence that they existed.

In a little while, he had taken a coil of fiber cable that Old Sammuron had carried and tied the dead Drog to Goronzo's neck. The old man smiled and said, "At last the roaring in the tunnels is not so loud." They began their return trip to the Grand Cavern.

In the hopes of finding sanctuary in the eastern wall, Jendai and Grentana decided to use the same sunny morning to explore that section of the cliff. If it was reasonable to move the enclave, they wanted to be sure that it was possible for the salamander to negotiate the icy precipice of Eastwall. The impending war weighed heavily on Jendai, ever since he had met Hallidan and seen his condorg. Now he believed Old Sam. There was a roaring in the earth, and answering it would require extreme measures.

He and Grentana both rode Calaranz, as they had not been able to find Goronzo. They were completely unaware that the other salamander had followed Raccoman and Sammuron, but Calaranz was quite capable of carrying them both. In fact, Jendai actually preferred riding double, since Grentana had to cling to him tightly, as if her life depended on it. Grentana's fright did not delight the woodbearer, but her embrace did. As the salamander raced down Westwall, Jendai spurred him to a faster plunge for the joy of feeling Grentana tighten her embrace.

The sun in the canyon shone in gold contrast to the dark corridors of the enclave. No sooner had Calaranz begun her plunge to the canyon floor than Jendai opened his arms wide and, with his face full into the wind, sang:

We fall from the sky, as the planets fly,
And run the precipice—scanning walls
In the thin bleak air, where the falcons dare
And the children whimper and old men cry—
Swimming cliffs where daring calls.
Hai-hai-hai! I'm bold Jendai—
Tracking granite, scanning stone,
Holding life in steady hands
Astride the mighty Calaranz.

The swift wind made him swallow much of his melody. Grentana drew down behind him so that the onrush of air would not choke the tuneful descant she sang behind her Moonrhyme lover. She sang as they plummeted outward and downward, and her song agreed with his:

Holay-hai, holay ho-hai!
Hold to the life in the windswept sky.
Holay-ho, holay ho-hai!
Cling to the man who's called Jendai.
Holay-ho, ho-lay, ho-hai!"

She squeezed him so hard, she forced a second verse from him. Jendai began the verse just as Calaranz slowed to cross the snowy floor of the canyon. Snow flew out on both sides of the salamander. Her mouth opened, and she shot a stream of red fire into the blue shadows of the lower snow. With fire and snow flying all about them, Jendai sang:

I carried wood while the summers flew.
Five hundred years, the red fire grew!
Old Sammuron called me from many—
To bring the cask of Selendrenni.
And the black stones broke,
In the fire and smoke,
And the broken fragments burned our hands.
But the stones must die, when the flames leap high!
Goronzo lives—and Calaranz!

When Calaranz started up the shaded cliffs of Eastwall, the lovers laughed, and Jendai called over his shoulder, "I love you, Grentana."

"I know that!" she cried. Inwardly she was glad, for she knew now that she loved Jendai, too. She was not as certain of her love as Jendai was of his, for she had been married before and he had not. She knew that although her husband was dead, she must not let her affections rush unguarded.

"Well," he called back, interrupting Grentana's reverie as Calaranz scaled the cliffs. Both of them were looking straight into the sky as Calaranz climbed upward. Jendai pressed his body full against hers and Grentana found herself warmly crushed between the high back of the saddle and the Moonrhyme's strong body.

"Well? Well, what?" asked Grentana.

"I have said I love you and—."

"Please don't make me respond now," Grentana pleaded.

Nothing more came from the riders. Only the sound of Calaranz's claws digging into the icy surface of Eastwall broke the crisp air. Up they rose. Grentana was glad that Jendai looked ahead. She was also glad for the cold air of Eastwall. It cooled her burning cheeks.

Calaranz suddenly stopped. The salamander looked into one of the lowest windows of the labyrinths of the east cliff. Both Jendai and Grentana peered around the animal's wide neck. There, on the snowy ledge inside the open window, was a tiny drift of snow, but since every window held such a drift, there seemed to be nothing unusual here that would cause the salamander to stop.

Then they noticed that right in the center of the drift was a single boot print. The boot print turned inward toward the inside of the cavern. After they had examined the print, what next caught their eyes were the remains of an old campfire. It looked as though there were smoke smudges on the stones that arched across the upper portion of the window.

"Here, Calaranz," said Jendai softly, patting the salamander on the shoulder.

Calaranz obeyed and slithered into the opening. The pair dismounted. Jendai lit a torch, still finding it hard to believe that anyone had managed to enter the lofty windows of Eastwall.

"Who?" was the only word Grentana could speak. Her thoughts followed Jendai's exactly. No Moonrhyme would be here before winter was ended. The boot print turned inward, too, therefore their captive must still be here. Their captive? Why was he a captive any more than they were?

"What if—?" Grentana paused. "What if there are more than one? What if they are Blackgills?"

Yes, Blackgills," said Jendai distractedly. It seemed that the boot print must belong to a Blackgill.

The track was small and had to have been made by either a Canby or a Moonrhyme. Since Moonrhymes never came to Eastwall in winter, the boot must have been worn by a Blackgill—hopefully, a lone Blackgill. If the Blackgill were in the service of Parsky, he must have been sent north to spy on the enclave. Perhaps Parsky had sent a drone to chart some secret way of arriving at Westwall through an undiscovered passage.

"Yes, that has to be it," said Jendai.

"What has to be it?" asked Grentana.

"It must be a Blackgill spy!"

Though Grentana hated to agree, she felt that Jendai was right. If it were one of Parsky's Blackgills, he was sure to be armed. Neither Jendai nor Grentana were. They both hoped that whoever had left his high and snowy footprint would be afraid of Calaranz, even if he were armed. Calaranz was their best hope of survival now, and they vowed to stay close to the salamander as they moved into the cavern.

Jendai took a torch from Calaranz's saddle box and ignited it before they proceeded. In every adjoining passageway, they thrust the orange flame of the torch, but saw nothing.

When at last they had advanced a great distance, they became afraid of losing their way. They stopped. Both of them knew what would happen if they lost their way in the unfamiliar tunnel system. They were now at so great a distance from the window through which they had entered that they could no longer see its light.

"We must go back, Grentana," said Jendai.

The section of the cave in which they now stood was near the joining of three other black labyrinths. The other tunnels picked up Jendai's sentence and flung the echoes of his voice through a thousand stone corridors.

"We must go back, Grentana!" shouted the corridor to the left.

"We must go back, Grentana!" reverberated the inner honeycombs of the tunnels to their right.

"Grentana," persisted the echo, refusing to drop Jendai's last word. "Grentana . . . Grentana . . . Grentana. . . ."

"Grentana!" said a loud voice. It was still an echo, she thought. No, it was too loud for an echo.

"Grentana!" It was her name, but Jendai had not spoken it.

"Grentana, Grentana!" The joy flung itself from passageway to passageway.

A small form emerged from the dark cave. In spite of the great salamander, the stranger ran directly toward the couple. With arms wide open, he went directly to Grentana, still crying as if in a delirium.

"Oh, Grentana, I am mad with joy!" he shouted.

"Grentana, I am mad with joy!" came the first echo, and a thousand echoes repeated, "Mad with joy!"

The torchlight now fell full on the stranger's face.

"Ganarett!" cried Grentana and a thousand echoes: "Ganarett . . . Ganarett . . . Ganarett!" The echoes swam and crossed and reverberated and returned as the pair embraced, "Grentana . . . Ganarett . . . Grentana . . . Ganarett!"

Jendai's heart felt leaden. Worst of all was seeing Grentana kiss Ganarett in wild joy. All joy died in the woodbearer as he turned away.

Yet Grentana, even in the ecstasy of their delirious meeting, could not fail to notice that Ganarett was now a Blackgill. The last time she kissed him, his gills had been gray.

Fifteen Star Riders had received a commission from Ren. They turned in the night sky and settled like a falling constellation north of Demmerron Pass. Hallidan and Raccoman had been given complete charge of the riders.

Hallidan took them to the top of the cliffs by night. The knights had rarely felt such bitter cold, but they were forbidden a fire. Hallidan knew that if Thanevial had already emerged in Eastwall, a fire atop Westwall would be clearly visible.

Velissa and Raenna had monitored their descent through the scope at the Blue Observatory. They had seen the Star Riders meet in the southern sky over the shadowy bulk of Maldoon. Then through the scope, they watched the gathering of stars separate into two fields. The largest of the star fields moved off to the southeastern horizon, just as it always did.

The smaller star field traveled in splendid bits of light across the dark red cliffs east of Canby. Within an hour, the moving star fields had traversed the eastern horizon and were settling low over the tall granite sentinels of Demmerron Pass. Like Maldoon, they were but shadowy shafts in the blackness.

Velissa had the eyepiece when finally the moving stars drew close together and settled as a group upon a northern summit. It was a magnificent spectacle! Never had any of the Graygill star-watchers seen a starfield land on a mountaintop.

Soon the bright convergence of light, which had clustered like a fiery beacon on the mountain above the cliffs, began to dim. Velissa knew that Hallidan and the other Star Riders were covering the bright bodies of their mounts. And even though she perceived the whole event through a telescope, she knew that across the snowy miles the condorgs shivered in the blackness of the cold night.

On the lonely mountain, Hallidan drew a long, folded blanket from underneath his saddle. He threw it across Zephrett and the translucent light of his mount was contained. The other knights quickly followed suit, and the condorgs slept in darkness. The Star Riders huddled together in the thin and biting air of the mountains, without the pretense of fire.

"What shall we do tomorrow, Hallidan?" asked Mandon.

Only one set of triplets had ever survived birth in Rensland. All three of them had become Star Riders and all three of them were now given to Hallidan's command. Mandon was one of them. Manden and Mandin were the other two, though it mattered little which name was used to speak to any one of the three. All three were identical, and any of them would answer to whatever name was called.

"Tomorrow, Mandin," assured Hallidan, using the wrong name, "we descend to the enclave."

They had brought fiber rope and heavy cabling. Best of all, the Star Riders had brought fifty extra fire-glass swords. They were so newly forged that they emitted a fiery heat even on the mountain top as they lay sheathed in their fiber scabbards. These swords would have emitted too much light had they been unsheathed. Now piled in the middle of the shivering knights, they gave some comfort against the savage cold. The swords were of the length that Raccoman carried and were intended as a basic arsenal for the Moonrhymes. Hallidan desperately hoped that he and Raccoman would have time to train the Graygills, if only minimally before war broke out in the tunnels.

"There will be fifteen knights and fifty armed Moonrhymes against somewhat less than a thousand Drogs. The odds are overwhelming, but we also have Goronzo and Calaranz."

"Goronzo and Calaranz?" asked one of the other riders, rubbing his hands together to keep them warm.

"They are the fire salamanders. They have destroyed nearly a whole army of catterlobs. I believe they will do well against the forces of Thanevial."

The men knew the fight would be rigorous, but they were determined to make the Graygill world as secure and free as their own proud citadel. They knew there would be no peace for either world so long as Thanevial lived and controlled the power of the Singreale.

"Why these containers?" asked one of the knights, as he kicked a fiber-clad, glass-lined pail. There were five or six more of the odd containers lying in the snow.

"Have you ever heard of fire eels?" Hallidan asked the inquisitive Star Rider.

"No," answered the Star Rider, still staring at the strange pail.

"Or the Ice Fields of Selen?" asked Hallidan.

"No," replied the knight, who now had begun to study Hallidan's face circled with the bright light of stars.

"Never heard of the Selendrenni?" Hallidan seemed to be evading the knight's questions in an attempt to stimulate the interest of the others. He wanted to stretch the revelation as far as possible to take their minds from the cold.

"No, no," repeated the knight.

"Well," said Hallidan, "perhaps if you have not heard of the Selendrenni, then neither has Thanevial."

Hallidan smiled broadly. His white teeth glistened with strange confidence. Then he said, "I mean to recapture the Singreale for our beloved Ren. It may be that the Selendrenni will help."

The night was so cold that sleep eluded them all. They often rose and walked just to stay warm.

"Hallidan," asked Mandin, "what of Parsky?"

"Maldoon is already broken. The catterlobs are nearly gone. The Iron Destroyer is useless in the canyons. It will be a little matter to deal with Parsky once we have dealt with Thanevial."

They understood Hallidan's objective and pledged themselves to saving the enclave.

"Does Ren rule here . . . in the land of the Moonrhymes?" asked one of the Star Riders who appeared as a dark silhouette against the starry sky.

"Ren rules all of Estermann—all this planet is his, as we are his. Ren would have this entire world serve one light—that of Singreale."

The triplets began to sing the old anthem of their alabaster city:

Here is the land where truth is king.
Here is the land where justice reigns.
Here is the land where Singreale sings.
And men live free forever.

The tall men stood on top of the icebound mountain and their song drifted among the stars.

Love cannot let
  A dying man
Pass lightly
  Into night's long black.
Love reaches out
  Into the blades
And, pleadingly, turns
  Handless back.

CHAPTER VIII

Sammuron's Gift

NEITHER VELISSA nor Raenna could sleep. Raenna's thoughts were with the stars that had settled on the mountaintop. In the Blue Observatory, she watched the dying embers in the fireplace. Again and again, her mind wandered to the ice-covered peak where a lonely vigil of half-frozen men waited among the stars for the coming of the dawn. One of those men might have come to her, except that he was committed to the liberation of the enclave and the recapturing of Singreale for his king.

Velissa's thoughts, meanwhile, did not rest atop the icy enclave but within it. She feared that the hordes of Drogs had already burst into the tunnelrees. As far as she knew, her husband's small fireglass sword was the sole armament of the entire settlement.

Both of the women were glad when they saw the moving starfield settle on the mountain. This simple event told them two things: that Ren had sent aid and that Hallidan was alive and well. Velissa dared to believe that her husband was also safe.

"Velissa," Raenna asked, as she studied the last embers of her fire, "do you believe in praying?"

"Of course," said the Graygill. "Do we not always pray?"

"Yes," Raenna agreed, then hesitated. "But I don't mean the mere blessing of loaf and yeast."

"I pray everyday for the life and safety of Raccoman," said Velissa. She was lying on her side in her makeshift bed. Like Raenna, she studied the glowing embers and the orange shadows they cast.

Raenna turned her eyes from the fire. Through the window, she could see the last few stars in the winter constellation that the Graygills called the Grand Dragon. When she had looked at the stars for a long time, she turned in the direction of the darkness around Velissa's bed.

"But who do you pray to?" she asked.

"My father taught me to pray to Singreale," said Velissa.

"The stone? The diamond?"

"No," said Velissa. "The diamond is but a symbol of his unusual power."

"But wasn't Singreale once King of Maldoon?" The wife of the Star Rider was confused.

"Yes, there was a king named Singreale, but they say he came from beyond the Nebulae that ring the Stars of Life. Singreale was not a man. He certainly was not Graygill nor a Titan. He is a spirit that swells from galaxies to Nebulae. He is the essence of all living things and passes every breath of being through his own spirit, and all of it burns like a beam of radiance through his universe and settles in splendor in the diamond that Thanevial now controls."

"Velissa, would you pray for my Hallidan?"

"Yes, of course. . . ." Velissa faltered at the pathos in Raenna's voice.

"He will not hesitate to give his own life itself while Thanevial lives. He believes that the arch Drog must be stopped no matter what the cost to him personally. Velissa, he will fight Thanevial to the death, if necessary."

"Why so strong a grudge?" asked the Graygill.

"They were once twins."

"Twins!" cried Velissa. Raccoman knew, but had never shared this with Velissa. None of the other Star Riders ever brought it up, for they knew the pain it brought to Hallidan to have it mentioned.

"His brother's rebellion against the king of Rensland has torn him with such feelings of remorse that he will never rest until Thanevial is dead."

"I, I, I. . . ." Velissa stammered terribly, trying to measure all that Raenna was saying.

"Velissa, I'm afraid I must be honest with you. Hallidan did not return to this continent because of his special friendship with you and Raccoman. He came to settle an old score with his twin. One of them will die—perhaps both."

Raenna stopped. Velissa felt she could hear her sighing in the brokenness of her soul.

"Velissa, pray for Hallidan," Raenna said at last. The Graygill turned her face to the wall and prayed silently to the spirit that soared through the universe and yet collected in the magnificent diamond that Thanevial now controlled. Yet Thanevial did not control the universal spirit to which the two women now prayed for the security of their husbands, and this gave them comfort.

"I once took a stand for usefulness before all of the Miserians in Rensgaard," Raenna told her friend. "I am still convinced that every life has to have meaning."

Velissa listened and agreed, but said nothing.

"Velissa," Raenna continued, "I believe we must act to save the unspoiled lands from Parsky. Our husbands are occupied with the enclave and cannot help us, but we must take steps against Parsky or he will set another people of peace to quarreling and war and death."

To Velissa, the whole idea of their trying to stop the desperate Parsky was unreasonable. It was not at all unreasonable to Raenna, who had slain Drogs twice the size of Parsky. However, they both realized that they must act soon, before Parsky could reach the simple Sundal star-watcher and his family.

"Velissa, if you are afraid, I will act," said Raenna.

"*We* will act. I am not afraid," said Velissa. "Even now, our husbands act with valor and we must do all we can for the Sundals."

"Parsky rides alone," said Raenna, with a smile. The fire flickered.

The Moonrhymes were astounded when they saw the size of the dead Drog that Goronzo had seized on his vengeful descent of the Paladrin Shaft. The women and children gathered in the Grand Cavern to see the slain beast-warrior.

A loud lament arose. The men sent their families to their individual quarters while they sought the best plan for holding such a formidable enemy at bay.

"I do not believe that the Changelings will attempt to climb the pit again," Raccoman told them. "Their encounter with Goronzo must have left them confused about the nature of the enemy they face." Then Raccoman stopped speaking. He waited for any one of the Moonrhymes to offer his thoughts, but none of them did. He began again.

"Still, I believe we should station two of our fastest Moonrhymes in level four to be sure that the Drogs do not try to come out through the Paladrin Shaft. If they should see that happening, then they must quickly warn the enclave.

"Beginning now, hide your wives and children in the darkened tunnels you have chosen. No one must walk the corridors, except in response to a direct threat. I have a friend whose name is Hallidan. He should be in the tunnels soon, perhaps with reinforcements. I have reconsidered the matter of leaving the enclave. While I do not like thinking about it, the last war with the Drogs of Thanevial will likely be fought in these tunnels. We must make our defense here. We cannot evacuate!" It seemed as though Raccoman had at last settled the issue of attempting to leave Westwall. He now knew it could not be done.

While Raccoman was talking, Jendai entered the cave, causing a stir. Raccoman ceased talking, and Jendai began.

"We went to Eastwall on Calaranz. There we found Grentana's husband—Ganarett, the Blackgill!" His whole announcement tumbled out at once.

Ordinarily, such a report would have struck the enclave with wonder and they would have wanted to know all about Jendai's discovery. But this did not happen. Jendai was about to walk away when he turned back to tell them, "Grentana has gone back to Eastwall on Calaranz to bring the Blackgill here. They should arrive within the hour." Suddenly he noticed the corpse of the ugly, monstrous Drog, gleaming in the torchlight.

"What's that?" he cried.

"Our enemy," replied one of the Moonrhymes. Jendai's face grew ashen.

"They are here, Jendai," said Raccoman.

"Then the war begins?" asked the wood-bearer.

"The war has begun," agreed the Canby.

Lots were drawn. Two men took a torch to descend to level four and watch the Paladrin Shaft. Raccoman realized that the monsters on the lowest level must have already begun a trial-and-error search to discover other labyrinths that would give the remainder of the Changelings access to the tunnels of the upper levels.

Raccoman had no desire to lead the weak defenses of the enclave. However, all who lived there agreed he was by far the best choice. Now he counted on two things: the arrival of Hallidan and the swift, destructive powers of Goronzo and Calaranz.

Calaranz soon returned, bringing Grentana and Ganarett with her. Both of them were aghast to see the large Drog corpse and to learn that the army of the Changelings had now entered the tunnel system. Raccoman dismissed Grentana and Ganarett to Grentana's quarters and instructed them to remain there. Grentana's compartment was very close to that of Sammuron. It was inevitable that Jendai, who shared Old Sam's tunnelrees, would see the two of them enter her chamber. Just seeing them together inflamed him with jealousy.

Raccoman had lived through a most fatiguing day. He was eager to sleep, but when he entered his own miniature cavern, he found Jendai waiting for him.

"Raccoman," Jendai said in an urgent voice, "I believe the Blackgill is a traitor. How else could he have survived Demmerron unless he was already in the employ of Parsky when the battle occurred?"

"Do you have any proof of this?" asked Raccoman.

"Proof? The only proof you need is the fact that he is still alive while the other valiant men of Canby died at Demmerron." Jendai's words were hot.

"He's a man and he's alive. Therefore, by the code of the enclave, he must be allowed to live. We will be kind to him even in a time of war."

"I tell you, he's a Blackgill and an eater of meat. He must go! He will spoil all life in the enclave!"

Raccoman was about to speak again when they heard footsteps behind them. It was Grentana and Ganarett, making their way around Jendai.

Grentana could see that Jendai was upset. They passed without speaking. Something inside of Grentana longed to reach out and touch Jendai, for she knew how deeply he felt about her. But Ganarett, her husband, had been found, and she was committed to him for as long as he was alive. It was the code of the lost Canbies—and while Canby no longer existed, the code did.

Moreover, Grentana had no wish to abandon Ganarett. She loved him as she had loved him all through their young marriage. Now that he was alive again, the matter was settled.

As they walked down the corridor, Raccoman saw a coldness in Jendai's eyes.

"Jendai," said Raccoman, "give up your grudge against Ganarett."

"But he's a traitor, a Blackgill, a meat-eater!" Jendai declared, his face white with grief and anger.

"He's also Grentana's husband for as long as he lives."

The blood began to drain back into Jendai's face. "Yes," he said. His lips curled and he repeated Raccoman's words in a different way, "He is her husband for *as long as he lives.*"

Raccoman grew afraid. "Jendai," he said, "I was once a Blackgill and a meat-eater. It is not the color of a man's gills, but the state of his heart that needs changing. There is a cave in the ridges west of Canby. I went there once and was purged of my black gills and my need for meat. Ganarett need not remain a Blackgill. If we survive the coming war, we can take Ganarett to that cave and he, too, can be purged."

"He'll never change *as long as he lives,*" Jendai repeated.

It was clear from the venom in his voice that his grudge was deepening and that his hatred would soon be as deep as his hurt.

That night after everyone had gone to bed for an uncertain rest, Sammuron and Jendai sat up talking. Sammuron told Jendai of Estermann's primeval forest. Blind as he was, Sammuron could see that the enraged wood-bearer was not really angry that Ganarett had been found, but that he had lost Grentana.

The old man began his recitation as was his custom:

When the times of fires were yet an age away,
Before the season of the current gloom had come,
There lived a man and he was I—his vision bright.
And he could see a grumblebeak against the sky.

Jendai stood up, then sat again. He was impatient and wished to hear none of Old Sam's stories. The old fire-keeper continued, as though he had not heard the restless shuffling of his wood-bearer:

There was a Graygill lass whose village is no more.
But it was there before the storms of fire—
Yes, much before,
I tell you.

Jendai tried to give attention to Old Sam. Though his hostility had not ebbed, he loved Sammuron and would never walk out on the old man's stories, even in his current rage. A heavy tear spilled out of the old man's eye. The crystal drop rolled over the heavy pouches that separated his useless eyes from his withered cheeks.

Jendai watched the tear fall and catch a ragged crevice in the old man's face, then splinter into two drops. The odd division seemed to reflect the splintering of the wood-bearer's soul. He thought of Grentana and his own eyes filled with tears. Old Sam went on:

There were villages then—
And a hundred thousand Graygill men
Before the fire storms.
Women there were and every man
Could chose his own—
And never then was a man alone.

Jendai could not quit thinking of Grentana.

Each man was all a man should be.
Each day he took his family
And sang an anthem to the fields
That brought forth most abundantly.
Does it seem a lightsome thing—
That older men should cry?
Does it seem a lightsome thing?

The chanting now began to pick up the rhythm that Old Sammuron had used throughout his centuries of telling stories.

Does it seem a lightsome thing—hey-hai, a lightsome thing?
The fields were ours, as was the sun—hey-hai honny, sing!
The fields were white, the stars were bright—hey-hai honny,
Ho-ho-ho—say me no. . . . in the day before the fire.
Not a lightsome thing at all!

The rhythm of the story was beginning to flatten out. Old Sammuron could tell it was. He quickened the syllables and chopped the black air with his hands.

Do you want to know the lass's name,
My dear Jendai?
My lover's name was Geremenni—

Her attributes were very many.
And we talked long. She sang, too—sang, I say—
With a voice as sweet as cammonmay.
I loved her, my Geremenni.
We walked and talked
In the lilting sunlight,
Played our dreams by the laughing streams
Romped in meadows and the leas,
Woke ourselves to set our dreams—
Till the fire storms came.

Now the old man's blind eyes narrowed and the chanting grew morose.

Jendai—hai, can the sweet dreams die?
Hopes may burn till hopes are dead!
And the fears that stalk are the greatest dread.
For the fire storms came and the world burned,
And the villages, we later learned, were the
Charred remains of the searing rains of
The storms of fire with their surging flames.
Hai-hai-hai! I watched her die
And the Cataclysm swept the sky.
I wept, but when the whole world weeps
None sees a single person cry.
Oh, Geremenni,—gone I say
In a wall of flame swept faraway.
I was alone! I am alone. The world was dead.
And that long dead world may die again!

This was no story, and Jendai now knew the old man's hurt. He had carried the burden of his apocalypse for two thousand years. His blind eyes cried for a long-dead love. Though Jendai had carried wood for the old man for five hundred years, he had never heard this ballad. Still, the old man's love, dead by two thousand years, could not assuage Jendai's own anguish.

"Grentana!" cried Jendai. "Grentana!"

"Come, wood-bearer," said Old Sam with firmness.

Sammuron knew his pain and held him in his thin, old arms. He chanted softly as he often did when he sang to the children of the enclave.

Hai-hai, Jendai . . . there's hope for love.
My son, my son . . . there's hope for love.
Serve the future, trust and wait.

"My only love is now a Blackgill's wife—and will be as long as he lives," said Jendai. A tear crossed his face, and he stared into the embers of the old man's fire. "Yes, by Singreale," he said. He snapped his left fist with resolve into the palm of his right hand. "Yes—*for as long as he lives.*" Sammuron had released his embrace. Now he sat back and was afraid as he heard Jendai stand and walk away.

"No, no, son Jendai!" cried Sammuron. "Trust and wait!"

Grentana's joy could not be measured.

"But how have you survived the winters since the Battle of Demmerron Pass?" she asked Ganarett, when at last they were alone.

"I grubbed roots in the fall and—I cannot lie to you, my darling—I killed congrels and ate them. Do not judge my black gills harshly. I was hungry. I had to eat something."

Grentana knew from the color of his gills that he had eaten meat, but she could not bring herself to hate him for his starving defection. Still, she wondered if such severe circumstances would really drive a good man to the eating of meat.

"My poor darling," she said as she thought of Ganarett's struggle to stay alive. "How could I ever condemn you for eating meat? You were starving!"

Ganarett smiled. How wonderful it was of Grentana to understand. "Then you do not resent me?"

"You're alive and we're together. That is all that matters. Maybe someday, when the whole sordid war is over, we can move back to the valley and farm as we once did."

"No, my darling," Ganarett laughed. "No more farming for me. I want to be a hunter."

"A hunter?" Grentana was bewildered. "What's a hunter?"

"In the cave where you found me," said Ganarett, "I've hidden a bow and arrows."

"Arrows?"

"Listen, my dear, I've been practicing for more than a year. I can shoot ganzingers in flight."

"But why?" asked Grentana.

"Because I love the taste of their flesh. We learned a great lie in the valley. Vegetables and fruit are not the stuff of which great meals are made."

They were sitting side by side, and Ganarett had his arm around her shoulder. Now as he talked enthusiastically of killing animals and eating their flesh, Grentana drew away.

"No, please, Grentana. Meat is good."

"Meat is murdered animals!"

"No, animals are for our use. I will cook you a thick, rich congrel stew. You'll change your mind."

Grentana did not believe she would ever change her mind, and they both sat for a long time and said nothing. At last, Grentana turned to him again.

"But a year and a half, you've been killing and eating. Why—why did you not come to the Moonrhymes and beg sanctuary?" she questioned.

"At first, it was winter. I could not climb Westwall. By spring I could climb, but my gills were so black, I knew the Moonrhymes would never accept me." Ganarett was becoming uncomfortable.

"So you stayed in the Eastwall tunnelrees all this time," she said. "Oh, my poor darling."

"I have not gone out all winter," he assured her.

They embraced. She anguished over the long loneliness he must have felt. She kissed him and was glad to feel the bristles of his gills again across her face. Oh, he was home—home. They were together again. What did it matter if his gills were black? What did it matter if he ate meat?

She snuggled against his chest. "But if you did not leave the window all winter, how did you live?"

"Grentana, meat can be dried in the sun, just as we used to dry vegetables to be eaten in winter. All through the fall, I dried the flesh of congrels and ganzingers. I found a catterlob calf and killed it and—"

"A catterlob calf! However did you get it to the Eastwall window?"

"I quartered it, carried it up in pieces."

"But they're so large."

Ganarett shifted uneasily, as though he felt his answer had been too weak.

The question was dropped. No other answer came. Both of them were glad. The conversation had gone on long enough to suit Ganarett.

"Let's get to sleep, my darling," he said. "There will be time for a million questions later."

"All winter you have been alone, and we've not been together for two years since that fateful day you left to fight the catterlobs at Demmerron."

Grentana suddenly sat up. "How did you escape death at Demmerron?" she asked.

Ganarett laughed. "I'll tell you all about it tomorrow when we are not so tired."

Grentana smiled. "Good idea, but tomorrow I'll want to know it all."

"You shall," he promised.

They were both nearly asleep when Grentana spoke again. "Ganarett, when you become a hunter, promise me that you won't ask me to eat meat."

"I promise," he said. "But you would like it."

"Promise me," she insisted.

"All right, I promise."

"And promise me I won't ever have to watch you quarter a catterlob calf."

"I promise."

"And promise me . . . you'll never leave me . . . for any reason again." Grentana's voice was becoming irregular. She was falling asleep.

"I promise," he said as he watched her heavy eyelids close.

"You never went out of the cave all winter . . . all through the long . . . long winter . . . you stayed in Eastwall . . . and you never left. . . ."

She was nearly asleep, but it troubled her that her Graygill husband was now a Blackgill hunter. She slept uneasily, wishing so much about Ganarett had not changed.

One thing troubled her more than all else. If he had not left the cave all winter, then why was there a single footprint in the snow—a footprint that turned inward? The footprint could not have been more than a day old and had to have been made by someone entering the cave. Ganarett must have just come to the cave, she thought. Her mind was muddled by the delirium of sleep that would not allow her to put the heavy pieces of the puzzle together.

"You did not leave . . . leave the cave . . . all winter . . . but the footprint . . . I saw a footprint in the snow. . . ." She was neither asleep nor awake, and the question was lost to her consciousness.

Jendai also could not sleep. His fears enveloped him. The war of tunnels had not begun, but he had already lost everything. He took a torch and woke the sleeping Goronzo. He belted the saddle girth and led the salamander to a window of Westwall. The stars were still brilliant and his sleeplessness promised to be a special kind of punishment to Goronzo. The salamander would rather have continued sleeping in his own warm nest, but at Jendai's urging, he slipped out of the seventh level window of Westwall and raced down the cliff into the enchanting starlight.

Something drew Jendai to follow exactly the same course he had taken the previous day with Grentana. Goronzo rushed through the shadows that created grotesque images on Eastwall. In a short period of time, the salamander had reached the icy cliffs of Eastwall and, as he had done the morning before, hurtled up the cliffs. The starlight ran in silver ripples across the vertical surfaces of glossy ice. Jendai's hatred for Ganarett seemed to ease. The swift claws of his mount dug easily into the ice and released it just as quickly as he traversed the wall.

Jendai wished that Grentana could be there to enjoy the swimming ice and stars with him. He groaned to think that they would never ever enjoy it again as one. "Never, never, never, never, never," he repeated in his despair.

His melancholy flowed out as Goronzo rose to the very window where he and Grentana had found the single footprint. Suddenly they were there.

"Here, Goronzo. Turn in here—this window."

Goronzo sped on by it, refusing to turn inward.

They cut a full vertical circle on the wall of ice. Once more Jendai ordered Goronzo into the opening, and once more the swift salamander refused to comply.

"Why do you shy away?" Jendai asked. He was determined. With his boot, he kicked Goronzo in the side of the neck. The great beast stopped. Jendai grieved that he had been so brutal.

"I'm sorry, Goronzo," he said. "Please forgive me." He reached down to pat the injured section of Goronzo's neck. There was a little tear in his beautiful skin where Jendai's boot had cut through.

"Please forgive me," Jendai again begged the great salamander. He leaned forward and looked at the side of the gallant head. He had never seen his swift mount so bewildered.

Jendai felt awful.

"But why, old friend, will you not enter the cave as I commanded you?"

Goronzo began to move again. It now seemed that he would enter the opening he had twice before refused, but Jendai knew the salamander was acting contrary to his instincts. Goronzo was only entering the cave to please him, and Jendai grew afraid.

When they were almost inside, Jendai was horrified, for in the entrance to the cave, he saw a group of huge dark creatures.

"Westwall, Goronzo! Now!" he cried.

Goronzo turned his head in an attempt to obey, but he could not move swiftly enough.

A lesion broke on the side of Goronzo's head near his eye, and blood gushed out. The salamander turned quickly and raced upward, leaving a trail of dark blood on the face of the cliff. The starry ice dulled in the horrible wash.

Jendai had reached over to console his mount, when he felt something warm on his shoulder. His tunic was soaked. When Goronzo was a safe distance from the disastrous opening, he turned and flew down the icy wall. He fled the slopes and raced to the canyons.

Jendai was bleeding so badly now that he lost consciousness as the salamander raced across the snow. Fortunately, Jendai had belted himself in the saddle. Up, up, Goronzo raced until he came to the upper window of Westwall. As he slithered in, Goronzo bellowed. Old Sammuron felt his way along the corridor.

Goronzo wailed again. This time Raccoman awoke and rushed into the tunnelree. "What has gone wrong?" cried the Graygill.

A bloody scene greeted him. It took a moment for Raccoman's eyes to measure what had happened. In the wound below the salamander's eye he felt what he could not see—the shaft of an arrow. He grasped the shaft and pulled it out. The head of the arrow would have been as invisible as the shaft if it had not been coated with blood. Raccoman was relieved to see that the bleeding soon stopped and that Goronzo's eye was uninjured. He was counting on the salamanders to help the Moonrhymes defend themselves in the coming conflict.

Raccoman's face clouded when he saw the bloody shoulder of the unconscious Jendai. He stood upon the saddle girth and untied the fiber straps that held the wounded wood-bearer. As soon as the straps were loose, Jendai fell sideways from the saddle. Raccoman caught him as he fell and lowered him awkwardly to the floor of the tunnelree.

"Bring me a torch!" he shouted. One of the crowd of Moonrhymes standing nearby brought a torch, just as Grentana and Ganarett came running up. The bellowing of the wounded salamander had awakened them both.

When Grentana saw Raccoman bending over the wounded Graygill, she became afraid.

"Raccoman!" she cried. "Is it . . . is it . . . ?" Grentana could not make herself say his name.

"It is," replied Raccoman.

Grentana tore herself from Ganarett's embrace and ran to the unconscious form.

"Oh, Jendai, Jendai!" she cried.

Raccoman said, "Grentana, leave me a little room. It has to come out."

"What has to come out?" she asked.

"The arrow."

"There is no arrow," she said.

Raccoman said nothing more. He grasped the invisible shaft in his hand and pulled gently, being very careful not to break the weapon off inside Jendai.

Grentana was stunned as Raccoman pulled the arrow free. The arrowhead was covered with blood. She saw the invisible arrowhead made visible with the blood of a man she loved—and yet must not love.

She bent over the unconscious man and, with tears coursing down her face, she sobbed, "Live, Jendai! Live, Jendai!"

"Sammuron," Raccoman pleaded, "please make him live."

Jendai was ashen. The old storyteller approached and knelt beside his beloved wood-bearer. He laid his hands on the bloody chest and bowed his feeble old back over the inert form of the man who had kept his fire and brought the Selendrenni.

"Will he live?" asked Grentana. Ganarett studied his wife's tear-stained face as she pleaded for the life of Jendai, whose love she had once publicly denied, but now confirmed in his hour of death.

The old man did not answer Grentana.

"Jendai, I am old, but I offer you now the rights of the living," he said.

Hai-hai-hai—my son Jendai.
Your blood is mine.
Your hurt grows here upon my ancient skin—
As I take your wounds!

Sammuron had ever been a man of magic and mystery, but the Moonrhymes who witnessed what followed could not believe what they saw.

Old Sammuron removed his tunic and shirt. His skin was thin and blue and white, but his hands were not so frail as they appeared. He tore Jendai's shirt from his body. Jendai's silent young chest was vigorous and well muscled. Both the old man and the wood-bearer were naked to the waist.

"Jendai, my beloved, I give you the greatest gift I can give. For five hundred years, you have been my life. Receive from me now the life you served."

He lay down beside Jendai and grew silent.

The old man's chest began a labored breathing. Then Grentana gasped. A lesion broke on Old Sam's shoulder and blood shot from the ugly wound. At the same time, the lesion on Jendai's wounded shoulder closed. As if by magic, the wood-bearer's broken flesh had come together and sealed itself.

Sammuron's old chest heaved twice and then was still. At once, Jendai's chest began to move again. When the old man stopped breathing, Jendai opened his eyes. He lay there a moment and then sat up.

"You're alive, alive!" cried Grentana, throwing herself on the surprised Jendai.

"Oh, Jendai, how glad I am! I thought you were dead."

"Jendai lives!" shouted Raccoman.

Jendai looked to the floor and placed his hand upon Sammuron's bloody shoulder. He felt alone. The old storyteller was no more. His songs were mute, his wisdom silent as the snow.

An odd sleep
Overtakes the saint,
Whose nightmares
Offer ghouls and fiends,
While demons
Foul and fanged and clawed
Own rosy,
Undeserved dreams.

CHAPTER IX
Ganarett's
Treachery

FROM HIS LOFTY VIGIL, Hallidan watched the dark bulk that was Goronzo race through the canyon and up the icy cliff. He heard the wood-bearer command the salamander to turn into the opening. He saw the beast refuse and Jendai force the animal into reluctant obedience. He could see, as the salamander raced back to the enclave, that the rider, who slumped in the saddle, was probably dead. He saw the dark fluid wash the starry ice. But most importantly, he had observed the shadowy forms in the opening of the cave.

Two other knights were keeping the vigil with him. Together the three of them had watched what seemed a silent, unreal pageant on the cliff. But they knew it was all too real.

"Drogs," said one of the knights.

"They are in Eastwall," Hallidan replied.

"Are the labyrinths of Eastwall connected to the cave system of Westwall?" asked the other knight.

"Perhaps—probably," said Hallidan. Nothing more needed to be said. The bitter cold discouraged talk. Hallidan could hardly wait until morning. He had been gone for so long, he no longer knew the status of the enclave. The sight of the Changelings in Eastwall had completely unnerved him.

He took heart from seeing Goronzo run for refuge to Westwall. This was a good sign that refuge was still to be found there. Only morning would tell him for sure. The three knights looked at their sleeping companions huddled near the condorgs. The condorgs seemed to be resting well. They had adjusted to the cold north better than the Star Riders had. Perhaps the light that illuminated them from within gave them some defense against the cold.

Hallidan set two more of the knights to keep watch. Then he drew his cloak around him and tried to find a comfortable place on the rocky crag to get some rest.

His thoughts kept him awake, however, as his mind turned to Raenna. He had loved her for centuries, and now he knew that he had even loved her all those years when she had been married to Rengraaden. Never had he violated Raenna's former marriage, but he would always remember how happy he had been the moment he discovered that Rengraaden had abdicated his vows and left Raenna a Miserian.

He loved her as she loved integrity. Even after she discovered Rengraaden was a Changeling, she would not forsake him. Hallidan knew Raenna would never have killed Rengraaden if he had not menaced the Queen's child.

He felt lonely now. Their separation had drawn on for two long months, and there was still no indication of when it would end. The cold seeped through his warm clothing until it seemed he could never be warm again.

"Raenna," he thought, "when the war is over, I will. . . ," but then he interrupted himself. He knew his thoughts were not totally honest. It was not the war that he wished to be over. He still wanted to settle accounts with his brother Thanevial, now monstrous in both form and allegiance.

The cold had settled in around him. He brushed a small drift of snow aside with his gloved hand. The white powder flew in his face. In its swirling, he saw the green mists of Rensland rise. An ivory citadel thrust upward through the jungle. The sun was shining, and he and the stately Raenna walked the red eastern fields. He stopped and drew her to himself. They kissed. She ran through the dreamlike meadows and he pursued her. She hid from him, laughing aloud as he searched. She was more beautiful than he had ever seen her. The sunlight fell upon her beautiful gossamer gown. The sheer, filmy garment fluttered in the breeze and trailed in ripples behind her.

In dreamlike strides, Hallidan ran after her and saw her hide behind a caladena tree. His reverie was welcome as he laughed in the warm, elusive sun. His sluggish legs obeyed his heart. He came to the tree where she was hiding and slipped behind it with his arms open to seize her and draw her to himself.

A dark and horrendous form pushed him back.

Raenna lay on the warm earth covered in blood. The prince of the dying Drogs stepped on Raenna's form. His boot was on her silent chest. He threw back his head and laughed. His leathery face was ugly and demonic. Hallidan drew back in horror.

"Thanevial . . . Thanevial . . . Thanevial," he murmured in the delirium of his dream, and his words awakened him.

The cold of the mountaintop was now inside him. Above the frozen peaks, the morning starscape settled cold and ominous. There was nothing warm in the night.

Jendai was alive, but tired. An image of Old Sam's bloody torso camped in his mind. More than all else, he wanted to be free of that image, but it would not fade. "Sammuron, Sammuron, you have died that I might live—but to what end?" he lamented.

He could make no sense out of why Old Sam had chosen to sacrifice himself. The ancient bard had made Westwall bright with fire and chants and ballads for as long as there had been an enclave.

"Why, why did you reckon the life of your wood-bearer so important?" He grieved over the old man's death even more than he had once grieved over the death of his own father. For Jendai, Sammuron was more than a life—he was the definition of all life. Now Jendai felt the burden of being for the first time. He felt as if he had just been born. His newness made him look inward with shame upon all that he had been before. He felt a deep guilt for having hated Ganarett—a double shame, that he had even thought to kill him in jealousy.

He knew he had been wrong to take Goronzo to Eastwall at night. He relived his brutality to the beautiful salamander. He remembered how he had torn the beast's red skin. He saw again, in his penitent heart, the pain and bewilderment in the eyes of the gentle beast.

"I am alive, alive!" he cried in joy. "My past is behind me—I will not be the man I was!"

An unspeakable happiness now eclipsed his grief. He was loved by Grentana!

"Oh, Grentana, yours is the first face I saw when I awoke. However you feel about Ganarett, however long you remain the Blackgill's wife, if I never live to know you in marriage—still I saw your face. I know you love me."

He knew that Ganarett could not have missed Grentana's obvious concern for him. None of the bachelors of the enclave could have missed it either. Grentana had not been able to stop her display of affection for Jendai. All those Moonrhymes who had known a woman's love must have well marked the event. Jendai the Third, son of Jendai the Second, son of Jendai the First was loved as surely as Old Sammuron's tunnelree was warmed by an ageless fire.

"The Fire of Sammuron! Now who will keep it?"

Jendai's mind raced back to his life, his entire life of labor—the fire of Sammuron. Why the fire? Since the cataclysm, why the fire? Was it only to hatch the black stones that gave Goronzo and Calaranz a chance to be—or was there some other reason as well that the old man kept the fire going? Jendai could not find in his hardest thinking all the reasons for the old man's fire.

Still, it was not his to question. Sammuron was dead. The fire had to continue. If the old man believed the fire in the mountain was essential, then his life had acted out the fervor of his faith for two thousand years. There would be fire in the mountain—fire ever in the mountain—for as long as Jendai lived.

From where he lay, he could see the orange flickering emanating from Old Sammuron's room and knew the fire would burn throughout the remainder of the short night. He could also see the two salamanders, who always slept in the fire room, usually with their huge heads nestled in the glowing cinders. Goronzo and Calaranz were two good reasons for keeping the ancient fire alive. Though the salamanders no longer appeared to need fire, still they never tired of the flames.

At the moment, Jendai was not sure how long he or anyone else in the enclave would survive. The enemy had gained control of Eastwall, and they were now in the lowest levels of Westwall. The wood-bearer knew that all who lived in the Moonrhyme settlement must do everything possible to halt the rise of the Drogs to the inhabited levels of the cavern system. Yet what could they do? They had no weapons. Their sole defense lay in Goronzo and Calaranz, and Jendai's night on Eastwall had proved that even they could be wounded or killed.

Jendai's mind wrestled with a million thoughts until at last, in sheer exhaustion, he fell asleep. There were less than two hours till dawn.

A few chambers away from Jendai's tunnelree, Ganarett, the

Blackgill, waited until he heard the consistent slumbering hum of his wife. It had taken her several hours to fall asleep.

For a long period of restlessness, she had meditated on the meaning of her love for both the Moonrhyme and the Blackgill.

Ganarett stealthily slipped from his place beside her in the bed. He grabbed his boots and stole outside their chamber. Once a good distance away, he buckled on his sword and put on his boots. The tunnelrees were mostly deserted, so he went to a large workroom in back of the Grand Cavern and picked up ten heavy coils of fiber cabling. There were sentries at each hallway, guarding the entrance to every level of the enclave. He knew, therefore, his task would not be easy.

He felt confident he would have no difficulty finding his way through the first level of tunnels, for they were well marked. He entered the tunnel to the second level of caverns, but a sentry stopped him.

"It is the sixth watch! We have strict orders from Raccoman that no one is to pass through the tunnel system until the sun outside is fully on Westwall. Even then, no one is allowed to pass without strict orders from Raccoman."

Ganarett laid down the burden of the heavy coils of fiber cables. He said nothing.

The Moonrhyme was swordless, as were all Moonrhymes. The Blackgill smiled.

"I'm going to pass on to level two."

"You shall not pass," said the unarmed Moonrhyme as he positioned himself in the center of the tunnel.

Ganarett drew his sword and, in a single motion, thrust it into the Moonrhyme's chest. The sentry collapsed. The assassin picked up the coils of cable and ran quickly down the corridor. He killed the guard at level three in the same manner.

Before he came to the end of the last lighted level, he sat down and took a scrap of yellow parchment from his kilt. He had found a piece of coal near Old Sammuron's tunnelree, and now he used it to etch a command in broad black letters on the parchment. He knew Raccoman had a fondness for poetry, and he thus wrote the forgery exactly as he felt the Graygill would have done it.

To the last guard of level four:
Forsake your post—Who keeps the door of this enclave

Shall this outstanding honor save.
Be servant to all Moonrhyme men,
And call this message-bearer, Friend.
Lead this man who serves me, then,
And bring him swift to Paladrin.
Who heeds my words and does this message bear
Serves both life and Raccoman Dakktare.

Ganarett stuck the note in his belt, picked up the coils of rope, and started down the last of the lighted tunnelrees. After a long walk, he came at last to the end of level three. The inky darkness of the tube stretched blind and silent before him.

Ganarett surprised the last guard with his sudden appearance.

"You shall not pass!" declared the unarmed Moonrhyme.

"I have a note from Raccoman Dakktare that says I shall," replied the Blackgill. "Not only shall I pass, but the orders I hold say that you are to accompany me to the Paladrin Shaft."

"But why?" asked the dumbfounded Moonrhyme guard. "The shaft is already guarded by two Moonrhyme sentries."

"I cannot say. I only know I do not know the way and you are to accompany me there."

"But why do you want me to go?" The Moonrhyme persisted obstinately. The Blackgill began to lose his patience.

"Look, my good fellow," said the exasperated Ganarett, "do you obey our commander, Raccoman, or not?"

Ganarett wanted to kill the guard as he had killed the other two Moonrhyme sentries, but he thought better of it. This was the last of the poor sentries. Without him, Ganarett could not hope to find his way to the Paladrin Shaft.

"I will obey Raccoman—for whatever reason," the Moonrhyme relented. "Show me the order."

The Moonrhyme read.

"How do I know this note is not a forgery?" asked the sentry.

"Look, Moonrhyme, you're beginning to weary me," the Blackgill replied, already reaching for the hilt of his sword.

Suddenly the Moonrhyme noticed that there was blood at the top of the scabbard, and he was afraid. He did not want to believe the Blackgill, but he had no reason to doubt the note that spoke from Raccoman in exactly the way Raccoman would have issued such a command.

"All right, let's go," the Moonrhyme reluctantly agreed.

He took the last torch from the wall bracket and turned into the blackness of the burrow. The tunnel threaded downward into the heart of the mountain. Ganarett fondled the heavy coils of rope and smiled. The unsuspecting Moonrhyme, acting against sound judgment, led Ganarett toward level four and the Paladrin Shaft. The trip would take them two hours. The sun broke full on Westwall in less than one.

The knights greeted daylight with more joy than they had ever greeted any morning. Hallidan and the triplets loaded the condorgs and readied the suspension ropes. He knew there was no room to land the condorgs in the narrow windows of the enclave. He had already determined that the fastest way into the heart of the precipice dwellings would be to try the same method that he and Raccoman had once used to rescue the Paradise Falcon. They would suspend cables from the undergirths of the condorgs and swing into the openings.

Hallidan had decided to land two knights who would swing themselves into the enclave, then help to receive the weapons and, especially, the heavy bundles and fiber buckets. He sensed that his every move was being watched from several windows in Eastwall.

"It would be a miracle," thought Hallidan, "if the Drogs are not, even now, in the enclave of Westwall as well."

At sunup, the condorgs flew. Hallidan guided them to the upper windows of the enclave. They threw out the suspension cables high above the snowy crags of the canyon floor. The free condorgs began hovering in the bright warm air of morning. Two of the knights cautiously undid their saddle belts and threw a leg over the front of the saddle.

The height at which they worked made the aerial maneuver spectacular. The knights, displaying a smooth, athletic daring that did not stop to congratulate itself, acted with precision. Each man moved onto the rotating wing pinions of his mount. There, perched over the high void, each grabbed the saddle girth and swung his body into space.

The condorgs wavered only slightly as the weight of their well-muscled riders dropped to their undersides. Then each Star Rider worked his way down the thin, strong cables that were tied securely to the girth straps. Hand under hand, they dropped down until they hung like insects on golden webs that glinted in the morning sun. Then, gradually, they began to sway, each creating a human pendulum suspended from the underbelly of condorg.

Their mounts hovered steadily until the arcs of their swing brought them directly into line with the windows of the enclave. Swaying at an awesome height, the Star Riders propelled themselves squarely through the openings.

No sooner had the first two knights landed in the openings than their presence was cheered by a crowd of apprehensive Moonrhymes. Soon all the windows of the enclave filled with grateful Moonrhymes who smiled broadly at these beloved Allies.

The Moonrhymes watched with interest as the Star Riders moved their condorgs, one after another, into the hovering position. They began reciting one of Sammuron's old chants that they had learned in the fireroom as children:

Ho-ho-hai, and a welcome cry—
Our windows open into light!
The sun by day and the stars by night.
A thousand feet from the canyon floor,
Enter our windswept cliffs.
Welcome to the tunnelrees!

The chant was an old welcome that even the smallest children could repeat with enthusiasm.

The chant became a roar.

As each Star Rider landed in the window, the grateful spectators offered a volley of cheers:

"Singreale lives!"

The entire detachment of Star Riders had swung into the windows within a quarter of an hour. Each of the triplets brought a separate bundle, and their encumbered swings took a little longer.

Goronzo and Calaranz stuck their massive heads out of the openings and bellowed happily at the reinforcements. Their first appearance frightened the condorgs, but not for long. Hallidan was the last to swing in, and joy overtook the enclave in an instant. Singing broke loose, burying the chant. The anthem of the Moonrhymes was old and simple, and it had long echoed in pride throughout the stone tunnels. The tones of the anthem filled the enclave and floated outward from the face of the cliff into the morning sun:

From the high, white cliffs
To the canyon snows,
From the tunnelrees
And the mountain fire,
To the lofty windows
Of the star-blazed ice,
And the grain-filled fields
Of the Mooonrhyme shine—
The enclave lives,
The enclave lives,
The enclave lives forever!

It was a song of hope.

"Look!" shouted one of the Moonrhymes in a second-level window. In the distance, they saw a gathering of small specks set against the sky. The specks were rapidly growing in size and apparently coming straight for the enclave.

Hallidan grasped their meaning first.

"Miserians!" he cried.

"Miserians! Indeed!" cried one of the Star Riders.

"There must be fifty of them!"

"Ren is forever!" shouted another knight.

Raccoman and Hallidan embraced, though awkwardly, for the titan was twice the Graygill's size.

"Ren is forever!" cried Raccoman.

"Is there any word from Raenna?" asked Hallidan.

"None—nor from Velissa, but I believe they must be safe."

Hallidan felt the same. He knew that there was too much to be done in a short time to send anyone to see about them now. Yet both he and Raccoman determined that the safety of the two women would be their first order of business once the enclave was secure.

Raccoman and Hallidan turned to watch the cheering Moonrhymes welcome the tall Miserian warriors. They were indeed beautiful women. With more grace than even the men had demonstrated, they began the same aerial maneuvers. Once more, there was chanting and singing. In less than an hour, all of the Miserians, completely outfitted in light armor and with fire-glass swords, had entered the enclave.

Raccoman, after consulting with Hallidan, decided on a tactic.

Everyone—Moonrhymes, Miserians, and Star Riders—was ordered to the Grand Cavern. The Star Riders and Moonrhymes gathered up the extra bundles of equipment, and all moved to the armory.

Jendai brought Goronzo.

Grentana was puzzled at the disappearance of her Blackgill husband, but she knew that she must join the others. She brought Calaranz, and though she stood near Jendai, she found it hard to look at him. She realized that, only a few hours before, she had been all-too-obvious in showing her love. Still, they must work together. There was little question now that she had her own part to play in the defense of the enclave. If Calaranz was to be used at all, she must ride her, for she and Jendai were the only two who had ever ridden the salamanders.

They stood by their mounts, holding the light fiber saddles in their hands. As the crowd drew near, Jendai turned to Grentana.

"I am purged of my jealousy," he said. "I wish the best for you and Ganarett."

"Please, Jendai." Grentana did not want to talk about the matter. "Jendai, I am worried. Ganarett disappeared in the early hours of darkness—sometime just before dawn."

"Disappeared?" Jendai would have pursued Grentana's concern, but Raccoman Dakktare had taken the platform to address the unusual gathering of seven hundred Moonrhymes, fifteen Star Riders, fifty Miserians, and two fire salamanders. He raised his bright-red fire-glass blade to bring the crowd to silence. The force in his voice was made all the more strong by the fifteen Star Riders who had gathered in a stately semicircle behind him.

"Ren is forever! We welcome his friends!" As Raccoman gestured toward the knights and the Miserians, the host of grateful Moonrhymes clapped their stubby hands in applause. When the applause died, he began once more.

"There are Drogs in Eastwall, and we have reason to believe they may be in these tunnelrees. We believe there may be a thousand of them." Raccoman stopped talking and gestured toward one of the bundles that Hallidan and the knights had brought with them. "In this bundle are fifty new and very hot fire-glass swords. They were made at the glass foundry in Rensgaard. They are of the same length as the one I carry, so with a little training, you should be able to handle them. The first two swords will go to Jendai and Grentana. The other forty-eight to those of you who are unafraid to learn, as quickly as possible, the art of war."

Grentana wanted to protest receiving a sword, but she knew that her example was important to the enclave. Having been offered a chance to defend the enclave, one hundred men stepped forward to receive the forty-eight swords. Raccoman was glad that the Moonrhymes understood both the lateness and the gravity of the hour.

"We want the women to bring all the food and a great deal of water to this very room. We now believe that we can best fight the enemy by using the Grand Cavern as a base. The leader of the enemy is named Thanevial. He holds the Singreale, and this will be a very great advantage to him."

A murmur of displeasure passed through the crowd at this disclosure.

"One more thing!" Raccoman kicked a bundle at his feet. "In this bundle there are windfoils and welding equipment. I am going to fashion two crude and quickly crafted sets of armor to protect Goronzo and Calaranz. I believe that if they are properly shielded, they will be formidable allies in our defense of the enclave."

A cheer went up at the idea.

"Of course, Grentana and Jendai will have armor, too, so they will be protected as they ride the beasts." Raccoman kicked another of the bundles. "Here is your special armor, my friends," he said, looking at Jendai and Grentana. "It was crafted in Rensgaard. You must wear it at all times."

"Now there is much to do. Everyone must act as instructed, and—oh, yes, one more thing: those of you who do not fight must widen one of the upper windows to make room for the condorgs to land."

Raccoman knew this would be the bravest undertaking of all, but at his word, a group of twenty men left to find pickaxes and stone chisels. Within the hour, there was the ringing of hard steel on the soft stone of the upper ledges. The stone fell fast from the upper cliffs, for the granite was streaked with green shale and could be rapidly cut away.

Within another hour, Raccoman stared into the blaze of his steelfire torch. The strong wind foils fit quickly together. By noon, Goronzo and Calaranz were covered with sleek plates of metal that clung tightly to their bodies to allow them to negotiate the thin clearance they would face in the narrow tunnelrees. Raccoman was still a fine welder, and although he would have called this hasty work crude, the sleek metal shields were a testimony to his genius.

The salamanders now looked like steel serpents. Their giant jaws opened, and they belched streams of flame into the darkness of the Grand Caverns. Their appearance was terrible. The Moonrhymes honored them with a chant.

Hai-hai-hai to the strong steel bands
Of Goronzo and Calaranz!

The bodies of the unarmed sentries were discovered only a few hours after Ganarett left them. Raccoman understood immediately what had happened. It was not hard for him to figure who had committed the murders. All the time the murders had occurred, there were only two swords in the enclave—his own and the one the Blackgill had brought with him. Ganarett had come to the enclave and been welcomed in trust. Then he had killed two innocent men, and Raccoman knew that one more would die before any of the Star Riders could arrive to defend him.

The Blackgill would be heading toward the Paladrin Shaft. Suddenly, Raccoman grasped the real truth about Ganarett. He knew it would be a heavy burden for Grentana to bear, but Jendai, if he survived the war, would bless his burdensome word.

Two hours before the bodies of the murdered sentries were found, Ganarett and the frightened Moonrhyme who led him down the corridors rested somewhere in the fourth level. The Moonrhyme asked Ganarett what he intended to do with the coiled cables.

"I have special orders from Raccoman Dakktare. They are for me alone to know."

"There is blood on the hilt of your sword," the Moonrhyme observed.

"Be grateful it is not your blood."

"Is it the blood of my Moonrhyme brothers?"

"We will be going now—you have your orders from Raccoman Dakktare!"

The sentry lifted his torch. "This way to the Paladrin Shaft," he said.

Ganarett followed him. The sentry turned into a tunnel he had never traveled before. Because he knew that he could not trust Ganarett, he feared to lead him correctly. If he did, his life would end as surely as the lives of the other sentries had ended. He hoped to lead the Blackgill into the unexplored tunnel system where both of them would be hopelessly lost. After an hour of walking, however, Ganarett became aware of the deception. They turned the corner of a corridor and ran squarely into a stone wall.

"You have deceived me!" roared Ganarett. "I was a fool to trust you, but your deception will prove costly." Ganarett drew his sword. The Moonrhyme saw the hatred in his face. It was a desperate moment. Though the Moonrhyme knew there were few options, he preferred darkness to death.

Ganarett took two steps toward the Moonrhyme, who retreated two steps.

"I'll kill you, traitor," the Blackgill threatened.

"Then you will do it in darkness!" the sentry shouted as he plunged the torch into the wall. All light died at once. The blackness of the labyrinth swallowed them.

The Moonrhyme dashed by the Blackgill and into the section of tunnel they had just traveled. He ran to an outcropping in the black wall and waited. He knew he had an advantage over the Blackgill. His years of climbing Westwall had given him a strength in his arms that Ganarett could never know.

Thus the Moonrhyme waited, not even daring to breathe. In a moment, he heard the rapid footfalls of the angry Blackgill. When he sensed him nearby, he crawled out into the middle of the tunnelree. The Blackgill ran into him full force and fell. The sentry heard his sword clatter noisily on the floor. Before the Blackgill could find it, the Moonrhyme was on top of him. They struggled in the darkness until the sentry's arms found Ganarett's head. The Moonrhyme's arms had lifted his weight for two hundred years from ladder notch to ladder notch, and they were strong indeed! He tightened his muscular forearms around Ganarett's neck and would not let go. He pulled his grip tighter and tighter, while pressing his knee into the middle of the Blackgill's back. There was a loud crack. Ganarett's traitorous head fell to one side. His neck had been broken.

The Moonrhyme felt around on the floor until he found the lost sword. He stood and walked slowly into the darkness until he felt the cave wall. He knew he was near the place where he had jammed his torch into the black wall. He dropped to his knees and felt every area of the floor. After half an hour, his hand at last closed upon the torch. He was overjoyed.

He sat down on the floor with the torch propped upright between his legs. He removed two flint rocks from his pocket, felt the top of the torch, and then smiled in the darkness. It was still wet with oil.

He scraped the stones together. Sparks, hot and red, fell onto the oily head of the torch. The flame burned, orange and welcome. He stuck the flints back into his pocket and picked up Ganarett's sword. Nearby was the spot where he had killed the Blackgill. Ahead of him, he saw a huge hulk lying prone in the hallway, but the body was more than twice the size of the man he had just destroyed. When he came closer to the carcass, he saw at once it was not a man at all, but a monster. As the Changelings had once assumed other forms in Rensland, their disguised horror now stalked the tunnelrees of Westwall.

"This must be the enemy. This was my enemy!" the Graygill exclaimed.

The bald and leathery creature lay tangled in the ropes that Ganarett had stolen. His head was pulled backward. His neck was broken. His cracked face revealed the horror of his fate. His milk-white eyes were filled with blood. The Moonrhyme was grateful that he had slain the Drog while it was still wearing a deceptive form his own size. He had killed a little monster and a greater monster had died.

He walked on to the end of the unexplored tube. He turned upward toward the level where torches still burned. Within a few hours, he was back to the well-lit halls of the upper caverns.

"Ha-ha!" he cried again and again, dancing and chanting in the Moonrhyme fashion. "I have killed a Drog! I have met the enemy and won!"

A hero's grave
Becomes a shrine—
His coffin,
An eternal bed.
When no one living
Is admired,
It's best to
Imitate the dead.

CHAPTER X

The Strategy for Survival

RACCOMAN FELT LONELY. He knew not where to find Velissa once the war of the tunnels was over and when at last he would have time to look for her. He supposed that she and Raenna were still keeping their quarters at the Blue Observatory. Raccoman knew that Velissa would have been a source of strength to him now, but he could not in good conscience wish her to be there with him. He wanted their child to be born in the open country, unendangered by war. Neither he nor any of the others at the enclave guessed that several parties of hungry Drogs had already left Eastwall to forage in the snowy plains south of Demmerron Pass in search of meat.

By dawn of the second day after the arrival of the Star Riders, four or five of the Moonrhymes, skilled in working with wood, were building the wooden trestle. Its heavy form had already begun to emerge from the enlarged opening. The Moonrhymes had torn out a half dozen of the long candolet beams from the inside the Grand Cavern and secured them to inner pilings, wedged in with granite plugs. They used such boards as could be removed from the cavern dwelling and made a floor for the framework. The work was going well.

By the end of the second day, there were still no Changelings in the upper burrows of Westwall. Mid-afternoon of the next day, however, found a great many of them standing in the open windows of Eastwall. The openings in Eastwall were much closer to the canyon floor than those of Westwall. The enemies looked across the narrow canyon, which was still too wide for the arrows of Thanevial's archers to span.

Hallidan had sent a special, well-armed detachment of Miserians to guard the opening of the Paladrin Shaft. A great encampment of Drogs still remained at the base of the shaft. It now became impossible to tell which of the groups of Drogs were largest—those at the bottom of the Paladrin Shaft or those whose gray and leering faces now crowded out of the windows of Eastwall.

By the fourth day, the trestle timbers were in place and provided a strong, if hastily built, landing window for the condorgs. Unafraid of the heights, the condorgs now felt secure. The wide landing portal would accommodate two condorgs at once. The trestle was strong enough to support both the heavy animals and their riders.

On the morning of the fifth day, there were still no Drogs in the tunnelrees of Westwall, and Raccoman was growing increasingly uneasy. At first, the delay had been welcome, for it gave the time necessary to train fifty Moonrhymes in the elementary use of the fire-glass. There was yet no indication that Thanevial was in either wall.

The interim had allowed the Moonrhymes to organize a battle defense of the enclave, but Raccoman feared that during the postponement, the Drogs had leaped from Eastwall and climbed down into the canyon. There were still isolated farmers beyond Demmerron who had not perished in the destruction of Canby. These would be an easy mark for the parties of roving Drogs. Worst of all, Velissa and Raenna were only a few days from the snowy valley that the Drogs would soon discover.

Hallidan consulted with Raccoman. They both decided to begin a limited offensive against Eastwall and the Paladrin Shaft encampment. On the morning of the sixth day, Jendai took Goronzo to the top of the peak. Raccoman rode with him and brought back the first of the condorgs to land on the new bulwark.

Ten of the Miserians departed swiftly for the Ice Fields of Selen. Jendai instructed them in the art of capturing fire eels. Following a procedure much like the one that Jendai had first used, the ten Miserians returned within four hours, each with a sealed canister containing four or five of the Selendrenni.

By the repeated swirling of the canisters, the Selendrenni were kept in their vertigo condition, until, one by one, the ten canisters could be brought to the brink of the Paladrin Shaft. Raccoman and the Star Riders on guard there dumped the buckets of Selendrenni down the shaft. They fell as a gentle rain washed in the sparkling water that held them captive.

Their fall was spectacular. They burned and flashed like fiery flakes of snow. The cascade of fire illuminated the hostile hulks of the Drogs. Their hideous, upturned faces watched with wonderment, even smiling in an evil fashion, unaware of the nature of the Selendrenni and Raccoman's ploy.

Their wonder died quickly.

As the fire eels reached the bottom of the pit, the Drogs burst into flame and fire shot up the shaft. Raccoman could not see how many Drogs were burning, but a great many of them were aflame.

The wail was dreadful. The fire eels crawled back further into the undersea passage. Though it was impossible to tell how many Drogs they had destroyed, it appeared that perhaps as many as fifty were consumed in the fire storms ignited by the Selendrenni. The acrid sulphur fumes, typical of Drogs, produced a stench that even the heat of the flames could not dissipate. Several Drogs on the walls of the cave disintegrated instantly in the roar of the flames.

Raccoman's hope that the flames would force the Drogs up some unknown tunnel into an upper level of the enclave went amiss. The colony of Drogs at the base of the tunnel merely retreated from the bottom of the upper shaft to a safe distance where they could be neither seen nor heard. Now the enemy was unable to be located, and the whereabouts of Thanevial and the Singreale remained a complete mystery.

By the seventh day, the Moonrhymes had become most skillful in their use of the fire-glass weaponry. Raccoman had trained them in the tactic he had humorously called "defootilating the foe." Humorous or not, it was the most effective way for Graygills to face the denizen Drogs, who were twice their size. The Star Riders marveled at how quickly the Moonrhymes learned and how effective they were. Made strong by cliff-climbing, they could swing their fire-glass swords as quickly as the knights and much faster than Raccoman Dakktare.

The uneasy waiting began to have a visible effect on the knights by the beginning of the second week. Raccoman decided to try and stop the daily spillage of the Drogs into the lower valley. Two Miserians established a vigil above Eastwall. Whenever a Drog, or a party of them, tried to escape, the Miserians dropped a canister of fire eels on the party. A crowd of eyes in Westwall always watched the fiery display. When it happened at night, it became a spellbinding spectacle. The Selendrenni would spill down the white cliff, streaking it with fire. The Drogs would explode in flame whenever the fire fell.

By the second week of waiting, Grentana had learned a certain smoothness with the fire-glass sword. Out of boredom and frustration, Jendai and Grentana took the salamanders to the canyon floor and traveled as far as the stone pillars of Demmerron. They encountered only two encampments of Drogs, each numbering five. The armored salamanders spied them, and the entire tactic was over before the Drogs could even guess who their destroyers had been.

On the morning of the fifteenth day, the Star Riders were so bored with the waiting that they spoke of trying to launch a major siege of Eastwall. Raccoman flatly refused the idea, reminding them that they had to protect the enclave and that to weaken their ranks with such a move could be costly to their strategy.

The weather became warmer as winter receded. Most of the ice had melted from the shaded Eastwall. And all of it was gone from Westwall. A maddening silence caused even the Moonrhymes, who were neither warlike nor prone to impatience, to be on edge over the siege that would not come.

While Jendai was tending Sam's fire, he heard a sound in the wall—the same sound of roaring that Old Sammuron had heard. Raccoman was summoned. Both he and Jendai listened.

"The worst possible news!" exclaimed Jendai. "It sounds as though they are tearing the inner mountain apart."

"But how are they doing it?"

"I cannot tell, but they are not doing it with their hands."

The two men thought for awhile.

"The Singreale—of course!" cried the welder. "They are using the Singreale. Somehow they have found a way to use the diamond to extend the existing tunnel system to the upper levels."

"They will be coming through solid stone to the upper levels of our settlement. We have no way of stopping their progress at the lower levels. Our first encounter with them will come here in the very dwellings of our people," said Jendai.

Raccoman was disconsolate as he held his head in his hands and thought. "No hope, Jendai," he said. "We would have better fought them in the tunnelrees. The Star Riders were right: we should have attacked Eastwall. Perhaps that way we could have found the connecting passageways and located and stopped them on the lower levels. Now it is too late . . . too late!" Raccoman's lament slowed down as one who had suddenly received a stroke of genius, but is somehow slow to realize it. "Too late," he repeated, "too late, Jendai . . . unless."

"Unless!" the wood-bearer declared.

"Jendai, how long before they break through?"

"Who can say, Raccoman? They've been working on this tunnel for several weeks—maybe we have as much as a week."

"Jendai, Jendai, if you are only right. Of course, you are right—you must be, dear Jendai."

Give me seven days, and when the seven days are gone
Westwall will be safe, the Moonrhymes shall have won.

Raccoman had not spoken in rhyme for weeks, but now he was sure of himself, so sure that his jingle proclaimed his new self-confidence. He had a plan, and for the first time in months, he felt unburdened and light.

Jendai—wood-bearer for the decades past.
Listen to me, Jendai. Here in this humble heart,
the Genius is cast
That will stop the Drog hordes in the tunnels they now mine.
Hah-hoo, Jendai—I do feel fine!
Light comes knocking at our door—
I see the end of this black war!
Was ever there such a noble mind?
So great a brain as this of mine?
Hah-hoo—hah-hoo—hah-hoo!

The wide-eyed Jendai, who had not known the Canby Graygill for long, backed away from his mad exuberance. Raccoman's free laughter drowned the sound of the distant roaring. Then his laughter stopped as suddenly as it had begun. He grew sober as though he were retracing the cause.

"Jendai . . . Jendai." Now Raccoman was utterly solemn.

I again must hear you speak.
Are you sure we have a week?"

"It's a guess," said Jendai, "only a guess. Who could be sure?"

"But you must promise me." Raccoman became emphatic. He grabbed Jendai by the shoulders. "Promise me!"

"How can I promise you?"

"Promise me, promise me!" Raccoman shouted into his face.

"All right, I promise." It was an unusual promise based on nothing, but Jendai reckoned that madness needed only little arguments and small unfounded proofs.

Hah-hoo!
I'm the finest strategist and military man
Who ever graced the Moonrhymes' clan.
Come to me, Thanevial—
Hah-hoo, hah-hoo, hah-hoo!

Raccoman ran from the smoky darkness where the walls still roared. Jendai felt sure that the stress of war had destroyed the Graygill's reason.

Velissa could not know of the brilliant ploy that now excited her husband. She and Raenna had been occupied with a matter that had become urgent. They were not quite sure how they would go about it, but they felt that Parsky had to be stopped at all costs before his evil corrupted the unspoiled valley.

Their timing proved wrong. They had thought that it would take about fifteen days for Parsky to reach the Sundals. It took him forty. The trip was long, and while they had managed to fly the distance in only a few hours, Parsky traveled slowly. The drifts in certain parts of the candolet forest were heavy, and the huge lumbering catterlob moved forward only a little each day. Parsky rode better where the snow was light.

The days were becoming warmer west of the western ridge just as they were north of Demmerron. This was to Raenna's advantage, for the snow trench created by the catterlob made it easy for Raenna to find and follow Parsky day by day.

Raenna always flew at a great height so that Parsky often appeared as only a dark blot upon the gleaming snow fields. Such an easy surveillance allowed Raenna and Velissa to return to the Blue Observatory every night. They would build the fire and consider, again and again, their chances of stopping the one who hungered to spoil the unspoiled valley. They knew that the longer they waited, the better their chances would be of stopping him, for both Parsky and the catterlob would grow weaker as the trip continued.

The two women had rehearsed it all a thousand times. Each night when they finished dinner, they talked of two things: When they could join their husbands and how they could deter Parsky from his evil purpose. On the twenty-fifth night of their surveillance, they came at last to an understanding.

"All right," said Velissa, "but only if we don't try to kill him."

"Velissa, he has been responsible for the deaths of so many, why would you be reluctant to kill him?" Raenna, as a Miserian warrior, had less aversion to blood than her friend. Velissa, on the other hand, had seen too much bloodshed, and she did not relish the idea of deliberately killing Parsky, since she had conceived another way to stop him.

"Oh, Raenna, I know this will be a better way." Raenna had given reluctant consent to Velissa's plan for capturing the Blackgill rather than killing him.

Velissa ran and brought back a blue-steel, mesh netting. The women had worked on the net for weeks, using metal fibers that they had stripped from the centers of ginjon leaves.

Their hands were cut and torn in many places from trying to handle the fibers. They refused to wear their gloves, for each had only a single pair and these were needed desperately for high-altitude flying. They would rather cut their hands than ruin their gloves.

They talked while they twisted the fibers and, inch by inch, worked toward the completion of the net.

"We'll finish it tonight," said Velissa.

Raenna only looked up and smiled in agreement.

"Just the catterlob then?" asked Velissa.

Raenna smiled again. "Velissa, yes. Just the catterlob."

"But can we do it?"

It was an old question, but Raenna answered it once more.

"We, I," she replied. "I will do it."

"But will the fire-glass cut through the armor?"

"Velissa, I believe it will. I'll take care of that. You just do *your* part."

Velissa did not need to be reminded of her part. She knew it well.

Still, both women knew that their husbands desired them to stay away from the enclave. If the war to save the Moonrhymes failed, then the women would be able to escape to Rensgaard, where Raccoman's daughter—for he was sure it would be a daughter—could be born in peace. This was most important to Raccoman and therefore it was important to Velissa as well.

Even after months of separation, they felt sure that the enclave still stood and that their husbands and the Moonrhymes were safe. On the thirty-eighth day of Parsky's journey, Raenna and Velissa had circled high above the enclave and seen a condorg on the landing window. They knew that the beast would not have been there if the enclave had fallen into enemy hands.

While no official communication had passed between the women and their husbands, Raenna felt sure that Hallidan had left the condorg on the trestle of Westwall as a signal to his wife's surveillance that the enclave was safe. Each day as they returned from watching Parsky, Raenna and Velissa had checked the enclave to be sure the condorg was still there. Many times they yearned to land, if only for a brief moment, and see their husbands, but the whole world, it seemed, was at war. They felt sure that their husbands would not want them to be in danger if the war was not going well. Often they observed Maldoon through the telescope, and knowing that Parsky was no longer personally in charge of the fortress, they also wanted to do something for the widows of Canby. They decided, however, to limit their objectives to tasks that they could manage well. Thus, they made the unspoiled valley and its safety their one concern.

They had seen Drogs in Eastwall. However, since they never left the observatory at night, they had not noticed that the small campfires of the Drog parties were moving closer to the Blue Observatory by night. They were completely unaware that the Drogs had even left Eastwall and had come through the candolet forests to the edge of Quarrystone.

The Drogs had no idea that there was a Blue Observatory. They happened, by merest chance, to come in that direction, for they were mad with hunger. They had not ceased to cannibalize their own kind, but their appetites cried out for other kinds of flesh, which they always preferred.

"Velissa, it cannot be much longer," said Raenna, "until the fate of the enclave is settled."

The women were so intent on the fire that filled the room with dancing light that neither of them noticed the ominous visage which now peered through the ice-frosted glass of their west window. Both had seen the evil faces in a world where tropical jungles sank their roots into green lagoons, but they did not suspect that the Changelings now trekked the snowy trails of the Quarrystone Woods.

The face passed the glass and disappeared.

Had they not been listening to the crackling of the fire, they might have heard the crunch of large claws in the outside snow.

Condorgs hardly ever made noise, but Raenna's beast gave a sudden outcry. Then they heard it bolt to the sky. Fear gripped the women. What could that outcry have meant? In an instant, they pulled on their warmest clothes and strapped on their swords.

Raenna started for the door.

"Outside?" Velissa's tone questioned Raenna's judgment.

"It is the safest place! If there is any enemy, we'll be better to take our chances in the dark."

"But who can it be?" Velissa was struggling hard with the issue.

"Come," said Raenna, "we'll talk outside where it is safer."

They left the Blue Observatory. The crunching of their own boots in the old snow sounded like a roar to them.

They quickly retreated to the heavy shrubs that bordered the candolet forest. Soon they were inside the trees that stretched out like a protective and friendly coverlet above and far beyond them.

"Who can it be?" whispered Velissa.

"Well, it is either Blackgills or Drogs."

"Somehow," Velissa said, then paused, "I don't believe that the condorg would be frightened by Blackgills, but I know they fear the Changelings."

She had made her point well. Still, Raenna was not inclined to believe that the Drogs would have come this far through the forest, even if they had managed to escape the enclave.

"It cannot be Drogs, for they are not used to traveling in the snow. It is unthinkable that they could travel this far so fast."

"Shh!" said Velissa.

Both of them watched. A party of four Drogs entered the clearing between the outbuildings where the condorg had been tied by the Blue Observatory. They listened to their guttural chatter.

"*Chounga! Caladranga mogrunga*!" grunted the Drog who took the lead in guiding the others across the snowy clearing and into the Blue Observatory.

"Four of them," Velissa choked. "Oh, Raenna, what are we going to do?"

Raenna said nothing. The dark, leathery creatures were moving around the Blue Observatory. By the light of the fireplace, they could see the Drogs tearing the makeshift beds to pieces.

"Raenna, perhaps we could catch them inside and surprise them. We could attack them in an instant, and . . . no." Velissa already saw the error in her suggestion.

Raenna still said nothing, confirming Velissa's suspicion that her thinking was unsound. The two women could not attack a party of four giants and hope to fare well. The four Changelings soon wearied of their destructive games and once again entered the clearing.

"*Condungra!*" one exclaimed, gesturing toward the woods on the far side of the observatory.

"Good," whispered Velissa. "They are going to search the farthest woods first. But they know we're somewhere about, don't they?"

"I'm afraid so. It's only a matter of time. . . . wait a minute." Raenna stopped mid-sentence, overtaken by a flash of insight. "No, I doubt if it would work—it's too insane."

"What? Tell me," insisted Velissa.

"No, it simply wouldn't work," said Raenna. "But if it did, we could draw them into our web, one at a time, and—no, no, it's foolhardy."

"What, Raenna?"

"Velissa, what if you were to point your short fire-glass sword in their direction in the dark so that all they could see was one red pinpoint of light. What would that look like?"

"It would look like one red pinpoint of light, I suppose," Velissa replied, unable to see any genius for capturing Drogs in what Raenna was suggesting.

"But what if you were to point it at them and say in a gravelly yet musical voice something like, '*Hon chon em taken, taken en em tree.*' What would the pinpoint look like then?"

"An eye!" Now Velissa was excited. "Oh, Raenna that's a good idea! We could lure them into the darkness one at a time and—no, Grendelynden's eye was yellow. The fire-glass is red."

"The color discrepancy will go unnoticed by the dull-witted Drogs."

"You're right, of course. Yellow eye, red eye—it would be all the same to these dull fiends."

"Can you do it?" Raenna asked.

Velissa had known the voice of Grendelynden on darker and more hopeless nights than this. Half-whispering, she growled, "*Fora Droggynoggens soon a bee a Droggynoggens three.*" It was a good imitation. "But what makes you think they will come one at a time?"

"Fear, Velissa. There is no way that the leader would risk his own life until he had sent the others to investigate. Remember, the Drogs always obey their leader, and the leader never endangers himself."

It was true. The Changelings were predictable.

"Velissa, you stand over there. Do your best to make your fire-glass look like an eye. I'll stay here with my sword sheathed until one of the Drogs makes his way toward you. Then I'll attack him in the darkness from the rear."

Velissa moved carefully into position. By this time, the Drogs were nearly across the clearing at the far side of the observatory. Velissa pointed her short fire-glass sword toward them. The Drogs continued walking away from her until she spoke in a very convincing imitation of their ancient enemy:

Chon chon em taken. Grendelynden see.
Kumma kumma Droggynoggens, kumma en em gnee.
Kumma Droggynoggens four a bee a Droggynoggens three.

The huge denizens stopped in the clearing, turned, and stared at the red light radiated by the point of Velissa's sword through the thick foliage at the edge of the snowy clearing. How right Raenna had been.

"*Condungra!*" cried the leader of the other three. So saying, he shoved one of the Drogs toward the red blip of light.

"*Ammgank!*" protested the Drog who had received the unattractive command. It was clear that he did not wish to investigate the red eye and this threatening riddle that all the Changelings thought they had left behind in the grottoes of the lost lands. The monster turned to his commander with a set face. He would not go into the forest to investigate. He knew well that this invisible enemy tore the heads from those who kept lonely campfires in another world.

"*Ammgank!*" he repeated to the commanding Drog. He refused to go and investigate the belligerent, riddlesome light. His commander drew his sword. "*Condungra, condungra, condungra!*"

"*Ammgank!*" he repeated. The leader of the Drogs shoved the rebellious monster to the ground and raised the sword over his head. He was about to decapitate the disobedient underling.

"*Caladranga, muglank!*" The Drog whined now for a stay of execution. He had changed his mind. He scrambled to his feet, drew his invisible blade, and began walking slowly toward the trees where Velissa was hiding. As he approached the edge of the clearing, Velissa chanted:

Ammganken, kille danken—emma emma gnee!
Kumma Droggynoggee uglee Kumma inna play with me!

Raenna was horrified. Grendelynden would never have said anything so ludicrous. She found herself wishing that Velissa would not try to improvise so much. Fortunately, however, the voice sounded inauthentic only to Raenna; it sounded like the real thing to the terrified Drog.

Velissa covered her short sword with the fiber scabbard and the eye blinked off.

Reluctantly, the Drog crashed into the shrubs and then into the dark candolet forest. Velissa had stepped behind a tree and was completely invisible. The Drog advanced cautiously while the others listened. Finally, the Changeling was exactly where Raenna wanted him. She slipped up behind him and swung her red fire-glass through the body of her bewildered enemy. He fell in sulphur smoke. The yellow haze of death would have been more visible in the sunlight than it was now in the shaded starlight.

There was no scream. The hapless Changeling had barely gasped, and so the three who waited and watched the shaded clearing heard not a sound. Their milk-white eyes gazed and reflected confusion. Nothing told them their fellow had been slain. Velissa gagged in the draught of sulphur fumes, but forced herself to control the cough that would surely have alerted the Drogs.

In a second moment of daring, she stepped from behind the tree, pointed her sword at her enemies again, and removed the scabbard. The single red eye blinked on. Velissa croaked the kind of music she mimicked well. Her raucuous and cheerful imitation of Grendelynden floated on the night air around the red pinpoint of light.

Before Velissa began her chant, there was a nervous cry from the Changeling watchers.

"*Korrunkh!*" grunted the commander. The red eye of the adversary had triumphed. Neither of the remaining two underling Drogs wished to take the place of their vanquished counterpart. Their commander tapped one of them on the shoulder and then pointed in the direction of the red eye. The chosen Drog did not want this honor. He shook his head vigorously, nodding no and shouting, "*Ammgank!*" He would not obey his master. He turned from looking at the red eye.

The Drog in charge struck him in his ugly cracked face. He reeled backward. Still, the Drog remained obstinate. "*Ammgank!*" he declared with finality, when he had recovered from the blow. The Drog who had not been designated taunted the reluctant Changeling.

"*Caladranga! Condungra!*" he chided him for not obeying orders. As he spoke of the unobeyed command, he, too, pointed in the direction of the red eye.

"*Ammgank!*" insisted the disobedient Drog.

Both the Drogs began to chide him now, turning him toward the dark forest where the fire-glass sword winked off and on in warning. The reluctant Drog dug his heels into the ground and refused to budge. The other two shoved him forward to the edge of the clearing. His heels left deep ruts of protest in the heavy snow.

At this point, they released him, expecting him to enter the forest and deal with the red eye. He turned around and once more insisted he would not go.

"*Ammgank! Ammgan—*"

His last refusal was cut short by his commander, and his disobedient head fell with a thump into the snow.

Suddenly the last of the three underlings had a visage of horror pass before his eyes. He was peering into the dark forest just as he felt his commander tap him on the shoulder with one claw. With another claw, the Drog commander pointed toward the blinking red eye. The blade of his commander's invisible sword still dripped. The underling could not utter the word *Ammgank*. Rather, he drew his own sword and started into the forest.

"*Mukken Gunnka, droggy lunnka,*" Velissa began the taunt. Raenna could not believe how poorly Velissa now imitated Grendelynden. Not that Raenna had ever heard the small ally sing his half-melodious jeers, but the imitation was so poor that even she would not have been afraid. The terrified Drog, however, seemed unaware that he was hearing anything other than the Ally himself:

Mukken mukken boggen, boggen,
Hanggen to dem uglee noggen
Droggynoggen, soona droggen
Who will lose his droggy's noggen.

Raenna wanted to laugh at Velissa's improvisation, but the Drog was now in the heavy part of the forest. Velissa covered her fire-glass with its sheath and slipped behind a tree. The Drog advanced through the shadows. Once again, with precision, Raenna pulled her sword from the sheath and swung the red glass through the Drog's body. He fell lifeless in the snow before he could even cry out.

"*Galanka!*" The one surviving Drog had finally seen through the deception. He had recognized the flash of fire-glass. However, he had not seen the woman who bore it and so believed her to be a Star Rider. Fear overtook him and he began to run away from the edge of the forest. Raenna dashed after him. Velissa was amazed at how swift she was. Raenna quickly outdistanced her small Moon-rhyme companion in the pursuit of the Drog. She also quickly over-took the clumsy, awkward Drog who had stumbled in the deep snow. She challenged him in the clearing, only a few feet from the open door of the Blue Observatory. Raenna and the Drog began to trace circles in the snow as they encountered and menaced each other.

Neither spoke, and their silence unnerved Velissa. She had deter-mined that as soon as the fight began, she would stay as close as she could, for if Raenna should fail to kill the last Drog, she must move in. She tried to remember what her husband had told her: the only way a Graygill could stand a chance against a Drog was to "defootilate." She steeled herself.

"What are you doing?" cried Mandra.

The boy stopped and looked quizzically at his mother. He then looked down again and began sharpening a stick with a long knife.

"Abbon!" His mother, who rarely raised her voice at him, had called his name again, but she did not have to ask him what he was doing. Reluctantly, the boy laid down his sharp stick and his knife.

"Mama, I am sharpening a stick," he said.

"Abbon, did Mr. Parsky show you how to sharpen sticks?"

The boy nodded.

"But why, Abbon?" asked his mother.

"Because," said the boy, "he says you can build a snare to catch congrels."

"Catch congrels? But you can pick them up. You don't have to build a snare. The little animals like to be picked up."

"Mr. Parsky can't," Abbon replied.

"He can't what?" Mandra had lost the general direction of the conversation.

"Pick up congrels," said Abbon, who was having no trouble following his own reasoning.

"Is his back stiff? Are his hands slow?" asked Mandra.

"No," Abbon laughed. "They run from him. They're afraid."

"Are they now?" Mandra laughed.

"I think it's because . . . ," Abbon said, then stopped. "Never mind, Mama."

"Because?" Mandra knew instantly that Abbon was concealing something from her. "Abbon, why are the congrels afraid of Mr. Parsky?"

"He told me never to tell," said Abbon. "Mama, can I please sharpen my sticks some more? When will Mr. Parsky be back?"

"Abbon, look at me. Why are the congrels afraid of Mr. Parsky?"

The child burst into tears. He cried for a good while before he could get control of himself again.

"Abbon, there's something you're not telling me. Why?" Mandra was becoming firm. She took her son's shoulders sternly in her hands and demanded to know what he was hiding from her.

"He . . . he eats congrels!" Abbon had said it all at once. Then his face clouded and he broke into fresh tears. "Oh, Mama, you made me tell, and I promised Mr. Parsky that I wouldn't tell you or Papa!"

"He eats animals?" Mandra was stricken in unbelief. "Did he tell you this?"

"Well, not exactly." Abbon was again unsure of himself. "Mama, please, I just want to sharpen sticks. When Mr. Parsky comes back, I want to have a great lot of sharp sticks ready for him. I have already sharpened more than a hundred."

"Where are they?" Mandra asked, then realized she was distracting herself. "Never mind where the sticks are, Abbon. Tell me, if he didn't tell you that he ate congrels, how do you know he does?"

"But, Mama, he made me promise not to tell you or Papa."

"Abbon, Abbon!"

"Mama, I know because he had me catch some for him, because they ran from him. And when I gave them to him. . . ."

Abbon stopped.

"Go on," Mandra wanted him to stop, but she knew he must not. "Go on, my son," she repeated.

"Well, when I would give him a congrel, he would turn his back, and then, Mama, I would hear the congrel scream. And when Mr. Parsky would turn around again, his face would be all red, and he would smile and thank me. At first, I didn't like to catch congrels for him, but then he told me that he would bring me a nice present for doing it and that someday I would enjoy eating them just as much as he did. He said even you and Papa would like them if he cooked them in a stew."

Mandra shuddered.

"I can show you where we always went to eat." Abbon turned and walked away from the house. Mandra stood firm. Abbon looked back and waited for her. "Come on, Mama. I'll show you. There's a place not far from here. You'll see—it's full of fur and bones. It's the place where Mr. Parsky always eats. Someday he's going to show all of us how to eat meat. That's what he calls congrels now—meat. Isn't that a funny word—meat?"

But Mandra did not think the word funny at all.

She looked at Abbon and grew afraid.

The Sundals were unaware of Parsky or the Valley of the Canbies. They had never heard of Maldoon or Demmerron. They knew only of the candolet grove that flanked the eastern border of their land and stretched to such a distance that none of them had ever dared to presume they could cross the ocean of red trees. Parsky had taken weeks to cross the candolet forest, but he had done it because he knew there were no other options open to him for the living of life.

The salamanders had destroyed nearly all of his catterlobs, and they would no doubt return in the spring to complete their work.

The drones would not be able to stand against the beasts that only the Moonrhymes controlled.

Parsky was aware also that he was being watched from the sky. He didn't know who was watching him, but his mind went back to the first report of Sky Riders and he decided that the little men who rode the stars had to be the ones who were keeping him under surveillance. Because he knew he was being observed, he decided on a radical action.

Further, he was now hungry, and he knew he had to reach the Sundals, if he was to survive. As Castledome forest once had died, now Maldoon was dead. He had no choice. He needed a new kingdom and he knew exactly where his reign would begin. He had one friend in a distant valley who brought him meat—a little boy who admired him greatly.

Sobbing leaves
A lonely dark.
A crying child
Can hurt the gloom.
Where lie
His parents' silent forms,
He gives his heart
To be their tomb.

CHAPTER XI

The Blazing Paradise

THE MISERIANS' attempt to use the Selendrenni to clear the Drogs from Paladrin had no lasting consequences. The Drogs still controlled the undersea passage. Now the Star Riders, following Raccoman's strategy, decided to secure the bottom of the shaft.

Hallidan found the going hard in the low tunnels. He could not see how the Drogs managed them. Worst of all, he was revolted by the odor of the partly eaten carcasses, which drifted up the Paladrin Shaft, making the air unbreathable in the close tunnels. Their stench took away his breath.

Goronzo and Calaranz had paved the way for the Star Riders with their intermittent surprise attacks on the Drog encampment that had returned to the bottom of the Paladrin Shaft. The Star Riders had gained control of the area at the bottom of the shaft by using a strategy of lightning-quick attacks. Two knights would ride the salamanders to the bottom of the pit and then leap off, fighting fiercely as other knights dropped from the upper edge of the tube, lowering themselves on strong fiber cables.

The salamanders would return to bring four more knights to the fighting area. This entire maneuver was carried out with such speed and precision that the encampment of Drogs was soon forced back into the tunnels. The knights outfought the Drogs in spite of the monsters' hunched posture, which should have given them the advantage in the low tunnelrees.

At last, all fifteen of the knights were at the bottom of the Paladrin Shaft. Hallidan fought tirelessly at first, but after a while the confining stone passage began to weary him. He let other knights squeeze past him in the stone tunnels to take up the hand-to-hand combat.

The low tunnelrees made it difficult for the Drogs to swing their long, invisible blades. The knights' fire-glass swords were much shorter and therefore worked much better. Unfortunately, the heat of the fire-glass caused the knights to become fatigued with the sweat and grime of the heated combat.

The scarcity of light at the bottom of the pit posed no real problem. In fact, it was scarcely noticed in the tunnelrees. The glow of the fiery blades was more than adequate to light the stone enclaves and burrows of their close battle.

As numbers of the enemy fell, they had to be pulled out, Drog by Drog, to keep the tunnelrees from becoming congested where the knights had to pass.

After a week of fighting, the Star Riders had gained only a small section of tunnel that would have taken barely two hours to walk. On the seventh day, however, Hallidan's troops achieved a breakthrough. The undersea tunnel that connected with the Paladrin Shaft opened into a large chamber. At this point, the fighting became fierce. Hallidan's misgivings mounted. He knew that the first two or three knights who broke through into the large cavern would be in great jeopardy, for they might be surrounded by the enemy in the large chamber.

Hallidan personally assumed this risk along with two of his best Star Riders. No sound came from the Drog that Hallidan faced as he hacked his way out of the tunnelree and into the spacious room. Then, Hallidan felt the full force of the Drog's sword, for the open area gave the monster all the room he needed to swing his long invisible sword. Hallidan pushed each thrust to the length of his blade and arm. Then, with a ferocious plunge, he drove the glass blade deep into his opponent's chest. As the slain Changeling stumbled backward, Hallidan kept his back to the wall and moved into the chamber.

He was quickly followed by half a dozen, then a dozen more knights, who formed a square of fighters. The Star Riders worked to cut through what appeared to be a hundred Drogs. Although the knights were well outnumbered, they fought with determination.

It was not long before the tide turned against the Drogs. Only two tunnels fed into the open cavern, and the dull Drogs had allowed themselves to be maneuvered away from these exits. Their every chance of escape was cut off. A yellow sulphur haze filled the cavern as the monsters fell. The odor of dying Drogs was overwhelming. The massacre must have amounted to at least a tenth of Thanevial's subterranean horde. Only three of the twelve knights had been killed. Three others had received minor wounds.

The dead knights were transported to the Grand Cavern on the backs of Goronzo and Calaranz. Wherever the ceilings were low, the salamanders had to flatten themselves to crawl through such structures without dislodging the bodies of the fallen heroes. Beyond the Paladrin Shaft, most of the tunnelrees were high enough to allow the burdened salamanders an unobstructed passage.

Hallidan decided to leave only four knights to occupy the chamber and thus block the Drogs' only entrance to Paladrin. While he tried to decide which of the two tunnels to enter, Hallidan heard a very faint and distant roaring, not unlike the louder roaring that Old Sam had long been able to hear from his cavern in the upper levels of the enclave. Hallidan decided that the faint roar was coming down the tunnel farthest to his right. He took his knights and edged forward out of the large enclosure into a low passageway that resembled the one in which he had just fought.

Since the opening to the left was the only other way Drogs could enter the cavern they had just claimed, he instructed the knights who remained behind that one of their number should always be stationed fifty yards down that tunnelree. This would secure the cavern in case the Changelings should try to enter from that direction. One man could defend the narrow tunnel against an army, if he needed to, and the knights would take turns guarding the cavern.

As Hallidan proceeded down the burrow, the distant roaring began again. He felt sure he had made the right choice as he listened. The single column of Star Riders advanced through the narrow tunnel with such light as their blades afforded. Then, all of a sudden, the passageway exploded into spaciousness.

The room in which they found themselves looked as though it had just been blasted into being. Debris and rubble were everywhere. Indeed, the knights had to search the area to find the outlet directly across from the one through which they had entered.

Once again, they filed out of the open cavern and back into a short, narrow passage. A short while later, they entered yet-another newly blasted cavern filled with debris. All of their blades together could scarcely provide illumination in the huge, vaulted chamber.

"But what could have blasted such a room?" asked one of Hallidan's knights.

The distant roaring shattered the stillness in an ominous reply.

"Something is blasting its way toward the surface," said another of the knights.

"Singreale." Hallidan had barely breathed his reply.

The going went much easier now. The knights covered the debris-strewn trail in such good time that they knew they must soon overtake the Drog host. They all had agreed to Raccoman's plan for the looming battle of the enclave.

Hallidan, however, was having second thoughts about Raccoman's plans, for he wondered what he would do when he at last encountered the army of his evil twin. He had so few men, while Thanevial had more than just an army. He had the Singreale as well.

Raccoman waited in the Grand Cavern. Slowly he organized the Moonrhymes into two fighting forces of twenty-five men each. He and Hallidan had picked their moment carefully. When Singreale exploded its final rays and Thanevial broke through the stone walls of the Grand Cavern, Hallidan would move into a rear-guard position while the Moonrhymes and the Miserians swarmed from the front.

Now time seemed to drag as Raccoman and the Moonrhymes waited. The roaring grew nearer. Hallidan had been gone for two long weeks, and they dared to believe that the Star Rider and his men were not only alive and doing well, but were now approaching Thanevial's rear guard.

Raccoman was depending upon his blitzing tactic to save them from the invading Drogs. More menacing than the size or ferocity of the Changelings, however, was the fact that they held the awesome Singreale, whose rays had been blasting the stone labyrinths into greater caverns through which the horrendous army swarmed the underearth.

Raccoman could not understand how the demon horde could breathe, for the dust from the constant explosions would surely be a choking ordeal to survive. Nevertheless, the Drog denizens, covered with dirt and filth, stomped and clawed upward through the heart of the great mountain.

Raccoman and the Miserians intended to launch an offensive in the open windows of Eastwall. Raccoman had some disagreement with the women over the nature of the battle tactic, however. Both the Graygill and the Miserians agreed that the tactic would have to be a lightning-quick maneuver to succeed.

Raccoman had never been able to admit it, but the tall women nettled him when they disagreed with him and became pushy about their viewpoint. Being half the stature of both the Titans and the Miserians, he always felt the sting of their orders, for their size alone seemed to leave him no choice about obeying them. Still, it was the tall women whose disagreements he found most unpalatable.

A quarrel had erupted between him and Merigh-Ren, the leader of the Miserians.

"Try, if you can, Raccoman Dakktare, to see things this way," the Miserians told him. Raccoman hated it when these women spoke forcefully—and especially when they used his last name. Merigh-Ren continued, "We only need one of them and only for a little while. You can give us either one you wish."

"No, no, no!" the Graygill found himself shouting. "It would spread the war to three fronts. It's risky, especially since we have no idea how Hallidan is faring in the heart of the earth. I think we have only a slim chance if Hallidan can remain concealed until the precise moment they break through the wall. When that happens, we must attack from this side and he from his side. And we must have both of the salamanders, if we hope to wrench the Singreale from the hand of Thanevial."

"Just Goronzo!" Merigh-Ren demanded.

"No!" Raccoman was unyielding.

"Look, little one. . . ." Merigh-Ren's anger had permitted her a slur with which Raccoman could not deal. He turned his back and walked toward the dark wall of the inner cavern.

At this point, Jendai, who had overheard their conversation, decided to intervene.

"Raccoman," said the wood-bearer, "it sounds as though there is time." Jendai worked to soothe the Graygill's anger. "Why not station a sentry on the landing platform? He can signal us across the chasm if it sounds as though the horde is near to breakthrough. Then we can take both salamanders to Eastwall and establish a beachhead there."

"When you say *'we,'* do you mean yourself and me?" asked Raccoman. "The whole idea is out of the question."

"He means himself and *me,*" a voice replied. It was Grentana.

Now Merigh-Ren objected.

"Not you, Grentana—you're a woman."

Merigh-Ren seemed to have forgotten that she, too, was a woman. Grentana had only to clear her throat and raise an eyebrow to answer the indictment.

"Yes, but. . . ." Merigh-Ren faltered. She wanted to tell Grentana that at least she was a "big" woman, but she had already expressed her size prejudice once and angered Raccoman. She decided to be kinder to Grentana.

"All right, all right," Raccoman answered. "It is madness, but all right."

"The days themselves—our very hopes—are madness," added Jendai.

Raccoman knew they were right, but they still hoped that the final conflict could be won. He also knew that whether or not they won would depend on their ability to seize the Singreale quickly and by surprise. To do that, Raccoman desperately needed the salamanders at the moment of Thanevial's breakthrough.

"All right," he repeated, "but no more than one hour—then *be back here!*"

Grentana and Jendai wore their new, tough armor. No blade could penetrate it, but the stiff plates made it difficult to mount the salamanders. Raccoman had welded special footlocks in the armor of the beasts so that it was impossible for the Moonrhymes to fall or even be dislodged from their fearsome mounts.

The armored plates of the salamanders caused some of their swiftness to be lost. However, it was desperately important that they live, and to live they had to be armored. The beasts had become a symbol of survival to the enclave.

Some wondered if the heavily armored riders would slow the beasts down; they wondered if it might not be better for the beasts to fight alone. Still, even though the salamanders seemed intent on the destruction of their foes, they needed direction from their riders to fight effectively. Jendai and Grentana insured the safety of the beasts. Should the salamanders be wounded or outnumbered, their riders could turn them to flight and safety.

The Miserians dressed for battle. All of them went at once, hoping to push the Drogs into one tunnel where they could be held or pushed back by only a few of the Titan women.

One by one, the Miserians mounted condorgs and flew out of the window of Westwall. The brown-gray Drogs watched them go and supposed that they were all returning to the other land or were leaving on a mission of surveillance in the valleys.

After they had all gone, Goronzo and Calaranz immediately appeared together on the trestle. The Drogs still watched from across the canyon. The ice had all melted, and it was clear that winter had dissipated. There were still small patches of snow here and there, but the air had grown much warmer.

When the last of the Miserian condorgs had disappeared from that part of the sky which the Drogs could see, the fire salamanders made their move. Their armor, which would slow their climbing of Eastwall, did not prevent their rapid descent of Westwall.

The morning sun was so bright upon the granite of Westwall that the day seemed almost summerish. Under other circumstances, Grentana and Jendai would have enjoyed the late winter morning. Now, however, they steeled themselves for the ordeal ahead.

They raced their gigantic mounts to the floor of the canyon, which separated the enemies of Eastwall and Westwall, and then raced laterally and south toward the Sentinels of Demmerron. At first, the Drogs thought they were about to mount an attack on Eastwall, and so the ugly beastlings gathered to prepare a defense. Then as the mounted Moonrhymes turned down the canyon, the Drogs became confused. Why the salamanders and riders were armored, they could not guess, but apparently the two Graygills had no agenda with the beast-warriors.

Once out of the Drogs' sight, Jendai and Grentana turned again and raced up Eastwall towards a position directly above the Drog encampment. As they flew along the summit of Eastwall, Jendai noticed that the morning sun cast the shadows of the mounted salamanders in bold projections on the face of Westwall, which would have been all too obvious to the Drogs, had they been near the encampment. He and Grentana reined the salamanders back and away from the edge of the cliff until the landing platform of Westwall lay directly opposite them.

By this time, thirty condorgs waited behind them, with their wings undulating gently, yet powerfully, in an attack position.

Jendai raised his arms in silence.

His signal was well understood. Twenty of the women drew coiled ropes from their saddles, and each looped and tied her rope to the upper knob at the fore of the saddle. Gracefully, almost in formation, the women slid from their saddles onto the rotating wing pinions of their mounts. Grasping the ropes, they swung forward into space, dangling high above the desperate terrain.

Instantly, Goronzo and Calaranz rushed forward. Gently, the condorgs, with the swaying Miserians, followed. The salamanders plunged over the rocks and rushed at tremendous velocity down the cliffs and into the windows of Eastwall.

They had taken the Drogs by complete surprise. Half a dozen of the monsters at the front of the opening were knocked from the lip of the window. They fell, wailing piteously.

Just inside the cave, Calaranz grabbed two Drogs with her powerful jaws, decapitating them instantly. Goronzo grabbed two more and, with a whip of his armored head, threw them out of the window opening. The huge salamanders then tore into the other Changelings who were too far from their swords to defend themselves. A dozen were crushed beneath the strong claws of the salamanders. Twenty more were dashed against the walls of the high cavern in which they held camp.

Surprise owned the day.

The first two Miserians, dodging the carnage of falling Drogs, swung into the cave behind the vicious fighting salamanders. Then two more swung through as their condorgs flew on by the opening to make room for the next ones. In a moment of swift maneuvering, the lip of the cave held six Miserians. Those who first landed used their free hands to catch their sister warriors as they swung into the enclave.

Goronzo and Calaranz had so disrupted the Drogs that sixteen Miserians were able to land in the cave before the Drogs could regroup themselves. There were less than forty of them in this part of Eastwall.

A stroke of genius from Grentana now foiled the Drogs' effective defense. She had seen what appeared to be a large, metallic blossom floating only a few feet above the floor in the center of the cave. In the dim light and the salamanders' fury to rip through the Drogs, she'd had some trouble assessing the nature of this light metallic flower. However, in a moment of insight, she identified the nature of the strange blossom and moved quickly on Calaranz to act. The flower was a composition of the metal hilts of fifty swords whose invisible blades were sticking down into the cave floor.

The surprised Drogs ran to draw their swords for battle, but

Calaranz swung a forepaw into the blossom and sent the arsenal flying like a volley of darts into the dark interior of the cafe. Three Drogs were skewered on their own flying swords.

While the surviving Drogs groped about in an attempt to find their scattered weapons, the Miserians moved in. Their blades were furious, and the Drogs, unable to find their own swords, fell to screaming deaths.

Within a half hour, the enclave window belched sulphur smoke, and the Miserians were in control of Eastwall. The yellow death fumes of the vanquished Changelings drove the women to the window to breathe, and they gladly made way for the Moonrhymes and their mounts to race out into the sunny air and down the cliffs.

At the bottom of the canyon, Grentana and Jendai looked at the bodies of the Drogs who had fallen. They did not meditate on the hideous corpses for long, however, for they intended to keep their word to Raccoman to be back within the hour. The son of Garrod rejoiced to see them enter the Grand Cavern right on schedule. He was relieved that his master plan to capture Thanevial had not been endangered.

The Miserians in Eastwall found the tunnel by which the Drogs had entered the window cavern. The entire detachment waited, but since no other Drogs seemed forthcoming, they decided that only five women could watch the tunnel, while the rest could return to the Grand Cavern to await the breakthrough of Thanevial's hordes.

Back in Westwall, they all waited as the roaring in the earth grew to such violence that it shook the floor where they stood. Raccoman knew it would not be long. He forbade Jendai to remove the armor from the weary salamanders, insisting that they must be ready when the walls of the enclave exploded.

Raenna and Velissa rode their condorg past the place where Parsky had abandoned his mount. The snow had melted, but a heavy frost during the night had covered the carcass of the dead catterlob with white.

Raenna flew the condorg above the thinning candolet groves. They had to fly low in their attempt to track Parsky's thinning boot prints in the snow that crusted in the thawing and refreezing cycles of spring. At last, they lost his trail altogether.

A short flight later, they saw the rising summits that surrounded the Valley of the Sundals. They flew to the square observatory southeast of the Sundal settlement and landed the condorg in a clearing that prefaced the small square house. They knocked at the door several times, but there came no reply. Perhaps, they reasoned, the star-watcher and his wife and child had gone to the village.

As they crossed the yard to remount the condorg, lamenting that they had lost all hope of finding Parsky, Raenna looked down and noticed a toy telescope, smashed and broken. Neither of them had any idea why Abbon's broken toy should be so far from the house, and neither of them would have given the matter much thought, except that as Raenna was about to remount the condorg, she also noticed that the square scope was badly mangled near the end of the tube. Velissa noticed it at almost the same time and gasped. Lying on the patchy snow was an axe!

Something that had happened long ago and far away filled Velissa with fear. She remembered Uncle Krepel's scope—also smashed with an axe. Violent scenes of the party at the Orange Observatory flashed before her mind.

"Raenna!" she shouted. "We can't go back yet!"

Velissa left the condorg, ran to the square window of the observatory, and looked in.

"Oh, no!" she cried.

Raenna had barely reached the window, when Velissa ran to the door of the observatory. This time she did not knock. She tore it open and rushed in.

Raenna looked through the window into the room and saw Velissa. It occurred to Raenna to join her inside the house, but the drama was unfolding too quickly.

Mandra was lying face down on the floor. Hindra was slumped in a chair with his head hanging limply to one side. Raenna watched as Velissa touched the faces of the Sundal star-watcher and his wife.

Velissa's anguished expression told Raenna that the pair were dead. They stared at one another through the glass in bewilderment and grief—and both of them breathed a single, soundless word: *Parsky*.

Velissa felt a sharp pain in her head, and Raenna, still outside, saw her fall forward. An instant later, Raenna also saw Parsky's wicked face leering back at her through the window. He carried a huge bludgeon and was about to strike Velissa again when Raenna burst through the door. Raenna drew her fire-glass blade as Parsky swung his heavy club, but the ceiling of the Sundal dwelling was so low that she had to lean perilously forward, making her an easy mark for the Blackgill. Her sword found its way into Parsky's chest. However, as he fell backwards toward the center of the room, his club smashed into Raenna's arm and chest. The Miserian grimaced in pain and crumpled near the open doorway of the observatory.

Her arm was broken, her garment was torn, and her side was badly gashed and bloody from the Blackgill's crude blow. She was alive, but desperately hurt. In her state, Raenna could not summon the strength to get up and see to Velissa. She studied the small Sundal parlor from where she had fallen. The room was strewn with the bodies of her Graygill friend, the two Sundals, and the dead Blackgill. What a twist of fate that a Rensland woman should survey the carnage in such a distant place.

Velissa stirred. Her groan was music to Raenna.

Velissa rose on one elbow and saw the Blackgill's body lying only a few feet away. She struggled to her unsteady feet and staggered to the Blackgill. Then she fell on him and began crying and pounding his silent chest. Again and again, Velissa beat her fists upon him. Raenna could barely stand to watch.

Finally, Velissa put her hands to her throbbing head and turned toward Raenna. She said one word that would have passed for either a statement or a question.

"Dead?"

Raenna nodded, still holding her badly injured arm. She sat for a few moments longer before she managed to pull herself up and walk outside. Velissa turned from the ugly scene and followed. Neither of the women spoke as they walked in painful silence toward the waiting condorg.

They were about to mount the condorg when they heard muffled sobs coming from inside the house. They turned back to the house again as a small boy, his eyes wide with terror, stumbled out.

"Abbon!" they both cried at once.

The child, desperate for someone to trust, ran to Velissa. He embraced her so furiously that he nearly knocked her down.

"Please take me with you!" he begged.

The women knew he had flown only once and never very far, but they also knew the terror of the journey would never match the horror his own small soul had so lately witnessed.

"Please!" he cried again. "Don't leave me!"

A lantern had been catapulted across the Sundal dwelling when Parsky had hurled his club at the Miserian, and the oil from the lantern had been spilled. The embers of the fire that still burned in the observatory hearth ignited the fine trail of oil. When the path of the flame reached the lantern, it exploded.

"My sword!" exclaimed Raenna. She now remembered that she had left her fire-glass in the Blackgill's chest.

The flames from the spreading fire were already so intense that they could not retrieve the blade. The condorg shied nervously from the blazing house. In pain, Raenna climbed up into the fore part of the saddle, and Velissa mounted behind her. Then Raenna extended her good right arm to pull Abbon up between her and Velissa. Velissa thought of the huge net they had woven to snare the Blackgill. His own treachery had defeated their plan and cost him his life. As the condorg wheeled in its early flight, Velissa tore the net out of the condorg's saddle box and let it fall in a tumbling path onto the blazing roof of the house.

The trio turned east. Now Raenna knew they could no longer remain separated from their husbands. The condorg flew toward the Stone Sentinels of Demmerron Pass. Abbon's eyes were as wide as his fears. Never had he seen this part of Estermann. Never would he forget this day. Never, Never, Never! It seemed the fire that destroyed his distant house now consumed his heart as well.

When the wounds
Of dying lovers bleed—
Together,
Death is better fought.
Embracing,
Finally they see
That lovers die
But love does not.

CHAPTER XII

The War of the Tunnels

RACCOMAN WAS TENSE. The last three explosions had not been muffled. The stone walls of the Grand Cavern shuddered violently in the nearness of the tremors. The Graygill knew that the Grand Cavern would soon explode into debris before their very eyes. The dreaded confrontation for which they had long steeled themselves was about to occur.

The wall before them suddenly rippled. Solid stone trembled, then dissolved. The entire front line of Moonrhymes was blasted backward. Several were blown across the open chamber. A small boy catapulted by the blast slammed into the stalactites on the highest dome of the cavern. The intensity of dust and rubble confused Raccoman so that he could not tell where the Drogs were in all of the haze.

As the dust settled, the huge hulks of the Changelings appeared in the dim light of the torches. To the Moonrhymes, it seemed that the explosion instantly obscured all light. To the Drogs it seemed that the lights suddenly blazed on. In the dull and heavy haze, the Moonrhymes were disadvantaged, as were the Miserians who supported them.

Nonetheless, two things worked exactly on schedule. Hallidan and the Star Riders, who had waited in the lingering darkness, watched the wall give way and proceeded according to plan. Each of them yelled, "To the honor of Ren and Rensgaard!" Then, drawing their blades, Hallidan's small detachment rushed upon the enemy from the rear, cutting through the gray horde before the Changelings had time to turn around. The Drogs, who had expected nothing from behind, were slow to realize that they were now being attacked from two sides and that the stronger attack was from the rear. They turned. The entire army of beast-warriors seemed to number in the thousands, but Hallidan knew that there were probably no more than a few hundred left. His twelve knights fought fiercely. The Drogs turned and fought with equal fierceness.

The distraction gave the Moonrhymes and the Miserians in the Grand Cavern time to charge the vast hole in the wall of the cavern. The Moonrhymes then took heart and swarmed over the broken stones that had once been the beautiful wall of their great underground park.

The difference in height between the Moonrhymes and Miserians added another dimension to the Drogs' disorientation. Since their attackers came at them from two levels, they did not know whether to swing high or low. For awhile, the knights and Miserians were outnumbered ten to one. The Moonrhymes then added a confusing tactic to the war that allowed the knights a kind of advantage they could not have achieved without the little warriors. Several times, just as a knight was about to swing at the upper torso of a Changeling, the beast would crumble, having just been "defootilated" by a shorter foe.

The battle spilled over into the very heart of the Grand Cavern. The great room was so immense that it seemed that the fighting was outside rather than inside.

Jendai and Grentana were mounted and waiting when the wall caved inward. Although the explosion of dust and debris blinded them for a moment, their gallant mounts acted as though some nobler hands were guiding them. They charged straight for the center of the Changeling horde.

Thanevial stood exulting in the melee, having just used the radiant Singreale to blast away the last section of the tunnel that barred his assault on the heart of the enclave. He now turned with defiance to begin the extermination of his enemy.

He held Singreale aloft, and a radiant burst of flame from the tip of the powerful diamond caught one of the knights full in the chest, propelling him the full length of the cavern. The limp body of the knight struck the wall of the cavern on the far side, then ricocheted out the window of Westwall and fell lifeless onto the wooden trestle.

Thanevial blasted another beam from the Singreale and exploded some of the upper columns of stalactites from the ceiling of the Grand Cavern. The collapsing columns of stone fell on the thickest section of the battle. Although the second blast killed none of the knights, the falling stones claimed the lives of both Drogs and Moonrhymes.

Jendai raced forward on Goronzo in an attempt to sever Thanevial's arm. Had he succeeded, the arm would have come off at the shoulder, along with the Singreale. This had been Raccoman's original plan, but it failed. Thanevial saw the beast and its rider approaching, and he leveled the beam from the tip of the diamond. Had the blow struck the gallant Goronzo full in the chest, it would have killed him instantly. Instead, the beam gave him a glancing blow upon the breast plates and ripped away his armor. The courageous salamander received an instant and bloody wound upon his breast. Some fragments of the armor were driven deep into the wound, and Goronzo reeled and skidded into a wall. His bulk careened over the fighting bodies of the Changelings, and the loose plates of his torn armor decapitated one Drog and sliced into the chest of another.

Thanevial was poised to give Goronzo what would have been a lethal blow, when Grentana's sword smashed through the evil Drog's glove and sent the Singreale flying into space. Thanevial ran even as it soared and tried to mark the space where it would land. But he had taken only a couple of steps when Calaranz smashed him against one of the stone walls and sent him spinning backward into the midst of the fray. Across the room, Raccoman exultantly picked up the Singreale and cried, "Long live the Enclave!"

Three Drogs, seeing the diamond in his possession, rushed him, but they were too late. Raccoman tipped the point of the diamond in their direction as they hurried toward him and cried, "Save me, Singreale!" A triple ray of fiery splendor shot out of the diamond and knocked the three attackers backward with such force they never rose again. The beam struck them with a kind of blue fire that played upon their scaly forms just before they burst into flame.

The force of the power that had come so suddenly to his hand stunned Raccoman. He backed up against the wall of the Grand Cavern, for he knew now that no one must get behind him. He used the immense power of the Singreale to encourage the Moonrhymes, who were dying too rapidly at the hands of their overpowering assailants.

Once Thanevial realized he had lost all hope of retrieving the Singreale, he turned upon those around him, slashing at them indiscriminately and cutting wide arcs of death through the ranks of Moonrhymes and Miserians. The Drog was in a part of the cave that was so congested by war that Raccoman dared not aim the Singreale at him lest he kill his friends along with the arch foe.

Thanevial was a powerful and wicked enemy whom, it seemed, none could stop. The ruthless Drog lord advanced through the melee, cutting and killing in tyrannical fashion. Goronzo was still tending his own wounds, and Calaranz could not be moved through the thick of the battle without killing more of the Moonrhyme warriors. Grentana and Jendai had reined the salamanders to the side of the cavern and waited, watching the Drog as he advanced through the carnage, cutting and swinging. The small warriors folded into silence before him. Through the haze of dust there rose in Thanevial's path a blue hulk. As before, he swung his great and powerful invisible blade. It looked as though his sword would cut through a huge knight standing in his path. But it did not. His blade rang out against the fire-glass of a formidable foe, Hallidan of Rensland.

The two brothers had met at last. The grudge of a thousand years burned hot between them.

"My twin!" cried the monster Thanevial.

Raccoman watched as the two met. He knew that Estermann would not again experience the clash of such Titans.

"You should have stayed in the other land," sneered Thanevial.

"You should have loved Ren. Your treachery has ruined two continents!" replied Hallidan.

"I will kill you now as I tried to do in the shadow of the citadel."

"No, Thanevial. I, with the honor of Ren, will destroy you."

Both brothers knew that their fight would be in earnest and that only one of them would be left alive when it was finished.

Thanevial swung his blade again. It sang, unheeded in the air, and rang out again on the glowing fire-glass of Hallidan. The clash of blade on blade drew galleries of watchers on both sides. The Moonrhymes looked on with fear and awe. The Drogs welcomed the sight as a respite from the fatigue of the underground battles, which had been more demanding than the Changelings had anticipated.

The Drogs drew their blades and stood before that section of the Grand Cavern that led into the lower tunnelrees. Raccoman still held the Singreale high above his head and waited for any evidence that he should advance into the fray and risk losing his prize. Goronzo and Calaranz, with Jendai and Grentana, sat and watched as Hallidan and Thanevial swung their blades and dedicated each blow to the other's destruction.

Where Hallidan circled in the dust that had settled from the Singreale's blasts, he left his boot prints intermingled with Thanevial's claw marks. It was clear that both of the champions had the stamina necessary for their conflict and that both of them were well schooled in the arts of war. Their towering forms fought on in the brilliant light of Singreale, which lit the duel and threw their huge shadows across the small forms of the entranced Moonrhymes.

Thanevial was the first to show signs of weakening. Hallidan pressed his advantage for a quarter of an hour. Gradually, his evil brother began to back away. His retreat grew more rapid, and in a moment of clumsiness, he stepped on a stone that slid under his weight. He fell backward, but quickly sprang up again.

In one horrendous swing, Hallidan's great fire-glass sword knocked the weapon from Thanevial's hands. It clattered and skidded across the floor.

The Moonrhymes cheered. Their joy was short-lived, for one of the Drogs broke from the gallery of watchers and ran at Hallidan. He was only a small challenge for Hallidan, who wheeled and brought his fire-glass down upon the Changeling's head. In a red arc, the sword split the Drog's skull, and the beast was drenched in his own gore and sulphur fumes. However, the distraction of the charging Drog was costly.

Just as Hallidan dispatched the would-be assassin, he felt a crushing blow to his own head. Though Thanevial had lost his sword, he had picked up a huge jagged boulder from the rubble all around him and crushed Hallidan to the ground. Then he quickly went for another to finish off Hallidan's life. While he strained to raise the boulder above his head, to hurl it at the fallen Star Rider, the knight thrust his sword up and into the heaving chest of the arch Drog. Thanevial lurched forward in death, but the great stone that he had held was hurled down. It crushed Hallidan's chest.

Thanevial fell across Hallidan, then tumbled to one side. The stench of sulphur, so characteristic of Drogs, marked the death of Rensland's evil lord. A yellow haze floated above the stone floor. The Changeling-warriors stared in unbelief as their leader died. The ugly gallery of beasts thought that they were witnessing the impossible. The death of Thanevial, Lord of the Tower Altar, debilitated their slow wits. They saw the clear judgment of their race and grunted discord.

The Moonrhymes cheered, and their rejoicing echoed against the stone underlays and raced from each of the stalactites, which grinned like a thousand stone teeth in the mouth of the joyous cavern.

Hallidan was badly hurt, however, and the sight of his huge body trapped underneath so great a boulder now caused Raccoman to cry out:

"Jendai! Come quickly! We must help Hallidan!"

Jendai, mounted on Goronzo, quickly raced to the knight. With the claws of his forelegs, the salamander grasped the stone and raised it to an awesome height. When he reared, he exposed his unprotected belly, and one of the Drogs forcefully hurled his sword like a spear through the air. Its unseen blade penetrated the salamander, and red rained upon the knight and the floor around him. Goronzo, in turn, hurled the stone he had lifted from Hallidan into the midst of the Drog encampment, and five or six of the Changelings fell with his blow.

Three Moonrhymes took advantage of the confusion of the moment and ran out into the clearing where the knight and the Drog lord had so lately fought. They carried Hallidan to Raccoman. The Miserians and remaining knights and Moonrhymes then rushed upon the hordes cowering near the section of cave that led to the tunnelrees. The fighting broke out fiercely once again, and the air grew thick with the haze of battle.

Grentana jumped from Calaranz and ran to Goronzo. She grasped the hilt of the sword that still hung in Goronzo's abdomen. The invisible blade had been made visible by the salamander's blood, and when she pulled it out, more gore gushed forth. She knew she had to stop the bleeding. She ran to the body of the Drog lord and quickly pulled Hallidan's fire-glass blade from the corpse of the wretched Thanevial.

As she returned to Goronzo, he folded to his knees. His collapse was so sudden that it alarmed Grentana and she leapt back out of the way. As Goronzo fell, Jendai jumped from the saddle. Goronzo rolled to his side, and Grentana lost no time in laying Hallidan's hot, searing blade fully across the gaping wound in the salamander's belly. There was a frying sound as the flesh was cauterized. When the beast felt the sting of the burning blade, he started up, then wailed pitifully to see the hand of Grentana quivering with the sword that brought so much pain. Goronzo lay down and stretched his head forward.

"Is he dead, Jendai?" asked Grentana.

Jendai watched the heaving sides of the salamander. "Not yet," he replied.

"He must live," said Grentana. Her eyes filled with tears of concern.

"He needs rest, Grentana," said Jendai. "If he has the least hope of survival, he must be allowed to rest."

Grentana and Jendai ran for water to wash his new wounds, while another of the Moonrhymes went to console the beast. Another Moonrhyme began removing his armored plates, for it was clear by now that the armored plates were no longer necessary as the war moved to a section of the cave far from the wounded salamander.

Moments later, Jendai and Grentana returned with water and they were shortly followed by several other Moonrhymes who brought in buckets to help them. Even in the thick of battle, the compassion of the Moonrhymes for their mounts would not be stayed. Only when Jendai and Grentana saw that Goronzo was resting as well as possible did they turn to watch the Miserians, knights, and Moonrhymes moving in a hard triple column through the confused Drogs. They could see that while the Drogs were being killed in great numbers, the battle would still be costly in terms of the losses of their fellow Moonrhymes and the gallant men and women of Rensland.

In a moment of insight, Jendai exclaimed, "Grentana, the canisters—let's use them now!"

"Certainly," she agreed. "Now if ever!"

They rushed to the area of the cave where the shielded containers were stacked and found them seething with such energy that they were searing to the touch. In preparing to handle the sealed pails, they pulled on their gloves. Jendai picked up a canister, while Grentana mounted Calaranz. She received the Selendrenni from Jendai and courageously rode in the direction of the fray.

Grentana turned Calaranz into the battle, directly between the lines of Moonrhymes and Drogs. She clamped her knees and legs into the saddle and dropped the reins as the salamander flew forward at lightning speed. Her strong hands tore at the canister and ripped the lid away. The Selendrenni shot up and out over the leathery heads of the fighting Changelings. The fiery eels fell in a volley of flames into the Drog battleline.

Grentana returned Calaranz to the stockpile, and Jendai again handed her a sealed canister. Once more, she rode into the battle and released another volley of fire. The Selendrenni burned a second time through the terrified lines of Changelings.

The Moonrhymes and Miserians drew back. Terrified by the burning Selendrenni, they gave Grentana plenty of room to work. Again and again, Grentana returned to repeat her fiery onslaught. The Drogs were perplexed by the falling fire. They could not fight the fire eels with swords alone. By Grentana's seventh advance, the Drog horde was so decimated by fire that they began to retreat.

As they watched the spectacle, the entire encampment cheered. The Selendrenni, weakened by their long captivity, had burned themselves out before the dissipated army of Drogs finally turned to flee into the nearby tunnelrees.

Raccoman still held the Singreale as he cradled Hallidan's head in his small lap. He smiled down at his fallen friend.

"We're winning—we're winning, Hallidan!"

Hallidan smiled back weakly.

The Singreale gave the Graygill and the Star Rider the light they needed to foresee the end of the Moonrhyme war. This day's victory, Hallidan knew, would be heralded upon two continents as the end of an evil age.

"Hallidan," said Raccoman at length, "If Ren only knew that the age which brought ruin to two worlds is now drawing to a close."

The wounded knight turned his face toward Raccoman. "Raccoman . . . my ancient enemy . . . my brother is no more," he gasped. "He who set Rensland at war is dead . . . he is gone, buried in his rebellion, as surely as his Tower Altar was swallowed in the molten sea."

Raccoman could see that the Star Rider was breathing with such great effort that he could not long continue.

With the back of his unsteady hand, the knight wiped the blood from his chin. "Tell Raenna that I love her," he said.

Raccoman begged Hallidan to cease speaking and conserve his strength.

"I will take Singreale and touch his healing ray to your wounds and you'll be well," Raccoman said, knowing his promise was weak.

"I am dying, friend Raccoman. I cannot live . . . but I have died in a good cause. Please tell Raenna, I love her," the knight insisted.

Behind them, at that very moment, a condorg landed noisily upon the bulwark that prefaced the great window of Westwall. Velissa swung to the ground and grabbed the reins of her mount to lead the great creature into the cavern. She could hardly believe the carnage that greeted her. Awe and fear passed across her face as Velissa walked toward the brilliant light of Singreale, still leading the condorg. The light was intense in the dark enclave. It was a moment or two before she saw her beloved Raccoman.

The injured Raenna clung weakly to the saddle of the condorg, and the boy, Abbon, sat behind her, his childish eyes taking in more than they could measure. She slumped in a deathly vision that tore Raccoman's heart. Raenna's eyes slowly opened to the blinding incandescence of the Singreale. The dying Hallidan opened his eyes at the same moment. In seeing each other, both seemed to experience a momentary surge of strength.

"Raenna, my one love," Hallidan said loudly enough to be heard.

As the fires of the Selendrenni still burned across the hazy interior of the enclave, Raenna slid from the saddle.

"Hallidan, my darling!" she cried. She stumbled and fell weakly before him.

"Whatever happened to Raenna?" whispered Raccoman to Velissa, as they embraced in the joy that ended their own separation. Velissa knew that there would be a better time to tell Raccoman all that had occurred since she last saw him. For now they both sat silently and watched the aching finale before them.

"Raenna, I always loved you. I dared to believe that one day we would circle Mt. Calz above a distant valley . . . or have an asteroid all our own . . . I . . . ." Hallidan's breathing came hard now. "Raenna."

"My darling, it cost everything, did it not? But the honor of Ren is saved and Thanevial . . . ." Raenna paused before she asked, "Is Thanevial dead?"

Hallidan did not wish to waste his final strength speaking that treacherous name. He answered her with a nod.

"Raenna . . . I . . ."

"Yes, Hallidan," Raenna encouraged him as she rested her head on his broad chest and waited for him to speak.

He began again. The song that now came to Hallidan was one

that he had sung once before when he lay wounded in a cave near Mt. Calz. He realized that to sing it here would require the last of his strength. Still, it seemed to him a worthy way to spend his remaining moments.

Raenna, my love, when the fighting is done,
We'll saddle our condorgs and fly.
We'll sail past the seasons and circle the sun
And skim the dim reaches of sky.
We'll rein our bright steeds to some cosmic spire,
Embrace on dim planets flung far,
And lie in communion in warm stellar fire
And purchase our own . . . private . . . star!

Hallidan's lips fell silent. His song and life were finished. Yet if Raenna heard, she heard only in realms far above the Moonrhyme battlefield, for they both were silent now.

There arose from the Miserians and the few Star Riders left alive the anthem that the fallen had sung so proudly in another land:

O, come to the monarch whose splendor is white,
Whose glorious being is day,
Whose city of bridges is quarried in light,
Where dark is forbidden to stay.

Truth, peace and justice are ever his seal—
Honor his substance of might.
He's friend to the Falcon and Lord of Singreale,
His reign is as condorgs in flight.

Bring every knight and stand them as men—
Sing honor to Rensgaard and Ren.

Velissa and Raccoman wept, while Raccoman still cradled the noble head of the silent Hallidan in his lap.

The carnage of the battle scene was hard on Abbon. Raccoman studied the grieving child, then gently withdrew from the two sleeping Titans who had been his friends. Velissa pulled Abbon close, and he held Velissa as though his own heart could somehow be repaired by the strength he felt in her embrace.

"Raccoman," she said, "this is Abbon. He is a Sundal."

"A Sundal?" Raccoman asked awkwardly.

It was another story that could wait. Raccoman suddenly grasped all that Velissa felt, and for the first time, he really saw the child. He took the boy from his wife and pressed him to his heart.

A flood of feelings came over them both. By this time, Ren's servants had finished their anthem. Three or four Star Riders and twenty or more Miserians gathered with glistening faces around the silent lovers on the stone floor. Velissa surveyed the end of the war—the long war—and, choked with emotion, she sang an old requiem of pain and new hope:

There is fire in the caverns, and war on the plains.
We have fed our best souls to the foe.
Come all you lost men to life once again—
Ho-lolly, ho-lolly, ho-lo.

Empires spoil themselves
With hate.
Castles canker,
Moat and stone.
But hope descends
In citadels,
Where pain will never
Hold a throne.

CHAPTER XIII

The Return of the Guardians

"WAKE UP, MASSSTER ABBON!" said the young Denedol. He had been hatched only a couple of years earlier and so was not very long, nor could he speak very loudly.

"When he is older, he will be longer," Raccoman had promised Abbon.

"Unfortunately, when he is longer, he will also be louder," Velissa lamented.

This particular morning was cold, and Abbon had permitted Denedol to spend the night in his own bed. At first, Velissa had told him forcefully that beds were for people and floors were for serpents. She found it hard to make the point secure, however, since Abbon and Denedol had become such good friends.

Denedol had a gift for singing. There was even a kind of melody about him when he called, "Wake up, Massster Abbon!" Like all serpents, he was not fond of winter. Had he been left in the rocky dens of Demmerron, he would have hibernated all winter in a snakey knot with all of his brothers and sisters. Here with Abbon and Velissa and Raccoman, Denedol made it clear that he did not like sleeping in a knot, since it left him in kinks long after the spring thaw.

All in all, he was terribly grateful to be a household pet. Abbon never went anywhere without him, especially during spring and summer. When they first brought him to the Blue Observatory, he was small enough to ride in Abbon's pocket. Now he was growing at an alarming pace and was already as long as Abbon, though in maturity he would be twice as long and, as Velissa had promised, twice as loud.

He slithered out from under the covers and coiled in triple rings of brown upon the boy's chest. "Wake up, Massster Abbon," he said once more. When the child did not stir, Denedol decided he was through begging. The time had come for some off-key singing that never failed to rouse the drowsy and reluctant Abbon from the bed:

Abbon, Abbon, Abbon, will ssspend hisss life in bed,
With a ssserpent on his chessst and a pillow on hisss head.
Lazy Abbon, dussst your ssslumber—jump your groggy mind and wake.
Don't resissst me, Masssster Abbon.
A boy's bessst friend is still hisss sssnake.

The high squeaky voice of the juvenile serpent was so annoying that Abbon threw his leg over the side of the bed and stood up. He did not want to suffer through another verse of the serpent's song. In an abrupt move, he dumped the young serpent back on the bed, then hurriedly covered him and threw his pillow on top. He ran from the room and scampered into the open area of the home. A fire was already burning.

"Why did Denedol wake me so early?" protested Abbon.

"Because today Jendai is coming for breakfast," said Velissa.

Before either of them could say another word, they heard a dull thud in the next room. Denedol had slithered out of his prison of comforters and pillows and fallen noisily onto the floor. Abbon knew that he would race into the room in a moment.

A flash of brown appeared and slithered straight to Abbon. In a moment, it had wrapped itself around Abbon's ankles in a tight coil that was so strong the boy could not take a single step.

"Let me go!" cried Abbon. "Let me go, you striped strip!"

Denedol hated that name, and he clamped his thin coils tighter about the small boy's legs. "Let me go, do you hear?" Abbon wanted to kick free, but it was no use. When he tried, he fell down on the floor, catching himself with his hand and then lying flat. "Let me go, Denedol!"

"Sssee how *you* like falling on the floor!" said the determined Denedol.

"You boys quit fighting!" demanded Raccoman, as he entered the room. "Let him go, Denedol. He didn't mean to make you fall."

The serpent uncoiled and Abbon stood once more.

"Now, hurry and wash your face," said Velissa. "Jendai is coming today."

"On Goronzo?" asked Abbon.

"I'm sure," said the metal-worker.

Following the Moonrhyme War, the entire population had left the enclave, electing to live south of Demmerron in the plains. The once-happy caverns were now silent and eerie. The Miserians and knights had searched the caverns and burrows to locate and destroy the last of the Drogs. The same procedures were used to rid the land of those Drogs who had escaped from the burrows of Eastwall.

The reason for the Moonrhyme exodus to the plains came from the general destruction of the war. The huge piles of stone and loose rocks congested the tunnelrees and were nearly impossible to clear. Evacuation seemed the only logical solution. Grentana and Jendai, like the others, now lived in the plains of Canby.

When Jendai arrived at the Dakktares' home, he stopped in the snowy yard, and smiled. He was proud to see the progress that had occurred since his last visit to Quarrystone Woods. The new house, which occupied the same site as the old one, was not quite finished, for Raccoman worked slowly with wood. He would not have made any progress at all if some of the Moonrhymes had not helped him. Now the new house was rising in bright blue, a color that Raccoman had agreed to out of respect for Velissa's preference. When it was all done, it would indeed be a handsome house, with three fireplaces and a hall large enough to accommodate a hundred Graygills at once.

Jendai left Goronzo in the front yard and knocked on the door. Inside, there remained a lot of rough beams and unfinished timber. The house was less finished on the inside than it was on the outside. Still, it promised to be one of the best examples of Canby architecture anywhere. Raccoman had insisted that many of its inner furnishings be done in his favorite color. Such furniture as they had was yellow, as were the inner walls. Already they had spent two years rebuilding the mansion where Velissa had once lived with her father.

Jendai's knocking on the door woke Rahnah. She didn't cry, but she did whimper, and Velissa walked to the small crib in the corner of a yellow room and lifted her from the coverlets. A Graygill baby is a tiny wonder, and the little pink hands flailed in every direction. She was two years old, and it was clear that she would be walking early, possibly by her sixth year.

Right now, she was awake and hungry.

Velissa sat down to nurse her near the table. Raccoman showed Jendai to a seat and went to get the black bread and candolet tea. Velissa had been preparing a broth to simmer during the day so that it would be just right by supper time. Some of the vegetables, half pared and diced, still waited on the unfinished cabinet top to become a complement to the evening stew.

"Raccoman, your house is going well. Another year?" he probed.

"A little more, I think."

"Abbon's room?"

"Finished!" Raccoman replied proudly.

Jendai poured himself a cup of tea and sat drinking it, looking faraway.

Denedol twisted and ascended in a rippling spiral around Jendai's boot, then around his leg, until he finally reached his lap where he coiled and shivered. Jendai's clothing was cold. Jendai set down his cup, gently took hold of both sides of Denedol's coils, and returned him firmly to the floor. He watched the shivering serpent slither over to the fire and rearrange himself into a looser two-coil heap.

Jendai was picking up his cup again when suddenly his face lit up. He had just remembered the best bit of news that had come from Maldoon.

"Calaranz has given us three eggs this past six months."

"Three!" Raccoman was amazed. "Are they fertile?"

"I don't see why not," said Jendai. "And it looks like she is swelling to drop another egg. Not since before the cataclysm has Estermann known the mating of fire salamanders."

"Four eggs. Are you keeping them in the fire?"

It was a superfluous question. The incubator was the first thing he had ordered done when the Moonrhymes were rebuilding Maldoon. At the time, it had seemed to Jendai an act of faith. Yet he believed the day would come when Calaranz might give them an egg or two. Building the incubator had not been a difficult project. Jendai had taken the smelting room that Parsky had once used as a part of his foundry. He added a chimney to the chamber and reinforced the inner walls with special masonry that could stand the stress of the inner fire it would have to contain. The incubator had been fitted with pulleys and a steel mesh basket to position the eggs above the fire chamber. One by one, as the eggs came, they were taken to the incubator. Once again, Maldoon had a column of thin smoke rising from her turrets and domes.

Like the house of the Dakktares, Maldoon was unfinished. The castle was immense and would require the Moonrhymes' attention for half a century to bring it to completion. They had worked tirelessly following the war of the enclave.

The liberation of Maldoon and the Canby widows had made husbands of the Moonrhyme bachelors. There were nearly enough women to go around. Some of the women had led their new husbands back to the shattered ruins of Canby, where they started life again. A few of the dwellings there had been easy to repair, but much of the city was still in ruins, though all of the streets were now clear.

Most of the Moonrhyme men had decided to stay in Maldoon. The main walls of the fortress contained many apartments, and each of the old cubicles held a Moonrhyme couple. Life in the castle settled predictably, and a new sense of order gradually returned to the valley of the Canbies.

The Moonrhymes had never feared heights, having climbed the walls of the enclave for centuries. Thus, they easily climbed the upper towers of Maldoon and restored the smoke-smudged domes till they were again brilliant and gleaming gold. The broken walls beneath them stood in contrast to the splendor of the gleaming pinnacles. The Moonrhymes were such natural climbers that it was not unusual to see a young Moonrhyme leaning back against the spires of the upper turrets, soaking up the late evening sun. It was winter now, however, and the turret climbers would not risk themselves on the icy towers.

Jendai was lost in his reverie, thinking about the war and this pleasant land that was now returning to peace. Raccoman called him back to awareness. The table was spread, and Abbon was keeping a nervous place. Rahnah had finished nursing, at least for the time being, and was lying on the floor, cooing in the joy of the warm fire and waving her uncoordinated arms at Denedol.

"Raccoman, have you heard what Hanmla, the stone-cutter, is doing?" Jendai asked. "He began only a few months ago to carve the stone shafts of granite before the canyons to the north. He intends to make two colossal figures at the entrance."

"Raenna and Hallidan!" Velissa exclaimed, jumping ahead to the conclusion which Jendai had intended to bring them.

It was not hard to guess. The Moonrhymes held the Star Riders in great esteem and heralded them as the saviors of the enclave and of all life in the northern lands. The report brought joy to the Dakktares, and they continued discussing the project till Raccoman realized it was time for breakfast.

Raccoman stood at length, prepared to exalt the loaf.

"May I, Papa?" asked Abbon.

"Indeed, but we've a need for speed!" answered Raccoman.

"Raccoman!" Velissa gently remonstrated. She never liked to see Raccoman in such a hurry that he could not be truly grateful.

Abbon recited the exultation:

To the maker of the feast,
To the power of loaf and yeast,
Till the broth and bread have ceased,
Gratefulness is joy.

They all pulled their chairs toward the table and began to eat.

"The Star Riders landed again a month ago," volunteered Jendai.

"The reason?" It was the season of their Festival of Light.

Velissa smiled, remembering.

Jendai smiled, too, and said nothing further.

Raccoman knew his ways.

All right, Jendai—
Tell us why
Ren's Riders
Left the sky
Especially during winter.

Jendai waited still longer to pique Velissa's curiosity, and the silence grew thunderous. Raccoman had asked a fair question. The Star Riders and Miserians had taken all the condorgs and left after the Battle of the Enclave. They did not like the extreme temperatures of the Graygill lands, particularly the snows that so often fell on the Canbies. Now and then, however, they would visit to exchange reports of all that occupied the outer kingdom. The king's prince, Garrod the Second, was well, and the universal peace had restored the citadel to its former place in the sun. Even the molten Seas of Draymon were receding, and it was believed that the seas would continue to ebb for at least a thousand more years.

"Sometimes," said Jendai, "I wish I had learned to ride the condorgs, like you and Velissa."

"Never you mind—don't change the subject."

"All right, all right," conceded Jendai, with a touch of devilment in his eyes. "Here is what they brought!"

He produced two exquisitely carved replicas of the Singreale. They held no inner light or power of their own, but they were intricate in design and hung from braided silver. Velissa's eyes lit up.

"They are for you both," said Jendai. "Ren's Star Riders said the king had them crafted at the Festival of Light so that you would long remember your days in his kingdom."

Raccoman took both of the necklaces and then pulled the knot to the length of the cord. He got up, stood behind his wife, and slipped the cord around her neck. Then he leaned over her shoulder and kissed her, exclaiming:

Velissa, my wife—
This symbol of life
is yours.

Jendai stayed till evening.

The scope at the Blue Observatory was still serviceable, and they often used it to survey the night sky and to measure the rising and falling of the starfields. Jendai wanted Raccoman to accompany him on Goronzo for a trip into the far country. As Goronzo's chief attribute was speed, even in the snow, he expected that the trip, which would have taken more than a week each way on foot, would last no more than two or three days.

"Are you going to fetch the Selendrenni for Jendai's new eggs?" Velissa asked.

Jendai shook his head.

"We are going to the Sentinels of Demmerron," Raccoman replied.

Don't worry, my dear,
It surely is clear
We can handle our trek
Without fear.

Velissa was still a little anxious when Raccoman was away. She could never be convinced that the Miserians had tracked down every last Drog that had escaped from Eastwall. The last known living Drog had been killed more than two years ago by a Moonrhyme hermit. The Changeling had been weak with hunger and had lost its weapon, so it was no match even for the old man only half its size.

"There are no more Drogs. You and the children will be safe," Jendai assured her.

Velissa eyed the two great fire-glass swords that hung in a crossed fashion above the roughed-in fireplace. Sitting before the glowing weapons was a silver wind foil bracket that held the exquisite Singreale. Its cool but steady glow belied the slumbering force it contained. Having blasted a cavernous heart in the Moonrhyme mountain, it now waited till the ancient throne room of Maldoon was refurbished. Raccoman and Velissa knew that the treasure would not long remain in Quarrystone Woods.

The glowing fire-glass swords, however, were theirs to keep forever. They were the last possessions of Raenna and Hallidan, and they had come to be the treasure of Raccoman and Velissa. The fire in them was dying. In another year, the blades would be cool enough to touch, and in time they would become only the cold reminders of a desperate season in the epoch of Estermann. Velissa agreed to the journey:

All right—I'll be all right.
Two days and one night—
No more than that?

"I will be back," said Raccoman, excited that Velissa had put up no more protest.

Grentana never seemed to mind if Jendai was gone. Perhaps her unpleasant memory of Ganarett's passing had freed her from the need to know at all times where her husband was. Now Grentana occupied the apartment at Maldoon that had once been the royal residence of the dead King Singreale—and it was agreed that the Singreale would be guarded by the fire salamanders for as long as they should live and by their progeny after them. The beasts could be as gentle as congrels, but they would offer a fearsome rebuke if anyone tried to break through the castle walls as the Blackgills of Castledome had once done.

Raccoman kissed Velissa good-bye, and the two Graygills mounted the warm back of the great salamander Goronzo. Soon they were cutting a dark rut through the new snow of winter. Far to the east they raced, coming in but a little while to the ruins of the Orange

Observatory. Raccoman wondered why none of the Moonrhymes had settled at the outpost. It was still sound in the side walls, and it would have taken so little to repair the broken roof trusses and to make the old place a comfortable and commodious habitation again. It was as if the Moonrhymes, knowing of Krepel's terrible past, were afraid the old house might still be haunted by invisible demons that would lure its inhabitants into its ancient evil.

Goronzo raced on through the snow. He came at last to the western ridges. Sure-footed on the ice ledges, he sped forward into late afternoon. The beast seemed tireless, and by the time the winter sun was setting, they rested at the base of the eerie stone shafts at Demmerron. Far up the towering stone, Raccoman could see that snow was gathering in the sculptor's design. The noble face of the handsome Hallidan was already beginning to emerge. It would take the Moonrhyme sculptor the rest of his millennial life to set the Titan's body free. Raccoman sighed and said:

I somehow feel compelled
To climb these silent sentinels.

"And so we shall," offered Jendai. "But tonight we will build a fire and warm ourselves well before we snuggle in the snow and sleep."

Soon the fire roared at the base of one of the huge Sentinels of Demmerron. The second towering monolith stretched into the inky darkness laced with brilliant white. The two small men hovered over the orange flames that illuminated their faces with an amber glow there in huge shadows against the spires. The thin black smoke, rich with the fragrance of candolet bark, circled the cold icy stones and fled upward, threading its way through the stars before it disappeared.

Morning came swiftly, drenching the blue-white valley with gold light. At last they extinguished their fire and mounted Goronzo. When they were strapped securely into the fiber saddle, the salamander bolted up the stone shaft. Raccoman laughed and shouted:

I want to see Maldoon and beyond
From the haughty top of Demmerron!

In a brisk half hour, they were at the top of the shaft. Atop Hallidan's mammoth head, Raccoman now stared out over the new land. He was amazed at how large the sculpture was. From the head of the colossus, he could watch the incandescent sun rise on the entire world he knew. He saw the gleaming new Maldoon. He celebrated the valley that was free at last from all war. He saw the new conical roofs of the village that had been his fascination in boyhood. He surveyed the western ridges, then turned and watched the sun rise on the snowy, precipitous ledges of Westwall.

"Parsky," he said half-aloud. The name came up less and less frequently, but all that he now saw brought back again the treachery that had once spoiled the valley.

"Parsky," he repeated a little more loudly as he stared out over the distant castledomes in the silver ginjon forest.

Goronzo, who loved to sun himself at the heights, lay down and let his tail drape over the cold and shaded side of the stone spire. The riders unstrapped themselves and dismounted.

"You said the name of Parsky?" Jendai mused.

I did indeed—
My mind has gone to seed.

"Yes, what then?" asked Jendai in a confused interruption.

There was a world long ago,
Winter-washed and pure,
Where did those ancient kingdoms go?
Did we dream it, Jendai? Can we be sure?
Dare we dream a dream at last
That will evermore endure?

During the fifth winter after the War of the Moonrhymes, Collinvar returned with a female centicorn and a colt. The blue house of the Dakktares was nearing completion, and their joy at having Collinvar and his new family could not be measured. They enlarged the old stable and gave it a new coat of blue paint, for the old weathered barn had faded and had to be painted to match the house. They named Collinvar's mate Milliton and the colt Grendyl, after an old memory. In time, they all learned to ride again. Raccoman rode Collinvar now and Velissa rode Milliton. Grendyl was fleet of foot and a delight to Abbon.

With the passing of years, the throne room at Maldoon was restored. Ren had nurtured two new guardians to maturity. The young guardians had flown across the sea from the distant citadel of Rensland. It was exactly ten years after the War of the Moonrhymes when the falcons appeared. Raccoman found the majestic birds outside the Blue Observatory one cold morning in the season of the tilt winds.

Ah, my friends, what can I say?
What brings you this way?
How can I entice you to remain?
How can I bribe you to stay?

The White Falcon spoke as clearly as Rexel and stated his demands in one word. "Singreale."

I must not play as though my lips are dumb.
I knew you'd be here—I am glad you've come.

The Graygill went into his new blue house and came back with the diamond. The ancient stone was going home again to Maldoon. Mighty Ren desired that Singreale remain forever in the lands of the Graygills as a witness between continents. Denedol slithered along behind Raccoman in rapid and wriggling protest. He clearly did not want to leave, but it was his duty to become a guardian. To this end had he been hatched in the mystic caves of Demmerron.

The White Falcon extended a talon and received the Singreale.

The Black Falcon looked at Denedol and then spoke to the Graygill, "You know why I've come? The throne room is finished at Maldoon."

"I know," said Raccoman, "You can have him—though I suspect Abbon will protest."

Denedol had long known that the day would come when he would have to go. He coiled himself tightly about Abbon's arm, and when Raccoman reached down to unwind him, he quickly rewrapped himself around Raccoman's hand. He did not want to let go of life in Quarrystone Woods. It took a good bit of coaxing to convince him. Each time Raccoman uncoiled the serpent with his free hand Denedol merely coiled around that hand instead, forcing Raccoman to repeat the process from hand to hand. At last, he grew tired of his protest and allowed his thin, long body to be placed within the gentle talons of the Black Falcon.

With the diamond and the serpent in their talons, the two falcons spread their wings and set out in the bright winter air toward Maldoon.

The congrels that lived near the Blue Observatory appeared, and sensing Abbon's anguish at the loss of his friend, they begged him to play. Raccoman felt that something more needed to be done to comfort Abbon in his grief over Denedol.

Velissa, my dear, the tilt winds surely come tonight—
Let's take the children on their first real flight.

"But, Raccoman, it's so high, and they are so young—especially Rahnah."

We'll bundle them up and strap them in,
And we ourselves will fly again.

"Do you think they will be safe?" Velissa asked. She soon caught her husband's enthusiasm for the idea, however, and found herself packing bread and water. She served the infant Rahnah, who was walking now. They dressed themselves and rode the centicorns along the Southern road, traveling in a few hours to the site where the old barn had once stood.

Raccoman had welded a framework to a metal sledge, which he had used to pull the Paradise Falcon overland to the valley he so loved. There it was anchored down, until such time as he would need it.

He had also welded two little seats just a little forward on the deck.

The four of them rode the centicorns swiftly to the south of the new Canby. The children loved the cold. All Graygill children loved the snow and cold, and today these two would sky-surf for the very first time.

Abbon was excited. But the tilt winds tested the child's patience. He could barely wait until darkness came, but soon they were all strapped in and waiting in the cold.

Rahnah was too young to understand their silent waiting. Abbon had already asked a thousand times when the winds were coming, and a thousand times Raccoman had told him, "Soon!"

At last, they heard the sighing that quickly rose to screaming. The screaming sent the winter air into convulsions. The steel trestle on which they waited several feet above the ground suddenly shuddered. The wind slammed into the valley floor and drove power under their ship.

"Watch the children's faces, my dear," said Raccoman, as he pulled free the tethering cables. He stomped the stabilizer bar, and the edges of the beautiful yellow ship rose upward into night.

Abbon's bright eyes saw the wonder of the stars, and he stayed awake as long as he could. They sailed on through planets that faded in blue-white splendor and floated among the asteroids. The stars bumped against Velissa's blue cape and slid down her arms and washed the yellow wind foils in light. A tiny flake of light stuck to Raccoman's sidelocks. He pulled it free and placed it on Velissa's upturned glove. She blew it like a silken puff into the magic sky and laughed as freely as Raccoman had ever heard her laugh. They embraced, and when they parted from their kiss, Velissa could not help but compliment both his genius and the night sky.

My dear, you're the best of a marvelous lot.
I've said it before, and I'll say it again.
Your perfection is perfect—it's almost a sin.

It was a truth so obvious that Raccoman felt little need to reply. He turned the Paradise Falcon upward, and it skidded on a slippery field of icy asteroids. The craft thumped on some jagged air, and the little lights around them produced an enchanting percussion. The tempo was an intrigue. The night was alive with watching. With such a cosmic audience, Raccoman wanted to dance, but he dared not risk himself outside the fiber straps in case the wind died. The thumping slowed its percussion till it became more rhythmic. Raccoman pulled Velissa nearer and sang:

The thousand glittering eyes of night
Shall look the other way,
When we embrace on the edge of space
For a thousand years and a day.
And the stars shall trumpet the heraldry—
Proclaim what is obvious for all to see.
That I am of the substance all men should be.
The model, the heartbeat, the standard, the key—
The idol deserving of idolatry.

Velissa smiled at him.

The wind stopped suddenly, and the Paradise Falcon dipped only a little before it soared off into euphoria, plowing a glittering furrow into the night.